Th

Precious

Princess

of Wonderland

The
Precious
Princess
of Wonderland

JAMES PRINCE

Order this book online at www.trafford.com
or email orders@trafford.com

Most Trafford titles are also available at major online book retailers.

Printed in the United States of America.

ISBN: 978-1-4669-3323-1 (sc)
ISBN: 978-1-4669-3324-8 (e)

Trafford rev. 05/08/2012

 www.trafford.com

North America & international
toll-free: 1 888 232 4444 (USA & Canada)
phone: 250 383 6864 ♦ fax: 812 355 4082

Dedication

Dana, this book of mine is mainly you and me. As you will be able to tell, I am an opened book and this book is in your hands now. I also have beautiful dreams; some are more realistic than others. But as you can tell, the book and the songs are fifty per cent you. You personally don't have to like it. The way it is written is not important. The editor will take the story and rewrite it in better English than mine.

My lawyer told me that I have something to offer. He said this is fiction, the kind of books the most sold. This is not much, but still this is some hope. I never hid that I love you and maybe I should have, but personally I believe that if I didn't say anything, it would have been wasted.

I do love you and I always will. No matter what you do or what you say, it wouldn't change my feelings for you. No matter if you love me or not either. As a friend I'm asking you to be my friend and nothing else, sincerely.

No matter where you go or what you do in your live, don't ever say you're not loved, because you would be lying.

Once I've seen a strong and young man lift you up twice from the floor before he let you down and I thought to myself; he'll let you down sooner or later. I told myself then that I would lift you up too and I will never let or put you down. You are a Precious Princess to me and this is a thought I'm going to die with no matter what. I'm not good enough to pretend I am your angel or something like that, but maybe we can say I am a good friend of yours. If anything is hurting you in any way in this story, please Dana forgive me, because I don't think I can survive another war against you. On the other hand if we fight again, it would probably end up in another pretty song or another good book.

May God bless you always.

From James Prince, Gaston Lapointe to Dana
The Precious Princess Of Wonderland.
© Gaston Lapointe 1997-98

Notes

The real purpose for writing this story is not to make money, but rather to warn you about a continuous oncoming danger. The doors of heaven are opened for you and so are the doors of hell. So please, if you own a copy of this book, pass it around to your friends so they too can have a chance to find out. If you give it away it might just end up on a shelf or in a drawer where it doesn't help anybody anymore.

Not everybody will like this book and no one can write a book that everybody likes, but if fifty per cent of the people who read it likes fifty per cent of it, I would consider it a success.

Chapter 1

One day like many others in late August of 1997, something very special happened that will change my life forever. I have never entered in a bar for the last three years, but that day was very hot and somehow I was thirsty for a drink. So I went to a place where I can't stop going since.

The place was full to capacity, the music was very good and I had to wait quite a while before a waitress came along. I had to push one and another to make it to the dance floor. But as soon as I saw a girl in uniform I asked her for a rye and seven. The young woman told me very politely that Dana would be there soon to serve me if I didn't mind waiting a little bit longer. Polite and honest I thought. I kind of wondered if my thirst justifies the waiting.

A few minutes later came the shock of my life. It has been eight months since and at the time I began to write this story, I'm still in the same state of mind, meaning in love way over my head. Blond with brown streaks, absolutely beautiful blue eyes, five foot five, but all of those physical qualities are not what struck me the most. Just as soon as she said a word all of my emotions went blurry. Her tone of voice is something I remembered from way back, but at this point and time I couldn't tell exactly what it was. It was only a few weeks later that I found out the full impact of this discovery. I knew though it wasn't her physical attributes that attracted me towards her the most even though she is one of the most beautiful.

The teacher of my grade five, Francine is her name, a person who took the time and tried to find out what my problem or I should say my problems were. She kept me after school and with her I had the most wonderful quality time of all of my life until I met Dana. I was only eleven then and I was very rebellious. To her I was special at least this is what I thought then and I still think.

Two years earlier my young brother Jean-Yves was killed in front of my eyes by a drunk driver at age seven. I felt guilty for his death and this is the way I felt for the next twenty-nine years, mainly because I disobeyed my parents and I forced my little brother to follow me to the road to pick up bottles when we were supposed to go pick up raspberries and come back home right after. But the bees were too mean and this is why we went to the road.

When I came home crying following the accident to tell them my brother was dead, mom gave me a slap in the face thinking I have to come out of the shock. But this is not the way I took it then. I just felt hated to death and I remember wanted to die before mom and dad came back from the accident's scene, but neither the house nor the bridge was high enough and the little creek wasn't deep enough. I wished then I was the one who died and I almost jumped in the hole where they buried him. I often thought my dad hated me because of this accident.

Six years later at age fifteen I tried to talk to the family about my feelings following the viewing of a movie called: 'The Misunderstood Child.' I told them then this was my story. But they all laughed at me saying: 'Poor little Gaston.' Never again I talked to anyone about this story until after I took a human relation course. The teacher of the course made me spit out all of my anger, my shyness, my timidity and all hang up I had. One thing I can say is I was prisoner of myself for more then thirty years.

Mom was and still is a very good person, but with twelve kids behind her she never had the time poor her for all of our little emotional problems. The results were pretty ugly at time. She had to come to school up to seven times the same day just because of me. This is how many fights I had the same day.

Dad took me to the woods from two to three days a week where he was working already for two years in a row by then, plus two full summer holidays working from six to six, six days a week. I never had a summer holiday after this until I was on my own. The result of this was that I became way stronger than others for my age and size. At age eleven, I beat the heck out of a sixteen-year-old who tried to molest me. Who knows? Maybe it was the last time he ever tried to do something like this, who knows?

I could tell you a lot of stories about fights I had from early age until I reached my mid-twenties, but this book is not for this purpose.

I met Dana on August 30th 1997 at 10:30 p.m. and I left early after a couple of drinks. Not before holding her hand warmly though and telling her I will see her again soon. Soon it was. The next evening I went back to my new treasury to find out she wasn't working that night. It was a Sunday night and the long weekend of September. For this reason the bar was opened contrary to usual.

I felt heart broken and I was disappointed until suddenly I saw her trying to get the attention of a well built young man who seemed to me was playing hard to get. Tall and good-looking, he was with a friend and the two of them look like they were there partying and didn't care much for the pretty blue eyes blond young women.

She left the main room and I watched the young men for a few minutes who were womanizing with a couple of pretty girls. 'You deserve better than this.' I told myself. Right then I knew I had a purpose with my coming in this place and this wasn't just to get a drink. It sure didn't take me long to find out how right I was. I went to the men's room and when I followed the path Dana took, I soon found out she'd cried. When I approached her at the counter where she was sitting, I asked her when her next shift was. I knew then she wasn't in a mood for too much conversation. I also knew I love her all the more and I was ready to give my life for her and her happiness.

"I will be in next Tuesday." "I don't know if I can make it on Tuesday, I have to work till dark." "Oh yes, you will." She said turning around and looking at me with those sad beautiful pastel blue eyes. I felt my heart was melting like an icecream cone in a hundred degree hot afternoon under the sunshine and I said: 'We'll see.'

She had on a beautiful long dress which suited her to perfection. She at the precise moment looked like a princess. Precious princess I thought and I knew then there was no turning back, that I would carry this through eternity.

The next time I saw her, it was the following Tuesday I wasn't sure I could come. She seems to be more and more beautiful each time I see her. Her overwhelming smile put me in a state of mind I can't begin to describe. When I see her, it is just like I am in another world. Maybe just maybe she brings me to Wonderland. That's what it is, I told myself and this is the reason why I came here in the first place. I am to write I was told. Now I know the subject, the title, the principal characters of the story, where it began and that it will never end.

The Precious Princess of Wonderland! I also know I want for this woman all the best I could possibly give, time, money, myself, help of all kind day or night, it wouldn't matter what; I want to be there for her any time, anywhere. This is exactly what I told her this Tuesday evening. When I told her about the book I'm going to write and the title she exclaimed:

"This is my favourite movie." "You mean Alice in Wonderland. This is not the same thing. This here will be a book about you, the rest and me. It would be nice and helpful if I could take you out for diner. I will need some information, a few things I would need to know about you. I also want the story to be as close as possible to the truth." "You'll have to use your imagination. Isn't it what all writers do? Besides, I don't think my boyfriend would appreciate this very much. I am very much in love, you know?" "Yes, I know you are very capable of loving, it's written all over you. Do you know what Ronald Reagan often says?" "Not really!" "Well, he often says: 'May the best man win.'" "Oh no, no, no!" She laughed and it was almost a cry. "Don't you even dream about it." "Dreams are the best reality I know and when I finished telling you all about mine, maybe you will understand what I mean. In fact everything started with a dream, but, I'll tell you about it later."

She was quite intrigued by all of this and the only chance I had to talk to her was when I needed a drink and this is what brought me to drink a little bit more than I wished to. There was only one more thing to do and this was to write to her. So this is what I wrote to her at first.

'Precious Princess of Wonderland. I have known you only for a week young woman and already you have given me the nicest dream of my life. This is something absolutely priceless. Something that all the gold of the world couldn't buy. I know my thoughts and I can express them and I can't wait to know some of yours. You make me feel as if I was fifteen again and in love for the very first time in my life. My hope for a good relationship was endless then. It was a time when life was more promising, when faithfulness was more important and obvious to most people. We could also rely on it and it was the number one condition for a solid relationship back then. Today as much as I hate to say, it is scary to see what is going on. There is so many divorces and single parent families, one have to wonder what kind of generation is ahead of us.

Just a few months ago I went to pick up a friend and while I was waiting for him, a young boy from across the street, age four maybe five years old came to my car to talk to me. He said: 'My dad is not living with us anymore; he is living with another family in another house." "Do you see your dad sometime?" He said: "No." In a close to tears voice. I felt like getting out of the car and holding the little boy in my arms knowing perfectly well he needed it. But in today's world I couldn't do it without risking to be charged for doing it. So I told the boy to be very careful and that it was best he doesn't talk to strangers without the presence of an adult he knows.

'Some bad guys could take you away and you will be missing your mommy very much too.'

He seemed to understand what I was telling him and he went back to play with the other kids. The Lord seems to remind me of all my faults soon or later, so I can repent too.

Even though I always stay close to my children, they too grew up with separated parents. It might seem sometimes I throw the stone at somebody else, but this somebody is me too. Who is wrong and who is right, I don't think is as important as much as what is done to minimize the consequences.'

I gave this page to Dana and she responded by telling me this wouldn't qualify me to become a writer.

"Funny how things are, everybody else I showed it to was encouraging me to continue. It is true though it isn't them I'm writing about. Nevertheless, it is not how I write which is the most important, but rather the story I'm telling. I happen to think that ours is wonderful." "You're probably right, will see."

Coming out of the dance floor one time she said to me: "You were looking pretty good out there." "What did you say?" "I mean you were looking good dancing."

Another time I noticed her watching other people dancing and I could just tell she wishes she could do some of it.

"If you ever want to learn some of this stuff, let me know." "Let me guess what, you can teach me." "Yes and this absolutely free." "I'll bet you would." "I love dancing and I love teaching. I just happen to know that you would be a very good student to work with." "Sure." "You can trust me too. I would never take anything from you that you're not willing to give me, but on the other hand I will take everything and all of you if you let me to."

She smiled, she turned around and she went back to work. Besides coming to this place to see Dana now, I have started to take notes of what is going on around me. I've seen many married people with somebody else than their spouses. I've seen many of them going in and out with different partners too. Some are basically making it right there in front of others. If I wanted to I could take at least half a dozen women out of there every night I go. Some of them have so many that I doubt very much they have time to clean themselves between dates.

A young woman once brought her mom in there to celebrate the old girl's birthday and she came and asked me if I would ask her mom to dance. 'Sure!' I said and I did too, mostly because the young woman was pretty and gentle, so I couldn't refuse her, but her poor mother didn't know how to dance one bit and she had no rhythm at all. Good thing I'm not too easy to embarrass, otherwise it would have been a kind of a party for me too.

Later on I danced with the daughter and I asked her if she was happy after she'd told me she was married. She wasn't too enthusiastic about it.

"Do you want to be?" "Who doesn't?" "I can tell you one of the good ways to be."

She started to pull me towards her.

'This is not what I meant.' I told her gently pushing her back even though she was enjoyable to hold.

"Oh!" "You're a pretty woman alright and just about any guy would like to take you. You only have to choose, but I don't think this would make you happy." "What do you mean then?" "If you want to be happy young lady your best chance is to go home and love your husband and kids as you never did before."

She looked at me with a bit of stupefaction, she made a funny face and she said: 'I'm sure you're right and I will, thank you.'

She hugged me before she left, but this wasn't the same kind of hugs anymore and I could see hope in her eyes and a smile on her face. I sincerely think she'll be a princess before long.

Another time there was a gorgeous young lady sitting close to my table where I usually sit and when I asked her for a dance she said she didn't know how. I saw her earlier watching the dancers on the dance floor and I could tell it was with admiration. The conversation went on and she told me she came early to get dancing lessons. She told me there was a birthday party lately at her place and she had a dance with a good dancer and this gave her the taste for learning more. Then I invited her to come to sit at my table and we talked about different things, but mainly about the book I'm writing.

"Single?" "No, I'm married." "Where is your husband?" "He is at home babysitting our three kids." "I think you should be at home with your husband or your husband should be here with you."

She looked at me for a long moment and she asked: "Who are you?" "My name is Gaston and I'm writing a book on this kind of stuff." "Mine is Michelle and you are right, I'm a believer too and I should be at home with my husband, he is a good man." "Smoking begins with one cigarette, drinking with one glass and adultery like you here tonight. You're in the proper trap. I'm a retired dance instructor and I would gladly give you and your husband free lessons together in your kitchen rather than see you coming here by yourself. Everything which is on the shelf will sooner or later be taken by somebody, especially if it's pretty stuff like you. Think about this, would you?"

She said she will and she would look for my book. She got up and she shook my hand and hopefully she went home towards her family.

I told Dana a bit about the conversation I just had with this lady and she didn't seem to like the idea of me doing the preaching in this establishment.

'I didn't tell her anything she didn't want to hear Dana. In fact I think she left pretty happy with me and with herself. To tell you the truth, I never thought I would some day do some preaching in a bar either, if this is how you want to call it.'

There is this one guy, actually there are two. They are in their thirties and they hang around together quite a bit. So much that at first I thought they were gays. This taught me a lesson about judging others, something I should never do. One is six foot eight, two hundred and twenty pounds and the other is six foot eleven and weight three hundred and thirty pounds. The two are brothers and one time they were in front of me. One was six feet away from the bar and the other was at fourteen feet. The short one passed the beer mug to the other, but it was on top of everybody.

'Above all heads!' I told the tallest.

"You guys could be the best waiters. I wouldn't trade you for my waitress though." "This is just it, we would starve to death."

I asked the shortest once if he'd mind if I write something about them in the book of mine.

"Not at all! We are six in the family. My brother here is the tallest, my sisters are both six foot two tall, my father was six foot six and my mother is a short thing like you." "What about sex? How in the world can you kiss her at the same time without breaking your back?" "Probably easier than you shorty and this in all kind of positions too." "Well put little guy, I'll let you know when the book is out on the market."

I don't think I could have pleased him more by giving him a hundred dollar bill. I don't think he has any problems taking girls out of the bar either, for what I've seen.

I had a dream back in February of 1992, one I could call a bit strange. In this dream I was driving down the highway 97 between Kelowna and Westbank B.C. at 118.6 km.p.h at night when a cop stopped me. I rolled down my window and I asked him what was wrong.

"What is wrong Gaston is I had to stop you before you kill yourself." "How do you know my name?" "I know. Do you know how fast you were driving?" "I was driving a little fast I admit, but not enough to kill myself." "I'm not after your money Gaston and if I didn't stop you, you would be physically dead exactly one minute and seven seconds ago."

This is what he told me while looking at his watch. I looked at him a little puzzled and at the same time he stretched his arm and I could see inside his hand as clear as if it was on television the accident I would have had down the road.

"You were driving at 73.69 m.p.h." "Your radar must be wrong." I argued as I always do when a cop stop me for speeding.

"My radar is perfectly fine. I need you Gaston and I need you alive. I need you to write for me."

I laughed a little and I told him I couldn't even spell properly.

"There are a lot of people out there who can do this. You don't have to worry about this one at all." "I wrote a lot of songs, but that's it. What would you want me to write about anyway?" "What you are to write will be revealed to you in time."

Finally almost out of desperation I asked him: "Why me?" "Because you will do it."

On this I woke up, end of the dream.

During the following five years I kept watching and wondering what I could write. I even went to the church and I asked the pastor what he thinks of it.

'Wait till you know more, if God wants to talk to you again, this is his business.' He told me. I thought about writing comics or magazines, books like Superman, Spiderman or the Punisher, which young and older kids could pick up for a few cents and get messages of peace and love. Something I could maybe call: 'The King of kings, The Lord of lords and Hero of heroes.' Maybe later, who knows?

Just before I began to write this book I had a huge desire to read books as I never have before. From the time I left school until then I don't think I read three books. But then I got so hungry for reading that I read more than one hundred of them in less than six mouths. Then in this whole pile of books I read I realized there were many pages that didn't say anything. I could write the whole story of most of those books with less than ten pages except for one I considered interesting enough from the beginning to the end. It was then I believed I too could write and this brought me back to my dream.

I had to believe in this dream you see, because I had others before which became reality. Here I will describe a few of them and let you be the judge.

My dad was a fiddler. One I thought was the best in the whole country. As far as I can remember I always wanted to play as good as him, better or even play a little. While I was a kid I remember trying to learn, but the encouragement wasn't there. On the contrary, what I heard the most were things like:

'You have no ear for music, better try something else, you're boring and even worse, you'll never get it.'

As I said, my dad was a good musician, my sisters were good singers and good dancers. Who do you think I should have believed, all these great performers or the little me who knew nothing at all, especially about music?

The result was pretty discouraging also, no matter how many times I took the fiddle, I couldn't put two notes right in a row even though I tried for years. Regardless of how much I loved music and how much I wanted to play, nothing would come.

'You don't have enough talent. You wasting your time and you're polluting the air.'

Kids can be pretty mean at time and I was one of them too. Later on I tried the guitar and I had a little more success with it. I learned three sets of chords and I made my first song at age fourteen.

'It wouldn't be so bad if you could strum properly.' I heard them say. What a kick in the butt, slap in the face and a kick in the teeth at the same time this was. I should have learned karate instead, because I sure needed self-defense at that time. But the dream was still there and I never gave up wanting to play the fiddle.

One night at age fifteen I had a dream I never forgot, especially because the same one repeated itself two more times. I was in a square room by myself, just four naked walls with nothing on them, a hard wood floor, a single straight wood chair with me sitting on it and I was playing the fiddle as good as my father. Not only this, but I was tapping my feet along with it, this too just as well as him. Wow, what a dream. I got up and the first thing I did was trying the fiddle. It seemed that just a few minutes earlier I could play so good, I could still ear it.

Uh-uh, not so easy while I am awake, it looks like. I could even remember the tune I was playing. What a drag, but yet I wouldn't give up or rather the dream didn't leave me. I had the same dream again when I was twenty-seven and again at thirty-seven. But from then on I didn't have to dream anymore. The dream of my sleep, which is the dream of my life became reality.

I got up the morning after the third time and I told myself it was impossible I could play so well in my dream and not at all in real life. I got in my car and I drove the forty miles distance that separated me from my dad's place. Once there I asked him if I could borrow his spare fiddle. He came up with the stupid excuse about the fiddle did belong to one of his friend who died and his friend's son wanted it back, because his father owned it at one time.

"I'll tell you what, this guy is not here, but I'm here, let me have it and if this guy ever contacts you again for it, I'll bring it back as soon as you let me know." "On this condition you can have it."

After he tuned the fiddle up I took it home to study it, for I don't know which number of times this was. Three days later I was playing it I'd say pretty well too. I was so excited that I drove back to my dad's place to play him the tune I just learned. Only this time he couldn't say I had no ear for music anymore. After I finished playing my tune I looked at him and he seemed to be so surprised, I thought he was going to faint. He looked as if he had seen a ghost. That's how pale his was.

"You have been playing for years?" "No, three days!" "You didn't miss a single note. Who taught you?" "Nobody but myself!"

Once his surprise and my excitement settled down a bit he mentioned something about this whole thing being a miracle. He heard me play again six months later and he told me I have learned more in six months than anybody he knows did in twenty years. Wow, what a compliment. You could hardly get this out of my dad with a one thousand dollars bill, at least as far as I was concerned anyway.

There is something else to keep in mind though and this is the fact that in his days, being the only one who could play good music around would put bread on the table. I guessed that at first he saw me as a threat or competition too.

Maybe we all are like this in a way. We want to be the best. One thing I know for sure is I want to be the best for my Precious Princess.

The empty room of my dream I interpreted it as being the music studio. I was in to record my first tape back in 1996. It contains something like twenty tunes plus five of my own songs. I also made a song that year for my mom's seventy-fifth birthday call: Tango For Mama. Just as soon as it was recorded I predicted the song will go on the radio and it did. It was a little bit of a struggle to get it on, but it was all worth it.

I explained to the radio D.J that the family was celebrating mom's birthday and I made a song for the occasion and it would be nice if we could surprise her by having her to hear it on the radio. The man told me it was against the rules of the station to do this kind of things and it was out of his power to take this kind of decision.

'Nevertheless, if you want to leave the tape with me, I'll see what I can do.'

He put the tape in the stereo, listened to it for a few seconds and he asked:

"This was done in a studio?" "It sure was." "Leave this with me, I'll manage."

The next morning at around seven while I was getting ready to record from the radio one of my sisters called me all exited in tears and in laughter saying she just heard it and it was beautiful. She said she was so excited herself that she didn't know if she should laugh or cry.

The guy told me afterward people were calling to find out who made and sang this song. I was pretty proud of myself, overwhelmed and also very thankful to God who gave me all of those beautiful dreams which became reality one after another.

Another dream I had once which puzzles me a little bit is one where I play the fiddle on a big show like the Ed Sullivan Show used to be and I accompany myself with my feet on the piano. All of this for the modest amount of eight millions dollars. It might seem impossible at this point and time, but when you consider what a hockey player makes in one single game you stop questioning. It's not what you are worth I would say you get paid for, but rather for the number of people you entertain. Also what a million-dollars is today and what it will be in fifteen years from now are two different things.

As for playing the fiddle and the keyboard I already do this. At this point of my life I play the fiddle, the mandolin, the keyboard, the guitar and the banjo. I have composed over one hundred and thirty songs and I taught dancing for a period of twelve years. I had a school dance in Quebec called: Lapointe Du Plaisir and another one in Calgary called: The All Stars Dancing Music School Of Dance. Oh, I was forgetting, I also had a D.J service too, called: All Stars' D.J, also in Calgary. This last one was just because I wasn't busy enough with my equipment. I did all this having no ears for music according to a few members of my big family.

If you can take a little piece of advice I'd say; encourage anyone who likes to learn something that is good for the mind and the soul. As for playing the fiddle and the piano at the same time, I can tell you one thing, it is on the way. I built up a rig to the keyboard with pedals I can push with my foot and I can change the chords as I need, playing the fiddle, the guitar, the banjo or the mandolin. I'm having a lot of fun like a little boy by myself being a one-man band. The main advantage is that everybody shows up every time on time for practices. I got a two hundred-dollar keyboard that contains fifty rhythms, which is far more than I really need. As soon as I can control both together I will make a video and send it to a few television stations. What faith can do is unreal.

Just like my father said the first time he heard me playing the fiddle; 'it is just like a miracle.' I'd say it is the miracle of faith. The mountain I couldn't climb in twenty-six years without faith even though I wanted very badly I climbed it in three days with it.

From the first time I met Dana I can only count on my faith. Since I am fifty-four and she'll turn twenty-seven in August, there is a mountain of years between us. I still don't know how a union of this sort could be accepted in our society even supposing she loves me very much too. In the king's world, the monarchy I guess it is tolerated.

Since my writer's name is James Prince and she is a princess and I'm a child of a King. Maybe, just maybe there is a chance in a billion or less. But hey, this is enough for me to believe in it. Oh, I know some people would say I am crazy. To this I'd say it is better to be a little crazy and be happy than to be not so crazy and unhappy. It happened a few times in the last eight months when I lost faith for a moment. It felt so terrible that I was ready to cry. Then in those times I recapture myself and I say:

'There is a chance in a billion, maybe less, so quit being stupid and believe in it.'

Besides, I had another dream where Dana is surrendering herself to me with tears in her eyes. She is crying and telling me she fought all she could and she couldn't fight any longer. At this point still in the dream I held her arms and I licked all her tears from her face until she had no more. Then like coming out of a nightmare herself she tells me she has never felt so wonderfully in her whole life. All the fear she had known since she discovered she loves me was gone.

"Falling in love is always scary even more in our days and age, especially when there is a huge mountain between the two partners. I would like to hold you for the rest of the night and for the rest of my life, but maybe you should go back to work now that you're feeling much better." "I don't want to lose this wonderful feeling." "Now that you have it, it's there to stay. Certainly I wouldn't do anything to jeopardize it."

And then I woke up. Darn this was such a beautiful dream I wished I never woke up. What am I saying? Me above all should know that reality is far better than dreams.

Falling in love quickly as I did is probably the best. One thing is sure, I spend more time tasting this wonderful feeling that nothing else can replace. If I get hurt or even died from it, it is even better. I don't know a better reason to die than to die in the name of love.

Now, as I said before I couldn't stay away from her work place. The truth is I went to see her three and mostly four times a week and I still do. Yet it is far from being enough even though I consider myself very lucky to be able to see her like this. Each time I'm there, I'm having a couple of drinks and I wouldn't have any without giving her one as well. Whether she drinks it or not it is her business.

On the third week she came to me as soon as I got there and said she couldn't take it anymore. She was close to tears in saying so. I told her not to panic and to wait a couple of days that I would explain everything to her somehow. I was a little upset with myself for scaring her this way, since all I want for her in the first place is nothing but the best. I knew then I had to come up with something and very quick to gain her trust.

I got home early that night and I gathered all the pieces of idea of mine I could get together. I have some newspaper's articles with my picture on them that I cut down and I put those together with my business card. I wrote her a letter explaining she was a princess to me and there was no way I would let her serve me for a lousy $0.25.

"You're spoiling me." "Not as much as I want too. Can you imaging having Princess Diana serving you all evening for a dollar or a dollar twenty-five? Could anyone in his or her right mind do this?"

So, I put everything in an envelope, I wrote her name on it and I gave it to her the next time I went. As soon as I saw her I gave her my hope for peace. She took it and she disappeared into the restroom. When she came back with the most beautiful smile on her face I knew she was feeling much better.

"So, you are the hub cap man." "That's cheap." I said laughing. "Since everybody else calls me the hubcap king."

I am a king and you are the most beautiful princess on the face of the earth, I thought to myself. What a combination!

I realized though I was drinking way too much since I come to see her four times a week and I tried different things to cut it down. One of them was to get a large glass of seven-up to reduce the strength of my drinks, only it was making such a mess on the table that I quit, but not before telling her that if I keep it up, I would be an alcoholic before Christmas comes. Man, I don't like this idea.

I don't like going to those places either, but as you know we don't go there to drink milk or water and expect the waitress to make a good buck too. Besides, I have only one thing in mind, as a customer I mean and this is to be her best one.

There is already a mountain of years between us, plus the competition is huge. I've seen dozens of guys cruising around her. I've seen at least a dozen others massaged her back and neck. Oh, I'm sure they are only friends, but nevertheless, I have to admit it bothers me a little.

I can't blame them either for doing something I which I could do myself, meaning having some sort of physical contact as innocent as holding her hand. One thing I know for sure is I hope and pray I will never be jealous. I think jealousy is the worst thing that could happen to a relationship and make at least two persons unhappy. I'd say if you can't trust a person it's best you don't get together, even though you're very much in love. I also heard guys telling me how they fancy her. She laughed too when I told her about it.

One night I told Dana about the two beautiful pieces of music I composed. I told her I was inspired by my love for her. She asked me what kind of love I was talking about?

"You're not talking about sex, are you? Or are you talking about the pure kind of love?" "I'll tell you what kind of love I'm talking about sweetheart. I wish I was an angel of God and be able to look after you and protect you day and night where ever you go. This is the kind of love I'm talking about. I'm not talking about watching what you're doing either. I will never spy on you."

In our days and age nobody can blame her for being careful.

Out of the two pieces of music I composed I made songs, one is called; For Better or Worse and the other one is called; Everything's Yours Oh Lord. For better or worse always and forever, that's what my love is for you, forever are yours, my heart and my soul, my love will always be true. The kind that does come from above, compassion and fidelity, cleaner and purer than a dove, I'll love you through eternity.

This is just a part of it. I don't want to spoil you too much, too soon. This kind of deep feelings for another person I believe can only happen once in a lifetime. I know I always wanted to find the person I could live a lifetime with.

When I was a kid I learned a song I still sing some times, it goes to say: 'In my sweet little house in the valley, till the end of my life I will stay, my sweetheart on my knees, my children around my neck, in my sweet little house in the valley.'

I don't really know why, but my life hasn't been what I wanted. I had many dates, some steady relationships and I respected girls as my mom wanted me to, even though some of them didn't like this too much.

At this point of the book I asked Dana if she wanted to wait until it is all done or if she'd rather read some parts of it.

'I'd like to see some parts of it if you don't mind.'

I gave her this first part, which is about twenty-five pages and now, I am very impatient to know what she thinks of it, right to the point I can hardly sleep. What makes me so nervous? Oh, my lack of faith again. Also at this point and time I realized she has never said much, that she knows a lot about me and me very little about her.

Well, I know she's the most gentle kind-hearted person I ever met and I told her so. Is there all I need to know? To love her yes. To marry her, I'd say no. I know she's got what it takes to make me happy forever, but I also know I need to have what it takes to make her the happiest on earth.

The flower girl often tried to sell me a rose and then I tell her, it's not a rose I want for my princess but a rose garden.

During my agonizing waiting period I continued to write about a lot of things which didn't work to good in my life.

At age twenty-three I met a girl whom I thought could be the one mainly because she was in love with me and like most man I got hungry for sex. Did I ever pay dearly for this mistake. Of course she got pregnant against my will. Maybe sex was fun, but the consequences were disastrous. I had insisted she takes protection, but the first doctor she saw was catholic and he lectured her about what she was asking. It is as he said against all morals. For the pope maybe I told her, not for me. Three months later on I came to the conclusion we weren't suited and I suggested we part from each other.

'Not this simple!' She said then. 'I'm carrying a baby, you're the father and if you want to see it, you'll have to marry me.'

This was Hiroshima over my head, the biggest blow I ever received in my life. This was not at all what I wanted from early age. It has crossed my mind too that she had purposely got pregnant. This was not at all the little house in the valley kind of life I always dreamed of. I loved the children I was going to have in life long before they came to this world. Maybe it is self-esteem, I don't know, but I never heard anybody say this.

One thing I knew for sure is I was not going to abandon my child before he was born or at any other times. So as a result I married my child to make sure I know him and he knows me.

After six years of this life I felt like a prostitute in my own home. I was getting impotent by the day, trying to fulfill the duties of a married man to a woman whom I didn't love, at least not enough. Big problem! First of all, I was and I still am against divorces. I think when a man or a woman for this matter gave his word he should stick to it. I tried to love her, but I guess love is not something you can force on anybody, including yourself. I'm a sex lover like most Frenchmen and I didn't want to lose it even though it did cost me dearly. Lose it I was told was going to happen if I was to stay in my situation. My physician of the time referred me to a shrink when he realized I had no physical defects, not this way anyway.

'Impotency or divorce are your choices.' The latter said. 'The decision his yours.'

I guess I could live in sin continuously too like many people do, especially before I invited the Lord into my life, but for me anyway, this was probably the worst option. I won't go into the divorce's details, for one thing there is no need for it, secondly, who wants to know? There is only one thing I will say about it and this is because it could help someone else. My lawyer told me though it was the best one he ever performed. To this day I still don't know if it was because he wanted more money from me or because of a clause I asked for. The clause stipulates that if any of the two parties were to move further than one hundred miles away from the other, both of us would have to pay half of the expenses for visiting the children. This way I wasn't afraid anymore she could remarry and take the children who knows where, even in a foreign country. Legally she owes me more than twelve thousands dollars of traveling expenses that I never mentioned to her and I never will, except maybe to tell her that she can keep it.

All I will say is I managed for her to accuse me of adultery and this did it. I don't think there was a battle between good and bad either in our case. All it was I think is we were two incompatible people who got together not knowing any better and we cannot give what we don't have. What makes me say this is the fact we didn't have too much of proper directions in life. For this matter I also think we didn't know how to give directions either. What make me say this is the fact I have two grandchildren from my only son and they don't carry my last name. My son tells me also he wouldn't have anymore kids. It bothers me enough to talk about it. For me to have my family tree cut down, especially now the world seems to be against clear cutting and wants to save the forests. So much for the posterity I have anticipated in life. I told my son lately the only choice I had left was to remarry and have more children of my own, question of testing the ground.

'It would feel funny to have brothers and sisters younger than my own kids.' was his response.

"We are both responsible for this situation, aren't we?" "Partly, I guess." "The fact is right now I'm in love with a beautiful and intelligent young woman and we never know what may happen. I know for sure I wouldn't be in a relationship myself without the deep love bound to last a lifetime and beyond. Also for the first time in my life now I have the time to take care of a woman properly, children patiently and in an enjoyable financial position to do so." "This is great, enjoy your life." "Well, your are very important to me too and so is your sister. You are both grown up people and you have a life of your own. I still can be there for both of you for little you'll need." "Sure, be happy, you deserve it." "Thanks son, it is nice to have your approval too." "Are you having a big wedding or a small ceremony?" "I don't know yet. I'd better ask her if she would marry me first, don't you thing? Or yet ask her a second time for a first dinner, something I will do very soon." "Oh, you're not this far yet?" "She doesn't know anything about this at all. The only thing she knows is I love her, because I told her in many ways. In fact, I'm pretty sure this book I'm writing is the largest declaration of love in the world since Jesus. I might be in the record book of Guinness someday, who knows? This is said without pretension. I must be an extremist too and I never knew a thing about it. I do know though that I would lay my life down for her at any time." "Wow dad, I guess you really got it bad." "Yes Guy, I never experience anything so powerful in my whole life. I thing it is the unconditional kind of love I heard people talking about. No matter if she loves me or not, no matter what she does, I really believe that absolutely nothing can stop me from loving her." "What would you do if she is a lesbian dad?" "Well, I know she's not, but if this was the case son, I would get on my knees and pray until God Himself change her." "What if she is and doesn't change in twenty years?" "I might put a cushion under my knees, but I wouldn't quit even then, my love for Dana is forever." "I believe you dad now and I am convinced no one can discourage you from loving this lady. I promise you I will never try this again." "Great son, I'm glad you came to the same conclusion as mine."

I don't believe in coincidences in life. I believe everything happens, happens because it is meant to be. In a Bible's study once three years ago I brought up marriage was not meant to be like we know it today, that a common-law marriage was just as good as a conventional one for as long as the two partners were sincere and committed to each other for as long as they live. Nobody can hide forever, so they too have witnesses. Marriage the way we know it today exists only since the thirteen century and it was made by men mainly to control men and family. The two will become one flesh. The only way this is possible is when a man and a woman have sex together.

Can you imagine girls and boys of nowadays facing their Creator and telling Him having two hundred wives or husbands in a year or even having half a dozen the same day? If you ask them if they are married they say no way or never.

We were told: 'May each man and each woman have his own partner.'

Men and governments who wanted to control everything I think have really lost it now or maybe this is exactly what they were after, after all. Women have children who have on their birth certificates: 'Father unknown.' You can call it the way you want, but I call it the fornication race. Who is going to have who, how many times and how often. Maybe aids will be their trophy. Unfortunately it is often the inexperienced one who gets caught. You know what I mean, don't you? I talk about the ones who give themselves sincerely.

Last Saturday night I had decided it was time for me for straitening things up with one girl who comes to the dance and teases a couple dozen men, me included. I teased her like I never teased anyone before. Only one thing though, I'm afraid Dana saw it and she might have got a bad opinion of me. I'm sure I was looking like I was after this girl, which wouldn't speak to good for me at all. Looking like a dirty old man or a pig, I'm sure it's not the best thing to do to attract a beautiful young princess. She wasn't too much for smiling the rest of that evening and neither the following time I saw her. So I asked her if she was upset with me for something. She said no, but I don't know. I think I've got a good lesson out of this experience too.

My observation tells me the governments and the court system are responsible for most of the divorces. Forty some years ago if a woman had children and a husband who didn't work she had a better chance to have welfare if he was gone. (Separation) If she was alone with her kids, she had barely enough to support everybody. If the woman next door kept the same kids she would get four times more money than the mother for keeping the same kids. (Separation) If a couple was on welfare the same thing happened. If they stay together, they didn't have enough most of the time. If they separate each of them could collect a cheque. Before to get a divorce you needed a very good reason and now, one can put out her tongue and the other one gets it for mental cruelty.

The carpenter is the one who builds the houses, but with his own salary only he cannot qualify for a mortgage. So he has to send his wife to work to meet ends meet. Again this is a way to cause the separation. The result we see today is that our kids are raised by strangers most of the time. All this was calculated very carefully by the beast.

Up to fifty some years ago the man was choosing his wife. The marriages were lasting much longer than they do today. Today it is the other way around and the marriages don't last. Both men and women are calling the talk shows like Dr Laura to ease their conscience and to get a kind of approval for their divorce. They get it too, but on the Day of Judgment it is not Dr Laura they will meet. They will meet a faire Judge then, a Judge who told us not to separate what He has united.

Not only that, here I'll bring up a story of a man who is sixty years old, a man who have lost his wife six months ago through cancer. He is extremely vulnerable. He never did anything in the house, his wife always did all. She actually took her roll as a woman and wife very seriously. He doesn't even know how to do the dishes, nevermind the rest of it. He worked for forty years and he saved and invested millions. He was the head of his own company. He is a pretty good catch, I would say. Here comes the trauma. He met a pretty forty-year old lady. Oh yes, they call themselves ladies. She talks nice, walks nice, dances nice and even makes love nicely. There is no need to get married nowadays either, do we? Very common scenario, wouldn't you say? Here is the trap. She stayed with him under the same roof for six months and she can prove it, that's it. She earned half of what his got made and saved in forty years. The same judge who gives this to her will tell me and you that prostitution is illegal in our country.

This is not quite the King Solomon's wisdom, isn't it? Let me tell you what it is. It is another way to break the family down and discourage men and women to get together.

I don't know about you, but I sure can speak for myself here. The last two experiences I had were bad enough to scare me for the rest of my life, not counting a few other times that weren't too great either. It is a miracle if I am still in business and if I'm still alive.

A lawyer told my last partner she could get half of everything I own. Yet every hour she worked at my place including cooking, cleaning the house and making the bed she was paid for it. And I'm not talking sex here, I'm talking cash. Funny I didn't get anything for my contribution in this relationship. Sex even though it was not bad, I don't think was worth the forty-five thousand dollars it cost me and I was very lucky a common friend slowed her down. Besides, according of her reactions sex was better for her than for me anyway. It's not very often I had multiple orgasms like she did. It took me three years to find out she was after the money even though we were living under the same roof. Is this what they call; gold diggers? We are not to be judgmental, but can I be a bit realistic?

I discovered the whole thing a week before she left. Am I slow or what? We were passing by a multimillion dollars ranch when she told me she is going to own it some day. I looked at her a little puzzled and I asked her with whose money? I can see a bit of mine, plus some from our common friend who laid us down on her will, a pour lady made millionaire by lotto and her parents' will. At this precise moment it crossed my mind she had somebody else lined up already. I didn't say a word though knowing very well it is better most of the time. A week later she was gone. It wasn't too much of a surprise, because I knew she was a run away kid in her childhood as well as a wife by then. I was out hunting with a friend of mine that morning and she left like a thief. I was hurt, but at the same time I thought it was for the better. Two weeks later she came back with friends and relatives to pick up her furniture and the rest of her things. I had no problem with this at all. I even offered to help if it was needed. One of her relatives who assaulted me twice before, a karate expert was with them and he kicked the door fifteen feet away from the house. He insulted me, but I ignored him. I gave them the permission to go in to get everything which belongs to her.

I was sitting in my van in front of the house talking to a good lady friend when we suddenly heard the blast and we saw the door flying out. What went through my mind at a lighting speed was; there are three guys in my house all bigger than me and one of them who provoked me many times before and he would love to break my face. No point even trying to talk to him, it wouldn't do any good. I'm legally allowed to use a minimum of force to defend my property and myself. It was hunting season the fifth of October and I had my automatic 30-06 beside me. So I decided to put a bullet in it and to shoot in the air in a different direction and to give them the necessary warning. I told them I gave the permission to take everything that belongs to her in the house, but I didn't give them the permission to break the house. Well, her brother-in-law, the karate expert and kick-boxer, this skin head thought it was his duty to walk against me anyway, right to the point where I told him pointing my finger at him and telling him he was close enough. After I put the riffle away they finished loading their trucks and they went away. They called the police and they told them I had pointed the gun at them. I was arrested the same day and I was put behind bars. What can I say? Maybe something like; so much for having the right to defend ourselves and our property in our country, either you risk your life, your reputation or both. Also at this specific time I couldn't afford a lawyer, so I went to legal aid for help and I was told they couldn't help me. Reason number one, I didn't have a criminal record. Secondly, there was no risk for me to go to jail. In other word if I was a very bad criminal and if I had shot the animal, they would've helped me. Who said that the crime doesn't pay?

THE HUB CAP COLLECTION

The largest hubcap collection in Canada

Chapter 2

I have a good question for you people.

Where do you think your thoughts and your ideas come from? Now try to be honest and answer this for yourself before you see what I'm going to say. Remember too that I searched for over five years before finding the idea for this book I'm writing now even though I wanted it very badly. I also got the idea at a time when I least expected it and I wasn't looking for it anymore.

At the last exam of my graduation we were asked to write something on a book we never had a chance to read. All we had was the title. I had many songs written by then and I had a discussion about ideas once earlier with the teacher who is also the director of the school. I told him then that without an idea a person couldn't likely write something decent. He argued with me then. Anyway I could see all the other students looking around and wondering what in the world they were going to do. The teacher couldn't say anything before the time allowed for the exam was over. I laid my head on the desk searching for an idea from the words of the title. After forty minutes the teacher knocked on my head asking me if I was alright. I told him I was searching for an idea. He excused himself and I continued thinking. When one hour was gone, I was finally successful and I had it. I had only thirty minutes left then. I didn't have time to make all the corrections, but I had something written and this was the very best composition in French of all my high school. When the results came back to us two months later from the Ministry of Education, I had the surprise of my life. My average in French was usually around 65 per cent, just enough to pass. But then I had a mark of 76 per cent, thirty per cent more than the best one after me who had only forty-six per cent and she was the best student of the whole class. The Ministry of Education recognized their mistake and allowed a thirty points adjustment to each of the students, except for me of course. This would have given me 106 per cent. There is no justice, but this way it allowed the class to pass except for two students who failed anyway. All they had was the 30 per cent the government gave them. Without meaning it I proved to the teacher and to the class that my theory on ideas and thoughts was the best after all.

Coming back to my book, I was saying the idea came to me at the moment I least expected.

It was two years ago I asked in a church's meeting the same question. Most people said the ideas are within us. I told them then I believe if my ideas were from myself I would write the very best book ever. I would write the very best songs and poems with the very best music ever. If the ideas were within me I could invent anything I want and I will be super rich almost overnight. If the ideas were within me there would be no limits to my accomplishments. Some of them said we are like antennas and we were catching the ideas when they travel by close enough to us. I think this is close to the truth. How many of you never said to himself; why didn't I think of this before? Or, I should've thought of this myself. A lot of times I heard a song somebody else wrote and I told myself: 'I could've written this.' The thing is I had the same idea, but I didn't put it on paper and someone else who was more receptive than me did it. How many times did you say he or she game me this idea?

One time last year I had an idea while I was making breakfast. I thought at the time it was the very best idea I ever had. I was so exited that I was dancing of joy and praising myself about it, but I didn't write it down right away, because I was busy and I took it for granted it was mine to stay. Big mistake, now I wish I let my eggs burn, because for days afterward I tried to get it back and I couldn't. I even prayed to get it back. I tried to put myself in the same position I was in when this idea came to me without expecting it. It was just useless, the idea was gone no matter how much I tried and all the efforts I put in to get it back. It is so much gone and forgotten that even if I would get it again, I wouldn't be able to tell if this is the same or not.

'Your second best idea would have been to write it down.' My son told me. 'Yes son, but you see I had no idea it was going to go away.'

Do you see now what I mean? If we were in control or master of our ideas we would be able to do all we want. Bang, bang, books, songs, poems, inventions, if I am the master of my thoughts and my ideas there is nothing to stop me, right? The strangest thing of all is that since I had this discussion about ideas in this particular meeting, admitting my ideas and my thoughts were from God, I composed six beautiful songs with my best music to my taste anyway and I began to write this book. I also proposed three of my inventions to the government of B.C. I have to admit though I don't have much faith in our government.

I read something once where it said: 'Only a small percentage of people who have ideas benefit from them themselves.'

I am a carpenter by trade and one time I was building a house for a university teacher and I came up with a number of good and new ideas which impressed the owner and made things a little bit better. Only there was another carpenter on the site who seemed to steal my ideas all the time and take credit for them. I kind of got upset with this and I talked to Sylvestre the teacher about it. The latter said to me: "Let him have them. They might be all he's going to get in his life. You on the other hand are a man with ideas and you will never be short of them. You'll have plenty of them until the day you'll die." "Maybe so, but what good is it if they get stolen all the time?" "You'll get an idea for this too."

Six months later Denis, one of Sylvestre's friends bought an old hotel and he proceeded to make a huge house out of it. He chose the other carpenter I think because he was two bucks an hour cheaper than me. My wages were $12.00 per hour back then.

Thirty days later Denis asked me if I would come and look at what was done then. He told me the carpenter he hired couldn't finish the project because of a lack of ideas. The architects wanted too much money and he asked me if I had any ideas of how to finish the job. Within a half a minute I knew how to do it.

"I can do it but I need $25.00 an hour, two other men who listen to me and don't argue the orders plus a contract that pays me until the job is completed." "How do I know you can do the job?" "Simple, if I can't do it you don't have to pay me anything."

Four months later he had a house opening party with more than one hundred guests, which included architects, doctors, lawyers, general contractors, blueprint designers and the other carpenter who couldn't finish the job in the first place. The latter came to shake my hand and congratulated me.

"Job well done! I had no idea it could be done like you did it." "Oh, ideas are free, they come and go. I just happen to be lucky enough to have some at the right time."

May 15 1998

Today I am pretty sure I have to write the saddest page of this book and live through the saddest day of my live. I feel so hurt it makes me want to be the Jeremiah of my time. The last six days have been nerves breaking. I know now for sure that something is bothering Precious, only I don't know weather it is my encounter with the other woman or the part of the book I let her have to read. The last three days were almost unbearable. My stomach has been up side down and I feel bugs all over my arms and legs. I just feel a disaster is about to happen.

I went to see Dana two nights ago, but she wasn't working. I asked the working girl what happened to her.

'She didn't want to work tonight.'

This was the clue I was expecting. This girl used to smile all the time too, but that night, I didn't see a single smile on her face. I asked myself this question; is it this strange and scary to see a man in love nowadays? Is it this much outdated? Maybe it was for the best Dana wasn't there. When I walked in, the woman I wanted to give a lesson to about teasing others was in the lobby and she walked inside with me. The whole thing looked like she was with me and this could make things a lot worse. One thing I did though was to walk in front of her, something I wouldn't normally do. I came back home early that night to my son's surprise since there was nothing to hold me back in this place. I told him when he looked at me with a question mark on his face that she wasn't there tonight.

I went to my bedroom and I read over and over again the part of the book Dana has. I couldn't find anything in it that could hurt or scare her. I read it and I tried to put myself in her shoes. I always been in the open with her and I couldn't see what bothers her. There is nothing in there she doesn't know already right from the beginning.

When Christmas came I gave her a card telling her about my love for her and some jewellery. If I am going to call her Precious Princess, I am going to treat her like one as well. Nothing less than gold, diamonds, pearls and rubies will be good enough for her.

There was a specific necklace I looked for, but I couldn't find it, one that could really suit a queen or a princess. I bought magazines, I went to many jewellery stores and I couldn't find what I wanted for my Precious Princess. They could make me the one I like one man told me, only $36000.00. I told him I didn't mind the price, but I don't thing she would accept something this pricey as a first or a second gift. I feel I owe her so much that nothing is too good or too expensive.

She has already turn down a car one time, a mutual found investment on another and my life insurance I double when I first met her, because I couldn't get my heart to settle down. My age has nothing to do with this.

I just about fell down a cliff and this not very long ago while I was trying to retrieve a hubcap. Just a little one inch in diameter tree held me back from falling one hundred feet. What went through my mind at the precise moment is what I would like to do before I go.

Dana is studying to become a counselor and she told me this right from the beginning and I'd like to help her buying an office. I know how much it would've helped me to get a start in life. Oh she'll manage anyway no matter what and I know this. This is exactly what she told me too. One can't give this woman anything. Isn't it natural to want to help the loved ones though? I sure think so.

"This money is for your family." "My Family will have more than enough to fight over."

Last night I wasn't feeling too good about things. I felt there was something wrong in the air. I told my son before I left the house I was foreboding an encounter and encounter it was. As soon as I walked in I spotted Precious and I went to stand in her section. She used to be waiting for me with a big special smile and my drink in her tray when I walked in. But that night, she wouldn't even serve me. After ten minutes of waiting I went to sit further behind the counter still in her section. Then almost ten minutes later she brought me my regular drink and I pay her without giving her a tip and even without thinking about it. I asked her how she was doing, but she didn't answer me and she walked away.

I knew the storm was coming down on me with lighting, thunder, hail and I didn't know what else. I saw her talking to the manager and shortly after she came to sit beside me for the very first time.

'I don't want you to come here anymore. I don't want you to come near me at all, not here, nowhere. You're scaring me. I'm twenty-six and you're fifty-four. What you're doing is very close to stalking, if you don't quit I'll call the police.'

Bang, the gun just got unloaded and I'm the target.

'Ok, ok!' I said and she took off. I was expecting a storm not world war 3. I always thought I wouldn't hesitate to put myself between her and the bullet to save her life. But what if she holds the gun herself? I had more of the impression it was a cannon shut. There was absolutely nothing I could have done to stop it. The bombardment of her words coming out of her mouth was more like the bombs launched by a squadron of fighter planes. It seemed like hours to me, but evidently, it only lasted a couple of minutes. Each and every word was a dart that pierced me right through the heart. I should have died right then on the spot, but we can't kill real love, can we? Love will never die and I'm full of it. So Dana, you can get rid of me if you want to, but you will never get rid of my love for you.

Like I said in my song, I'll love you through eternity. Love is also what you are afraid of. I absolutely understand your fear too. I know you know I'm not a dangerous man except for the fact I'm full of love. So if you think that love is very dangerous, you have all kind of reasons to be afraid of me.

The fact is the whole society is having problems. More and more men and women are afraid of each other and they have a lot of reasons to be. I didn't even finish my drink and I didn't want to cry in her or anybody else's face, for that matter. It was the ladies' nights, sure they call them ladies and they were serve by half naked men, which didn't impress me one bit. I felt sick to my stomach and I left knowing that if I stay, I'll have some cleaning up to do and I wasn't in a mood for this.

Almost all the women of my relationship tried to dispossess me. To find someone like Dana is a real blessing. A greater blessing would be to find someone like her to love me back. What am I saying here? To find someone like her it's impossible. She is absolutely only one of a kind.

There was a man at my place three days ago who asked me what he has done wrong. He said he never cheated on his wife, that he always supported her and did everything he could do to make her happy.

'Don't question yourself anymore. You see, not only the governments and the courts of justice are corrupted, but also the whole society is. It influences everybody including my old parents.'

Forty-five years ago we saw isolated divorce cases. Now there are more than 50 per cent of marriages that end up in divorces and only 10 per cent of the other half that is happy. This means there is only 5 per cent of the whole population who is happy in marriage. 50 per cent of the population who promised to the most important person in their live to love and cherish until death do them apart. Not only they said and swore they will, but they also signed a contract to seal the whole thing. No wonder I can't trust anybody anymore. I can't take a cheque from nobody or make a deal on a handshake, because there is more than 50 per cent of the world which is not trustworthy. Not trustworthy with their own second half, nevermind being honest with me, a stranger. I don't really know if this many people feel they are dead or if they feel they are dying, but the stats are there to show us.

The new wave is to give a cheque, which is perfectly good, walk out with the merchandise, go to the bank and cancel it. Then if I'm stupid enough to take the matter to court, which takes around three years and cost four to ten times the value of the cheque that was given to me in the first place, all of this to be told by a judge: 'I'm sorry for your lost.' Because he feels sorry for the con artist who goes to say lying through his teeth he wasn't satisfied with the merchandise. The real reason a person goes to court is for the principal of it.

Only 5 per cent of the population is happy in marriage. Not much is it? This is the same percentage than the breaking and entry which are solved by the police not only in this province, but also across this country. Neither one of them deserve congratulations, do they?

Two years ago I called the police five times for stolen goods. No one showed up even once.

Ten puppies and a cage got stolen one time, a little Ford ranger another, registrations from the two vehicles we were driving a different time right in front of the house on a Sunday morning, a dune buggy and finally the four wheels and tires out of my 4x4. They were so nice, they left the front end of the truck in the dirt.

It makes me laugh when I hear on the news that the crime rate is down 12 per cent. Easy to believe when we know that only 10 per cent of all the calls are answered. On the other hand when I tried to defend the property and myself, the cops were there fairly quick. They arrested me and locked me up for about two hours. They released me the same day, but the crown decided to follow through. My lawyer said it was a waste of time and money for a lot of people. I'd say so too, especially for me. It cost me $2000.00 not counting all the trips to the courthouse and more.

The main reason they did pursued I told the lawyer is because of the nationality of the name on top of the accusation sheet. 'It makes sense.' he said, 'I never thought of this.' They also have another reason and this would be to try to put a criminal record on me, what resembles very much to the mark of the beast. (Mark of the system)

But there is worse. A young couple from Quebec who lives in Kelowna now was at my place today and they were telling me they had to pay more than ten thousand dollars in lawyer's fees to prove that what was stolen from their house belongs to them.

The cop who arrested me knew very well the real guilty party one wasn't me. He told me though something I already knew. He told me there were in the book of law al least forty points of law with which he could keep me in if he wanted to, but he said he wasn't interested to do this. The cop let me go, but the crown decided I was a criminal and for this reason I had to be persecuted.

I don't know how it is for others, but I moved to B.C. from Alberta in 1990 and in just about every trip I made back and forth, I was stopped by the police just because of the colour of the plate. When I had red plates I was stop by B.C. police and now that I live in B.C., I am stopped just about every time I go to Alberta. I have nothing to hide, but I find this pretty annoying, I'd say, especially because I can't get the visit of a cop when I get stolen and I need one. See, the cop on the road brings in money to the beast, but the one who could come to my place would cost money without any chances of income and they don't care for my lost.

It has been ten days since the encounter with Dana and the pain is still unbearable. I asked myself the same question over and over again. How a person could suffer so much and not die from it? Yet my faith wouldn't allow me to despair or cry.

I tried to find out a way to get back to see her without getting into trouble. If I didn't love her so much it would be so much easier. It's the takers a person has to look out for, not the givers. Love helps, love gives, love is patient, love waits, love hurts and love is wonderful.

I cannot forget though that I was in court not very long ago for defending my property and myself. To have a chance to win the case I would have had to drag my opponents in their own dirt. Since it is not a very godly thing to do, I thought it was best to cut it short. Also Jesus said to make friend quickly with my opponents at law as soon as I can. Matthew 5, 25. I chose a different option which was offered to me. This was to get out without a trial on a peace bound. The judge made me understand that if I do anything at all to disturb peace there will be an automatic five hundred-dollar fine and a criminal record. Having this much faith in the justice system as cold as just-ice, I was probably better off this way, having no risk to get it unless I make a fool of myself.

Since I want to go see my mom in Florida from time to time I better be careful. The judge asked me if I understood correctly. I told him I kept peace for over fifty years and that six months is nothing as long as certain people stay away from me.

Don't you have the bad luck to have a car accident either, especially one causing death, because by the time the investigation is over, chances are good you'll be charged and end up with a criminal record too.

As far as I know there are not even five per cent of women who knows much about cars or mechanic and maybe a weak ten per cent of men. I also heard that here in B.C. a lot of people need a lawyer to collect what is due to them from the Insurance they have honestly paid as well. You better get a good one too who is highly reputed, otherwise you'll be better go to the store and get toilet paper, because it really make you want to shit.

I followed a case on the news last spring of a man who killed the fire chief's wife in a car accident. The breaks were defective on his truck and he was charged. He got a four year jail term, same as another man who was convicted for stabbing his wife forty-seven times. Really????? Where are we going? The killer went South for two weeks and he got caught on his way back. Before he left he put the dead body of his wife in the trunk of his car and he left it there to rot. He got just four years for such a crime????????

The thing is if you have a criminal record the government, the court and the police have a grip on you that you can hardly escape. It is kind of the return of slavery for you. When I dispute my last speeding ticket in court the cop brought back everything that was against my driving record. It is just like you have to pay over and over again for your past mistakes, but for this time at least the woman judge told the cop she wouldn't hold my previous ticket which was three years old against me.

What about when cops do something wrong? I was coming down from Salmon Arm one time and a couple of miles before Enderby there is a down hill with double lines about five kilometres long. There was a fairly new car in front of me at 40 km/h in an 80 km/h zone. The road on my side was wide enough four three cars, but this old man would drive right in the middle of it leaving me with only two choices. This was to either be patient and stay behind or pass a bit on the double lines. The driver hit the breaks every five seconds or so and you could bet it was an elderly person who was driving.

You can imagine I was tempted to pass at least a dozen times, but some how I found enough patience to wait and to stay behind. We finally reached another road where I could pass finally, but suddenly there was an oncoming car speeding and then went the flashers and the siren. Dirty cop, I thought, you're supposed to fight crimes. I was saved by my patience, but nevertheless, the trap was well set up.

It happened again another time when I was coming back from Calgary. This time though it was a little bit different. The actual ticket giver was waiting down the hill. It looked even more of an old driver than the first time mainly because of the weather. The road was a little bit slushy in an early winter evening. The car in front of the line was holding something like forty cars behind. The driver hit the breaks thirty times a minute and he wouldn't drive more than 32 km/h, except where there was the first stretch of the road where we could pass him. There was a pickup truck between me and this first car. Finally after twenty-five minutes of extreme patience the pickup passed the little old man in the little white car and so did I. Guess what, the ticket guy was spotted just in the right place just at the right time. When the officer gave me the ticket I told him I was going to dispute it. He said not to forget if I do it, it could cost way more, even up to a thousand dollars. Sound a bit like blackmailing to me. Pay and shut up or else. I asked the woman judge later on about this and she just said, no way.

Shortly after this the truck took off, but not before I took the plate number though. Then I went after the little white car, thinking it can't be very far for he was driving so slowly. After sixty minutes at 100 km/h, I still didn't reach it. I wanted to get his plate number as well. No luck, but then came to my mind the first time a similar incident was done to me. Funny I said to myself, this guy who was driving so slowly now cannot be reach at all. We were in the Rockies and I knew there was not any transversal road. I hate to go back, but I hate even more to let what I thought was going on, going on. So I did turn around and I went back to the same long hill to find exactly what I was expecting. The little white car was leading a long line of other vehicles again. Any question about why I lost respect for this kind of authority? I came home that night and I wondered for a long time about what I was going to do with this information. The pastor of the church where I used to go to is an ex cop of the same police force and when I mentioned to him what I saw, he said the police is not allowed to entrap anybody.

So I wrote to the watch commander in Vancouver who wrote me back it was found nothing wrong doing in this particular officer.

So I concluded he was only executing the orders. I talked to someone from this region later on about the same cop and he told me this officer was moved away because of deaf treats. No wonder.

Did you ever wonder why cops in the West are regularly relocated? If he's a nice guy he might have a hard time giving a ticket to a friend and if he's a bad one someone wants to kill him. In both cases the beast would lose money.

Last year I was stop for speeding, well, 97 km/h in an 90 km/h zone on highway 33, now update to 100 km/h. I had just bought a little Hyundai two days before and knowing I have ten days to transfer the papers, I didn't worry too much. Well, maybe I should've, because there was a little error on the papers the cop said, which the insurance people couldn't find. But it cost me dearly anyway. The cop concluded I wasn't insured and he said he will throw the whole book at me after he told me to get my car off the road.

I guess he did too. My car was towed away $90.00 and he handed me a speeding ticket $115.00 and another one for none insurance $575.00. Considering I just paid $700.00 for the car, I thought this was a little bit excessive. I didn't think it was making sense how they could charge almost $600.00 for one day of none insurance when it cost $500.00 for the whole year to insure it.

I told the officer I had a truck and a trailer to come and pick up the car with another driver. To this he said the towing was already on the way. The whole incident happened fifteen minutes from town, but the towing and my ride arrived at the same time. Only it was forty-five minutes later. I found out later on from my friend Ray who owns a towing business that by law I had the choice of my own as who is to tow my vehicle. If the car had been towed to a compound yard I would've understand it a little bit better, but it was towed to my own place. I took the matter to court, but as you already know, you can tie them all together or wish to, because they all work for the same cause and this is to take your money away. All of this is done in a way it looks like they do it for the best of the community. The same officer told the judge he has been nice to me by calling for my ride.

While I was waiting for my ride I asked him for how much money he was giving tickets in a day. He answered ten to sixty thousand dollars depending on how dirty he wants to be. No wonder they want our guns away from us, because if they keep it up certainly some of them will get killed. A good man is not likely to kill a bad one, but a bad one will.

People can only stand oppression for a time before they wake up to it. This is only minor things I'm talking about here; there is a lot worse happening and a lot worse to come.

With all of the taxes they are collecting, you would thing there is enough money to run the country and to put some away for the bad days. I have the feeling they are installing guillotines to cut our heads off with.

Did you ever thing of what ten per cent of all the money earned in Canada would be? Then compare this to the number of politicians we have or we really need. No wonder every once in a while there is one of them who gets caught trying to get a bigger piece of the pie. Quebec (Shawinigate), B.C. (Bingogate)

Last year I predicted that within ten years just about all drugs will be legalized. The next day I went to have breakfast in a restaurant and what hit my eyes on the first page of the Province newspaper of Vancouver is an article about two Vancouver doctors who insist heroin should be legalized. Jeez I said, I hardly had the time to predict it.

There is a lot of talk about legalizing marijuana at the present time too. This I only give a year or two before it is done. When half of the population will be frozen it will be easier to put them down.

I also only give a year for the governments of the provinces of Canada to run casinos all over the country. Only forty years ago, if I was caught playing poker for money I was thrown in jail. What happened to our integrity?

At the time I started writing this book April 24/1998, I thought the rate of divorce was fifty per cent, but I heard on the radio on May 22/1998 it was up to sixty-five percent. I think the real percentage of gays and lesbians is pretty high too. This means the time of the devil is running out. The anarchy is at the door.

When governments have to overtax and punish the smokers, the drinkers, the gamblers and men who need a prostitute to pay their debt, there is something wrong in the system. Don't forget all of you people to thank all these bad guys for saving our country, which I don't think can be save anymore anyways. When they have to legalized gambling, drugs, prostitution and who knows what else. Don't you thing it is scary?

Leaders of our countries who allowed millions of babies to be killed every year before they even see the light. Sorry, this might be wrong because they, I am sure can see the light before anyone of us. The way I know my God, I'm sure He takes them with Him right away.

I don't think He can put up with what is going on very much longer though. One thing too, He always warns people ahead of time and maybe this is the real purpose of this book here. See Amos 3, 7. 'Surely the Sovereign Lord does nothing without revealing his plan to his servants the prophets.'

In the last three years there was a very big effort to pull Bibles out of the schools. The beast knows very well the students will open their eyes and find out about all this brain washing process done by churches and the knowledge will increase as it is prophesized by Daniel. See Daniel 12, 4. Now, I'd say it is just a matter of little time before it's done, since the government now has control of our children. Well, they can look at you, the children I mean, when you're mad and say: 'If you spank me, I'll put you to jail.' And yet be right about it. If I had said this to my dad when I was a kid, I wouldn't be here today to write about it.

Seventeen years ago in Quebec, I fought against the obligation to wear the seatbelt. I was saying and I still do that it was my life and my property they were talking about, that my taxes were paying for the roads and the hospital's bills, that my money was paying for my car insurance.

I should also be the one to decide what to do with my life, where and what to tie myself to. If I ever get caught with not wearing it, I'll go to court pleading I'm not to tie myself up to the things of this world. Besides, I don't think the law is constitutional either. I said it right on television; this was the end of our freedom in Canada. I said then that within twenty years the government will be in my own home with laws to take my rights away. Another thing is I hate it and I feel if I ever dive in the water with the car, it is the seatbelt that is going to be the cause of my death. In a head on accident it is also it that would kill you. If someone hit me in my driver's door the seatbelt is holding me in place so I can get hurt a little bit harder. So, what is left? In town maybe at thirty miles an hour or less and yet I would feel safer if I didn't wear it, so I could get out of the car and run if it was necessary to save my life. I'm pretty sure if they were reporting every death caused by the seatbelt, which it kills as many people as it saves or more, no one would want to wear it anymore. On one side they say cigarettes kill thousand of people every year.

According to the reports cigarettes kill more people than road accidents and yet there is no law to stop smoking. Money, this is what they make with both of those two laws. In fact that's all it is. They don't care about your life or mine, only the money they can make out of you and me. All of those laws feed the beast and in the mean time the lawyers, the doctors and all the professionals make big buck so everything is fine, right? All of this is perfect for them all, especially for the lawyers, because the robberies, the divorces, the accidents and many more bring them a lot of money and they are the ones who make the laws.

If a man uses a gun to kill a bunch of people, they say no one should own a gun. They are using this excuse to get all the guns registered and they will use the same excuse to take them away from us. What would they do if the same idiot took a car and drove it to a crowd, killing more people he could with a gun?

Anything can be a weapon to the evil one. One of the main reasons the seatbelt law was made is because it will make millions of criminals who are capable to pay the fine or have no other choice if they want to keep driving.

Now they are in your home and this much sooner than the twenty years expiration I was talking about and this with the gun's law, the burning law, the kids, the clothes line, the gas containers, the satellites and more.

If you'd kept the newspapers of the last twelve months and count the number of murders, it is enough to be scared. To see how many elderly people who got hurt and stolen for their lousy pension's money. To have this happening in our supposedly civilized country, it is unacceptable. It is probably linked directly to the none-spanking law. The whole thing can only get worst now that we can hardly raise our kids in the way of the Lord which included necessary corrections.

I have two children and they were spank only one time each and this was enough for them to understand I was the leader in the house. To this day they never forgot and I'm still respected.

The idea for writing those things down is not to depress you, but rather to make you realize things are not as flourishing as well as they would want you to think and also to warn you about the coming of the end time. I still don't know how they can put so many people to sleep and do what they do without a revolution. This is beyond me. I'm sorry, I think I know. They attack small groups at a time and all the others don't bother, because they are not concerned and they don't care for their neighbours anymore.

I bought a parcel of land three years ago, five acres to be exact. So I thought I was home finally after something like sixteen years. Huh, huh, not so simple I found out this year through a threatening letter from the Ministry of Transportation. The letter was telling me I was not allowed to cut the wire fence to make myself an entrance and to repair it immediately or they will do it and my cost will be around ten thousand dollars. I found out I needed a permit to go into my property, another one to bury my own poop in my own ground and this last one is $250.00. On top of this it is in the air that it will cost $5000.00 for a permit to drill a well in a near future.

How come I can't get the cops to arrest a thief with stolen goods in his hands or in his vehicle? One time I had my dog holding one of these idiots by the fence and I called the police. I was told to let him go that I wasn't allowed to do this.

Another time an officer came to take my deposition and when I was done, he said all the jerk has to say is he found the stolen goods in the ditch and he's on his way home free.

A big 240 lbs. bully assaulted me two years ago. There were two witnesses beside myself and the guy even admitted what he has done. After been locked up for a couple of hours, the police released him and told me they couldn't hold him for lark of evidences. See, he already had a criminal record, the mark of the beast.

Last year I saw a wreck from a neighbour and I offered to buy it.

"Oh, you can have it, I give it to you, just take it away." "Ok, here is $15.00 for your friend to take it to my place."

The only thing that was good on it was the rounded back window with what I would have like to make an aquarium. This old beater only had to travel across the road. Three weeks later the beaten car wasn't home yet so, I went back after church to find out what was going on.

"Oh, I took it to the dump." "My place is just across the road and the dump is ten miles away, what is the point?" "I won't go to your place."

"Well, James could've come, if you didn't want to." "James wouldn't go either." "James is coming to my place all the time. Then I guess it means you owe me $15.00." "I don't owe you anything." He yelled. "You sure do." "What are you going to do about it?" He asked in a threatening way. I was dressed in a $300.00 suit and he was in a tear off pair of jeans I gave him a couple months earlier.

"I won't fight you on your property, if this is what you want to do, but if you follow me to the road will see what happens." "Get out of here." He said.

I got in my truck knowing there was nothing to gain by arguing any longer. I started it and at the same time he grabbed a piece of 2x4 and he smashed my side mirror with it. My old nature would've been to put the cub van in gear and scare him with it or to get out and give him the punishment he deserved, but I guess I've changed. I backed out the two hundred feet of driveway with difficulty having no mirror for my side and pour eyes for the other.

I went home and I called the police one more time. I thought for sure this was an assault with violence and with a weapon. The officer listened to me patiently and when I was done, he told me to come down and fill up a written complaint. I went to the office, but it was closed.

I went down on another occasion and this time the doors were open, but there was nobody to talk to even though I waited at least a half an hour. I called three more times, but no one ever heard of anything about what I reported the first time. It seems to me that most of the criminals get away easily and the innocent people got charged wrongly.

Last year, a few days after I shut the gun in the air to defend myself and my property, I went hunting and this is something I was doing just about every day in October of 1996. This was the eleventh of October. I went to hunt in the Cattle Valley when suddenly at about four in the afternoon some big clouds came up and send me to my vehicle. So, I decided the best thing to do would be to drive slowly back home keeping an eye on the road and another one on the sides. I couldn't believe my luck when I saw a young three points buck standing just in the middle of the road along with a little fawn. There was a little truck ahead, a white Mazda I think just about out of sight. How fortunate for me I thought, this guy just missed this. I stopped the van as smoothly as possible, I got out of the vehicle with as little noise as I could and I loaded the gun hoping to see the buck one more time for they both have jumped on the right side of the road. I saw the fawn hopping around when finally at about four hundred feet away the buck jumped the road from the right to the left and down the field he went. I'm not too good at shooting on the move anymore, but I took a shot anyway. I thought I saw the deer falling down, but I wasn't too sure about this. While I was bracing myself to take this shot, I heard two different noises. One of them was a coming vehicle from behind my van not very far and the other one was a kind of a groan on the right side. So I unloaded the gun for safety, then I took a few steps towards the noise I heard on the right side of the road and then I realized I might just have gotten myself into a pile of troubles.

The truck stopped and the lady who was in it asked me if I had a hit. I told her it was just a target. There is one thing hunters don't like and this is to be bothered while hunting except maybe to help someone lost getting out of the wood.

They drove about a hundred feet and they stopped again I think when they too saw the little fawn. The man took his gun out, loaded it and I told him it was just a little one. The woman said he looks like he's missing his mother. Then the man walked in the bush and he found the dying mother, I guessed, he never said anything. He looked at me as if I was dirt and then he drove away.

After they were gone it was getting pretty dark, so I decided it was best I go home and come back in the morning to find out if I got the buck or not. The next day I followed the tracks the buck made and all I could find were some blood drops here and there. I returned home without stepping on the other side making sure no footprint of mine could be found there. I knew also this guy was sure I shot this animal and he will report me as being the killer.

I kept hunting after this, but only on a friend's farm. This is a place where I can count something like fifty deer a day. Doe are also crossing my own land almost every day.

Anyway, part of the worst came a few days later when the wild life officer drove to my place, especially because a piece of wild meat was left in my porch earlier by someone I thought was a friend or a hunting companion. I didn't pay too much attention to it, because I'm used to this.

I lived on Indian land in Westbank for six and a half years and I owned up to fifty dogs at the time. Some Indians and other friends always brought me meat and bones, so until the officer showed up at my door, I really thought it was no different.

Last week though when I opened a letter on May 23rd, four days after I should've been in court charged with illegal possession of wildlife. I know it doesn't look too good for me and I have the feeling I am going to pay again for a crime I didn't commit. Just the lawyer's fees are already a lot for a man without money.

My lawyer has already made three appearances in court for this matter and he still doesn't have all the information and the circumstances?

They can do this kind of things to you, mainly because nobody else cares. If you really lucky you might find an honest lawyer who will really defend you to help you rather than to make a big bunch of money.

This morning I was in court myself expecting to have the information. The lawyer who used to represent me moved to the US and I couldn't afford another one. Everyone of them wanted the $1500.00 plus taxes before any appearance. The judge said there have been three appearances already and they will proceed no matter what next time and my chances to win without a lawyer were basically nil. When I tried to explain the situation to her, I was told to shut up.

'Listen and get a lawyer.' The judge said.

The lawyer to whom I was referred to let me know he won't do anything unless he's paid in full before any appearance. It is a great society to live in. This judge didn't like me mainly because I told her before in the case of the ticket that what she was asking me had nothing to do with this last case. She wanted to remember where she had seen me and what for. I tried to tell her I talked to one lawyer and she accused me of lying when suddenly the lawyer in question showed his face in the little window of the door. He obviously was looking for someone. She motioned him to come in and then she asked him about me. To her shame he confirmed what I was telling her.

Coming out of the room together, I told the lawyer he couldn't have had a better timing.

'I would like to hire you.'

Then I paid him the $200.00 deposit he was asking to open the file.

On June 10 1999, I was in court to suffer my trial, but there was no wild life officer and no witness around. So Bill, the lawyer brought me in a little room and he said:

"Congratulation, you won." "I won, I don't think so." "What do you mean, you didn't? We won the case." "I mean exactly what I said, I didn't win anything. I was losing even before I step in this courtroom." "I don't understand you, the case is ours." "The crown is the government, isn't it?" "Yes, why?" "Well, when I paid you the $1710.00 for my defense, $210.00 went directly to the crown in taxes. Now if you take off $300.00 for your expenses for one or two phone calls of your precious work, which would be very generous. This would leave you with $1200.00 earned in less than 14 minutes. This would certainly put you in a 50 per cent income tax bracket. This means another $600.00 goes to the crown.

The government is happy, you're happy, but I'm not. The crown won you won and I lost nearly $2000.00. This is a lot of money for a poor and innocent man. I know you deserved a good pay for an honest days work, but the government, does it deserved what he got from me?"

The government got paid a lot of money for charging me wrongly.

Chapter 3

Talking about lawyers now, I really have to see mine again before my next move. I let my beard grow and I plan to take my glasses off, put a cowboy hat on, which I never do, add to this clothes I never wore before and go see Dana without her even knowing a thing about it. I feel a little bit like a cheater or a traitor planning this, but I don't really know what else to do. My son and my friends, the few of them who know a bit about my personal affairs advised me to stay put for the time being. But to me love is stronger than reason and if worse comes to worse, I won't be the first person put in jail for loving. Jail I don't mind it so much, because when I was locked up for a couple of hours before, I spent some of the closest time with my Lord ever. I have felt his presence every second of the way and believe me it has been a very short time. When I was called to get out, I felt I wasn't ready.

All this though wouldn't help me getting close to Precious and I know this. Besides, I need to put all the chances on my side. So to the lawyer I went. I wrote down all the questions before, for as you know at $150.00 per hour, you don't want to waste yours or his time in his office. I quickly drew him a picture of the situation, I asked all the questions I had in mind and I mainly paid very good attention to what he had to say.

He listened to me very carefully and then he said: "Harassment, this is what you're going to be charged with if you get caught." "Do you mean Brad there is no more room for romance in this New World Order? A person is not allowed to express love or interest for another one of the opposite sex?" "Not if this person is not interested and told you so." "Yes but, everybody knows if a woman says yes the first time she's asked, she's ticketed as being a loose one." "Only, if you persist there is harassment." "So, I am ok then, because if I ask her one more time for dinner, this would only be the second time." "Gaston, why don't you leave her alone instead of keep supporting me?" "Brad, love and the loved ones are the two things I believe really worth fighting for. One last question Brad, if you don't mind?" "It's the same price, go ahead." "Can you add this bill to the other one?" "No problem, but just bring me some money soon." "Brad, you're not brook too, are you?" "Oh, get out of here before I change my mind about giving you this break, would you?"

So after this discussion I felt farther away from my goal than ever. All I gained really is one more bill. A criminal record is what I fear the most. When you have one, the system sure has got a grip on you. You can't leave the country when you want to and every time they have a suspicion of some kind they're on your back. Besides, every time they need favours, they wouldn't hesitate blackmailing you to get what they need.

I had another option and it's the one I have chosen. Quite a bit more complicated, but it is probably a lot more efficient.

Remember what I said before a while ago that I composed two love songs thinking about Dana and I really think one of the two will be a number one hit on the parade.

What faith can do to you? For one thing it does push huge mountains out of the way. Great, I thought of having a very popular singer recording it and sing it for me where she works. Garth Brinks is first on the list. He's number one everywhere right now and I know for what he has done so far he would like this one song I have to offer him. It is good as or maybe even better than those on his last tape. I sang it to young and older people even though it is not in my language and each and every one of them said it was touching the soul. One other man said after reading it that it was very good, adding he was a published author. Wow, go for it Gaston, I told myself, what do you have to lose after all? Nothing but a song and yet you might gain the heart of the Princess. Just this thought was enough for me to go forward with my head down like a bull ready to remove anyone or anything which stands in my way. So along with my son I got on the Internet searching for Garth and where his next and closest concert will be.

July 17th is the one where I'll have to go to. I will need a lot of luck to be able to get close to him as well. If it is as everyone says, I almost need another miracle to accomplish the task. But hey lately, miracles and me seem to be found together quite often.

Oh sure I could use a few more, but don't get me wrong, I am very grateful for the ones I've seen so far. First of all I have to get two tickets, because my son too wants to come along. I also have to send the music partitions. The 17th is only forty some days away. Could this be possible? Well, I really think so, if not I wouldn't be talking about it. Guy told me I was pushing my ambitions and maybe my luck a little bit too much.

'Maybe so, but I rather fail by trying too much than fail by not trying enough. See, this way I can live happy with myself no matter what the result is. Besides, I already know if it is meant to be, it will be.'

First thing first! I got to get the song copyrighted. No time to waste. The very first thing to do is to put the song on a tape along with the writing and send it to myself by registered mail. Next to be safer is to repeat the process and register it this time at a notary public; it costs only $20.00 plus taxes. Then if I can, I'll get it registered at a copyright company. The importance of the latter is if for some reason the song gets stolen, the company will be there to fight the battle for you. This would be much cheaper than the lawyer's fees.

So the work registration forms are on the way after I made a phone call today. At first I was told I need to be a member to be illegible. Then I was told I could only become a member if I have music on the air, as radio, television, theatre, or film etc.

'This is exactly why I want to become a member.' I told the woman who was talking to me. 'I want to protect myself against whoever could steal my stuff.' This is the rule for all of our members, she insisted. At the time where everything seems to be hopeless I mentioned having registered some songs with BMI Canada years ago. Then she told me that if I am registered with BMI Canada I am automatically registered with Socan. There I was arguing to get something I already have.

Amazing things do happen all the time and more so it seems if we keep observing what is going on. In writing down most of what did happen to me and what's happening every day, I can count an enormous number of amazing things to say the least. I know a lot of people who told me it was strange, but I told them not to me anymore. Someone is watching over me and He knows what He's doing better than I do.

Saturday August 1st, two weeks after the Seattle Garth incredible concert, this was for me the first one of this magnitude. There is one thing beside a lot of hope I should've taken with me and this is some earplugs. Only two days before Dana's birthday there was another concert in town with a special guest. It was sure one I wouldn't want to miss for the world. It was advertised like so: 'Special guest in town for a special cause. All profits will go towards a children counselling office building. Tickets sold in advance at town centre. Three shows on the agenda. First at 8:00 p.m., second at 10.00 p.m. and the last one, but not the least, because of a special announcement from Garth himself at 12.15 a.m.'

The first show went on very smoothly and so did the second one. I was introduced as being one of the crew, so I got to hear and see the show all three times. Nobody recognized me in my special Mexican outfit. It was packed over capacity I think and most people were concentrating on the show. The only ones who were really moving around were the waitresses because of their intense work. But then my heart went absolutely out of control when the announcement began. Garth said:

'This new song you people have applauded so generously here tonight has been written by a man in this community who could only been inspired by the Lord. This fabulous song was written about a young princess whom he loves desperately and she reminds him a teacher he had when he was still very young and she helped him with his troubles when he was a kid. This is why he gave me this beautiful song in exchange for this show in this establishment, because he knows she's here tonight. She is to be the counsellor and the owner of this building called: Princess' Children Care Centre.'

While Garth was still talking, I saw Precious holding her mouth with her hands and I feared for the worse while I walked towards the exit not knowing exactly what to expect. I don't think I could survive another war against Dana either, but I didn't mind dying after an experience of this kind, especially seeing her again. I passed beside her on my way out thinking maybe it was the last time I was seeing her. Tears were pouring out of my eyes just as they were pouring out of hers.

When I was walking still I heard Garth say a cheque of $62500.00 was there for the princess to put towards her office. I heard something else too.

'Gaston, Gaston!' This was her voice alright, but this was in my head right?

'Gaston, Gaston, is this you?'

I stopped, I turned around and I looked at her and I said:

"I should've known I couldn't fool you. I am on my way out, there is no point calling the cops." "Don't be so foolish and come here, I got something for you." "Only if you promise to have dinner with me."

She walked towards me and she gave me a hug that was worth all the pain, is gone. Then I heard another announcement this time that was concerning me. Garth was telling the crowd that such a song could not be taken away from the person who wrote it, at least not by him. He said he would be honoured to record it as a singer and he sang it one more time.

Both Dana's secret and mine were kept as it was at least from the public. We both listened to the song once more and for the first time; I felt there was a bound created between us which could not ever be broken.

Everything's Yours Oh Lord

Everything's yours oh Lord.
My heart, my soul, my life.
All my sufferings I put within your hands.
I understand. You are the consoler.
The Mighty Lord of all.
You see my heart in tears.
You know about my fears.
You know that I'm sincere and I love You.
Almighty Lord of all.
I have known so much joy.
Now everything's destroyed.
Give me back to enjoy a love life too.

2
Oh come and help me Lord of the impossible.
Once You have changed the heart of a lion.
Unto a fawn's.
And You are the healer.
Oh Mighty Lord of all.
If it's against your will.
I know that You can heal.
My heart seriously ill, easy for You.
Almighty Lord of all.
Listen to my prayer.
I know You can tell her.
Cause all of the power, belongs to You.
Second part spoken and back to first then end.

"It is totally beautiful Gaston. How could you write such a song?" "I have no explanation other than it could be from real love's vibrations.

Excuse me Dana, but there is someone to whom I owe thousands of thanks and so do you. You should go pick up your cheque too." "I don't want this money. I don't deserve it." "Oh don't give me this now. The hundreds of people who came here tonight paid this money for the kids in need. If you do love children as I know you do, go." "But you?" "I was only an instrument just like these people on the stage happy to do so. I'll be right back." "Wait Gaston, I think it is too dangerous for me to go home with a cheque this big and at night." "Smart thinking Dana, besides, you want to keep your identity safe as well." "Smart thinking too!" Both thumbs-up.

"Then, I'll pick it up for you and we'll meet at your convenience at your bank, how's this?" "You're an angel." "I knew it, but I'm sure glad you have discovered this too now." I said laughing for the first time in months.

On this note I painfully walked away from her towards the stage wishing the last ten minutes would've last forever. I grabbed Garth's hand warmly and I told him he would be invited to the inauguration of the office building.

'And to the wedding, I hope.' He added.

"Let me make a prediction too Gaston, I know it will happen." "It is not the most important." "Then what is?" "Her happiness is."

I picked up Dana's cheque telling him a few words about her identity and privacy. He trusted me on this and we made arrangement to meet the next day.

Then I walked back to Dana and to this day, I don't know how I did it, because my heart was pounding like a compactor at work. I felt it was enough to shake the whole town square and whoever is in it. I lift up my hands calling for hers and, forever friends I asked? She gave me hers and she said: 'Forever friends!'

Then she gave me another hug. I was still looking like an old Mexican man and I couldn't help thinking about the Beauty And The Beast. At least now I know she's not afraid of me anymore. This alone was worth twenty years of hard labour and made me understand why our patriarch Jacob worked fourteen years for Rachel, the woman he loved.

What real love can do? Not much can stop. I saw that Dana was very tired and personally I was totally exhausted.

"Would you like to come with me to meet the band tomorrow morning?" "I'd love to, but it will take me at least a week to recover from this." "I'm sorry Dana, I didn't mean to do this to you." "Yes you did." "I mean to wear you out." "I don't remember having lived this much emotion in my whole life for this matter." "Neither do I. I don't remember any deal or anything at all which has been as exhausting or have been this much of a nerve wrecking."

So I said good night to Precious and I went home wishing I had the whole next day to sleep in. Can't be this lucky a-a-all the time, can we?

After an hour of turning around and around I remembered I had a sleeping pill somewhere and I thought I'd better take one even though I don't like it very much. Tomorrow is another day where I'll need all my faculties, so a good rest is what I need the most for now.

I met Garth and the rest of the group for brunch at the Grant Hotel on Sunday morning. Oh how I wished Princess would have been there with the rest of us too. So far only a very few sure friends know who Precious is and no one knows for sure who and what she is to me except her and myself. If any indiscretion was committed it didn't come from me. How much did she tell, I have no idea. The brunch was terrific. Everybody was in a superb shape; at least this was the impression I got.

None of them seemed to be curious about anything except Garth who seemed surprised to see me coming in by myself. He said:

"After what happened last night Gaston, I was sure Dana would've been here with you this morning. I would have loved to be introduced to her." "Sorry that you are disappointed my friend, but it goes to say we can never be sure of anything or not much. But you'll meet her soon, I'm sure." "Was she the gracious one by your side when I sang the last time?" "Shtt, discretion, remember?" "Everyone here can be trusted Gaston." "You must be some kind of magician on top of being a good singer. All good musicians together and trustworthy at the same table, this got to be rare."

They all looked at me with a healthy laugh and one of them said:

"Flattery won't get you anywhere." "Good, because I already have been too far." "No more problem, is there Gaston?" "No Garth, just a heck of a time getting some sleep, that's all." "Yes, it must have been quite a time for you last night, wasn't it?" "Yes it was stressful, extremely emotional, exhausting and absolutely terrific. You guys were terrific too." "Thanks Gaston." Came out almost from every mouth at the same time.

"So you have decided to record the song I vaguely heard you say last night?" "No doubt at all after a response like we had. This song is a hit before being out, especially once we know in which context it was written. Each and everyone in the whole world need to hear it. To tell you the truth, I can't wait to read the rest of your book too." "It's an eye opener and a lot of people are not going to like it." "Too bad for them, it's true though that there are a lot of people who don't like to be awaken in the morning, but then, they can read it at night, can't they?" "I suppose so." "Just keep your good work. You and I know they're better wake up to the good news now than never wake up at all." "Thank you Garth, all encouragement is beneficial to me and I appreciate it."

Then we said good bye and assured each other to communicate all the information through Email in a near future.

"This brunch is on me guys." "It is already taken care of Gaston." Garth said with a big smile.

"It is part of our accommodations, so you just don't worry about it, ok?" "Alright then, I'll leave you with this and will talk soon."

Then I went home thinking about Precious and how she must feel today. I hope she's with some good friends who believe in love too. Hopefully some who are not entangled in the fornication race! I know I am surrounded by these and my only strength is coming from the Lord. I too would like to cuddle up every night with a warm and beautiful woman to release to tension of the day. I too was entangled in this race and way too many times. Although, I have never been as happy as I have been in the last twelve months. I feel as if I had a bath for the very first time in my life. Feeling clean, light and more, I can't begin to describe how it is as if the words weren't made yet. Many times I prayed God for Dana to experience the same happiness and to get the same protection. For this reason I know she'll be alright.

I also know the next few days will be very significant for the rest of my life. I sense something very big is about to happen. I can't help being edgy from head to toe even though I think I am ready for any eventuality. I sense the persecution is about to begin, she will need help and that most everybody will be running for their own life. See Matthew 24, 20. 'But pray that your flight will not be in winter or on the Sabbath.'

The deadline for registering guns is 2003 and my guess is that by then all guns and Bibles will be forbidden. Penalty for either would be beheading since jail cost too much and the word of God can be spread out even there.

The new guillotines will be almost like the CT scan they have in hospitals, except when people will go through it, they won't come out of it alive. They will have their head cut off and the rest of their body will be thrown in the incinerator, which is already a big tool in hospitals. No one will even get the aches; it's going to be a free incineration.

I personally carry the word of God in my heart and this is what I suggest to everybody now. Get the book and try to memorize as much as you can. This is the only way not to be fooled by the liar.

Remember too that if you surrender to the Lord, He will fight your battle with and for you. It is not what you know that save, but your faith and love for the Saviour. The day He is coming back as a King is near. He is not coming back to punish the believers, (His people) but rather to avenge their blood. Hallelujah, Hallelujah.

The ones who should be afraid are the ones who are against Him, especially now they know the devil is running out of time.

Two days ago I had a visit from a friend who told me after a bit of talking that it was scary. I told him it should be scary only for the ones who don't believe in the Lord.

Knowing what I know about God, I wouldn't want to be his opponent or against Him in any way, shape or form. It is just like it was said once: 'What men can do to you is nothing in comparison.' Kill me, if it is the will of God, I'd be with Him and the sooner the better.

Go after my loved ones, then I will be like a mother bear when her cubs are threatened. With the power of the Lord in me, I will chase the demons all the way down to hell if I have to.

I know I'm in for a big war. The love of most has already cooled of. Who cares about what happened to you or to me. Already millions of babies and an incredible number of elderly people have been killed in the last twelve months alone. If this is not alarming, what is? Yet everything seems to be normal to most people. Is the whole population sleeping or what?

'Parents will kill their children and children will kill their parents.' This was predicted a couple of thousands years ago. It is just a matter of time until the children will sign to get their parents terminated on a suffering hospital bed and vice versa, all this to the joy of the governments. The children will probably change their mind if they find out they can't get the inheritance if they sign.

Maybe it is already being done. I would like to know how many diseases and sicknesses and how many people who are being treated in hospitals today directly caused by fornication, drug and alcohol in our country. How many hospital beds are taking away causing a hard worker and a decent person with a heart disease to wait months to get in sometimes till death?

On January 2 1998 I was in the hospital for a hernia surgery after two years of waiting. The next day, I was kicked out as if I was an undesirable. Living all by myself in a shack with no power and no water wasn't the best of situations in this condition.

Not very long ago, I took a drunk to the hospital who swallowed pills while he was drinking. He called me and he asked for my help. He said he had some hallucinations and he was afraid to die. They kept him in the hospital for seven days. He's been there dozens of times already.

I really would like to see somebody very honest, somebody who no one and no money can buy investigate what exactly is done with our taxes in this country. I'd bet you he couldn't do it without risking his life.

Listening to Barry Clark on the radio the other day, I found out that Preston Manning had broken all his running promises. I thought he was a man of integrity.

It is as if no matter who gets there, when they get there, they are not the same anymore.

Same thing goes with the PM Jean, the same Barry said about: 'He got me to shake my head and for the first time in my life being ashamed to be a Liberal.' He was making allusion of the blood scandal. All these victims the same Jean didn't want to help.

Talking about Barry Clark, listening to him and to Dr Laura every day can give you enough information to write a large book. She often talks about the six hundred God's commandments they have in the Judaism religion, her religion. I wonder about this one here. 'What God has united may man not separate.' Times and times again I heard her tell a caller to leave her or his partner for drinking problems and a lot of other reasons than adultery. This is Antichrist.

Two days ago I visited an old friend of mine. He is eighty-nine years old and while he was looking for some gospel cassettes to give me, I asked his wife who is ten years younger if she was ready to let him go. She said yes making a face as if she couldn't wait for this to happen. I couldn't help thinking about what was said in Matthew 24, 40 - 42. 'In these days out of a home one will be taken and the other left behind. Out of a field one will be taken the other will be left.' Two minutes later my old friend put his hand on my shoulder and he said:

"Brother, you and I know where we're going, aren't we?" "You bet we know and this won't be soon enough, will it?" "No, no, I can't wait to see my mom again and to see Jesus." "Thanks to Him for giving us this hope. Thanks to Him for getting us on His side. When I was a young boy, the few times I had a chance to play soft ball, I remember the two leaders were taking turns to pick the players, each of them trying to form the strongest team. Most of the time the two teams were pretty well balanced and if they weren't, they would simply start all over.

I think this is exactly what the devil is trying to do right now and I believe he thinks having a pretty big team right now. I thing he is getting ready to challenge God on a big scale by the look of things. This is going to be the son of perdition lost and end. Praise the Lord for this. I am so happy to know I am on the good and strongest side, aren't you? Let's pray for others who don't believe in Him."

I saw my friend old lady try to hear what we were saying. Just before I asked about her husband she told me she didn't believe in this stuff pointing out all his cassettes and books from preachers. I was sad mainly for my friend.

I remember one time in the middle of the night holding a dying puppy on my laps and telling myself close to tears I was hoping having as much luck on my dying bed. Having someone loving you is almost a luxury nowadays. No this is wrong. Having someone really loving you is a great blessing nowadays, this is what I should rather say.

Tomorrow should be a great day, because I'll be able to see Dana again and I am very thrill about it. The only thought of her brings me so much joy and happiness. For some reason I have never despaired from seeing her again.

The only time I was going to cry over her, the power when out. It was as if I wasn't allowed to. My electricity is powered with an inverter connected to a running car battery. So I was this day sadder than the usual and while I was singing the song: Everything's Yours Oh Lord, at the phrase that goes to say everything's destroyed, just then the power went out cutting off the light and the computer. The car had run out of gas and to my surprise, all my tears had dried out too. It was as if I was told by God: 'Man of little faith, can't you trust me?' Just like Peter when he started to sink in the water. 'Don't you know if I want you to have Dana or if I want her to love and to be with you this will happen no matter what you say or do.'

Since I became God's child, I'm always asking Him to guide me accordingly to His will. So now I can only do what King David did, this is praying to God His will and kingdom comes, so everything will be fine. As for the book as I was told, I would know what to write when the time comes.

On August 4th I met Dana at her bank to deposit the cheque.

"Hi you, you look absolutely splendid. I can see you have had a good rest." "It was more than needed." "Oh, I know that working and studying all at once is not the most restful thing to do. But you are intelligent and very capable, so you'll make it, that's for sure."

Her smile and her warmth can cure any child in distress or any man's broken heart, I'm sure. After we were done with the banking and walked out I asked her if she had time for a coffee.

"Sure, I have some studying to do later, but I'm off work tonight so coffee would be welcome." "Tim Horton's or a place more private? Since we should talk about your future office, discretion would be the best at least for now." "I agree with you, we should go where it is more private, but don't you forget this, this is not a date. Forever friends, remember?" "I'll be damned if I do anything to break our friendship. It is to me the most important gift I ever received, so please, don't you worry?" "Ok then, let's go." "Do you know where Smitty's restaurant is?" "Sure, I'll follow you."

We both drove to the restaurant in a beautiful sunshine. It was a wonderful day full of hope and promises, because for the next hour or so, I will be sitting and talking with the Precious Princess. What a blessing, I thought to myself.

Once there we decided for a seat at the back since there was nobody close by.

"Do you think since it is getting close to suppertime we should get a meal?" "On me then." "Please Dana, I don't want to sound too macho, but please don't take the last of my pride away from me, ok?" "Next time then!" "Next time if it's ok with you I would love you to do me the honour to accompany me to a very important birthday dinner." "Maybe, whose birthday is it?" "It is the birthday of the most beautiful Precious Princess I know." "Hum, I'm not sure if I want to do this." "Oh come on, be a good sport. Don't spoil it, tell me you will." "Well, yes, but, nothing extravagant then." "No, this will be something simple coming from a friend, I promise." "Then, if this is the case, I accept." "This is settled then.

Would you like an aperitif?" "Please, thanks." "I'll have a red wine and than a spaghetti à l'Italienne." "This sounds wonderful to me too. It does feel like too much spoiling for one day. Gaston, I still don't think I deserve all this. This money, it is a huge amount, you know?" "Well, let me put it this way Dana. I'm not too sure either if you deserve it or not, but this is not the point. The point is the kids deserve it and they also deserve and they need to be in touch with you." "So you did all this for the kids?" "This too, but I did everything mainly because I want to be your friend and to be in touch with you." "Nobody deserves a friend like you." "Well, I think you do and I also think I deserve for you to be my friend." "You sure earned it, I should add. This spaghetti is good and so is the wine Gaston. Did you come here before?" "Once or twice, as far as I can remember." "Alone?" "A couple of times with my son I recalled and a couple of times alone. What ever is behind me has been buried pretty deep now and I only have the future to look forward to." "Well put, I've deserved this." "As far as I am concerned pretty lady, to me you deserve the best, all the best. If this includes telling you all about my past, you will find more than enough in the book I am writing. The story that yourself triggered. I owe you so much I don't think I could ever pay you in full." "What do you mean?" "Well, I mean the book, the songs, the music and the happy hours I spent watching you brought me to Wonderland over and over again. I would gladly give all the money I earned since I was eleven if I had it in front of me for this again." "I didn't do anything." "You didn't have to. You are what triggered the whole thing in my mind, in my heart, in my life. It is not yours or my fault, it just happened. Call it an act of God. This is what I did." "You seem to know and to love God very much." "This my sweet friend is the very best thing that ever happened to me. See, God is the reason why you and I are here together having this wonderful chat right at this minute." "I don't understand, I thought you simply wanted to be with me." "This is right too, but you see, we couldn't be here together if this wasn't his will too." "I think we're here together, because we both wanted and we both decided to come here." "Ok then, tell me why you have been in some situations you didn't want to be? Now, don't tell me this never happened, because I won't believe you anyway." "Yes it did. So you are telling me this was the will of God if I stormed on you that night?" "You bet it was." "Excuse me, but you better explain this one to me, because I don't understand this at all. You love God and He must know it." "Do you know what happened to Job? He loved God too and yet there was not a better man on the face of the earth." "Yes, but why?" "Well, I don't know all the answers, but do you see, this song written by my hand." And I paused for a few seconds.

"What is with this song? It is beautiful, but what else?" "You see?" I said with tears in my eyes.

"I don't think I could've written it without this deep pain you caused me that night and do you see too? Nobody but you could cause me this much pain." "Oh Gaston, you mean this was God's fault?" "No Dana, I mean this was God's purpose. Besides, in my desire to pay you back my debt I was drinking way too much and I was spending the money I couldn't really afford." "Oh Gaston, I'll give you back this money." "Would you really humiliate me this way Dana?" "I'm sorry Gaston, I didn't mean it this way." "Dana, I know and I told you before that you are the most kind-hearted person I know in this world, but thanks anyway. I'll be just fine. If God wanted things to be any other way, He would've given me different ideas. Would you care for dessert?" "Oh my God, I can't believe this; we've been here four hours already. No dessert thanks, but I really have to go now and this was very enjoyable." "Do you really mean this?" "Gaston there is something you must know about me, I only say what I mean to say." "Oh stop this, I already love you too much, you perfect specimen." "I got to run now right away." "Just one sec, would you? I need your address to pick you up on Saturday night." "Huh, huh, I wish, but Saturday night I have to work, remember?" "How could I forget? Sunday night then, is six o'clock alright?" "Six is perfect Gaston, I'll see you then." "Hey, I know you're late, but please drive carefully, would you?" "I'll be fine, don't you worry. Here is my address."

She hugged me and she left leaving me with a bit of nostalgia. I have the feeling it will always be like this when she'll leave. I feel a sort of emptiness. Every night

I went to see her at her work I felt the same way when it was time to leave. I always looked at her three or four times from the doorway before going home, thinking it might be the last time. It is as if the best part of me is left behind. Maybe this is what it's all about, the two becoming one. Things are different now though, thanks to the Lord of all, Who healed my heart the only way it could've been healed.

Chapter 4

Only five days to prepare a unique birthday party for a unique princess. Everything has been in my head and in my heart for quite some time now. The question is, can it be done in such a short time? Anything is possible if it's the will of God. This much I know and I think it is his will.

So I paid for the supper and I went out hunting for the things I need to celebrate Precious as she has never been before. I didn't care if I had to sell everything I own to do it. I just want it to be something she will never forget as if it is the very last thing I'll ever do.

So here are the places to go and I wrote down. First is the jewellery store where I noticed once before a unique gold, diamond and rubies article to match with what I already gave her. Next, the very best choice restaurant in town followed by the car rental company. After this it is the carpet store. I feel like I am doing general contracting again. Only this time I think I am building an ever-lasting relationship. I want a relationship which couldn't and which wouldn't fall apart. What else now, let's see? Oh sure musicians, this is very important too. This is an easy one though, because I have a lot of friends and acquaintances who play music. Only one thing though, I'm not too sure yet of what kind of music she likes the most. This and a lot of other things I need to discover yet. Since it takes almost one half of a marriage lifetime to know your partner, might as well start right away. Too many older people told me already they don't recognize their loved one anymore. I heard them say things like: 'I thought I knew her.' Again I heard: 'I can't believe he could do this.'

At the same minute I was writing those lines a customer came in and I shut down the computer to serve him. There he is this young seventy-two years old man. To my surprise he started talking about his life and mainly about his divorce.

"You wouldn't believe this, but just when you came in I was writing about this kind of things." "I'll tell you some divorce's stories. I suggested to my wife one day that we should try to quit either smoking or drinking. I couldn't believe her reaction. She asked me whom the hell I was to tell her what to do or not to do. This is how it has all started. Now she has decided she wanted the divorce shortly after this. I said ok; let's sell everything and both take half, so we can go our own way. Fine, we shook hands on it and everything seems to be alright. Huh, huh, three weeks later I got a phone call from her attorney saying: 'You're not leaving; you have to come to your divorce trial.' Since I have decided to come West I came West anyway leaving to my oldest son who is fifty years old the power of attorney down in Ontario. Half would've been fine, a quarter would've been fine too. She got the house plus everything that is in it, the money and half of my pension too. All I have worked for all my life is gone, just like that and there is not a thing I could do about it." "You must have promised her right from the beginning that you will give her your life. Now it's done."

He couldn't help himself laughing on hearing this. I must have heard enough of similar stories to scare off an army and yet this wouldn't stop me from remarrying. I don't mind losing everything to Dana anyway since I want to give her everything I possibly can. So, I kept organizing the birthday surprise as I first planed.

There are only two more days to go. I can hardly contain my excitement. I never even thought of doing something like this. Since I met Dana everything in my life have different dimensions. This book I'm writing, the songs good enough for the hit parade, my love for her and the music which seems to come directly from heaven. There are also three inventions I proposed to the B.C. Government. But I have to admit it; I don't have much trust in them.

I once prayed along with pastor Tony of Beaverdell for me to have the chance to play music for the Lord in this world and then next in heaven. I think Beaverdell is smaller than Nazareth was at the time of Jesus. I kept being so busy in the last twelve months, no wonder I had no time for unhappiness. This is something I learned seventeen years ago at a human relation course. The speaker said: 'The key of success and happiness is to keep so busy that you never have a moment to see what others are doing wrong.' I think it is the truth and it isn't. How can you be happy seeing your neighbour in need? Right though if you are too busy to see, you simply don't see it. This makes you a blind, which Jesus spent so much time and efforts to heal.

I guess I'm not too busy after all, because I can see a lot of things that are going wrong around me and around the world. But for now anyway, I have enough on my hands and mind with my life. Thirty-three hours to go before I will pick Dana up for dinner. Somehow I wish I could sleep it all. I can hardly control my patience with my surrounding. Even my customers at time looked at me as if the fire was pressing me somewhere around.

Five o'clock p.m. Sunday August 9th 1998

Here I was at the car rental talking to the chauffeur about the route to take and a few more details as how to approach the princess and all this. At 5:30 I sat on the back seat and I prayed for everything to go smoothly and for strength, calmness and wisdom. I felt I needed more strength for this than I would need to beat ten men at once. Once at the given address the chauffeur, John his name, got out and he came to open my door. I stepped down and I walked to Dana's door and then I rang the bell. When I looked in those beautiful blue eyes something like a strong electric current went through my whole body, but surprisingly I survived it.

"Hi Precious!" "Hi Gaston! What is this and where are we going?" "This, my dear friend is a courtesy car or a limousine, whatever you want to call it and it is now probably the only time in my life when I have the unique and proper occasion to ride in it. This is the first time ever I am riding with a princess and I didn't want to do it in my old beater." "So what are you going to do next? Let me walk beside the car, because I am too precious to sit in it. Your car or mine would have been just fine." "Please Dana, just this time so you can tell your children later on about what happened today, ok?" "Alright then, but no more of this stuff. I'm just a friend, remember?" "No, rectification, you're just a precious friend and gorgeous. I don't want to press you Dana, but this guy out there is waiting for us. Shall we go?" "Yes, where are we going?" "It's a place called the Kingdom and I have very good references for it. Do you know it?" "Not really, but I think I heard of it too." "Well, after tonight both of us will know what to say about the place." "A limousine just for me, I can't believe it. Look at the size of this thing." "Don't worry Precious, you don't have to drive it or I wouldn't be riding with you." "Gaston, for what I heard from you, you would go anywhere with me even if I was driving a school bus." "Touched right to the heart. You are absolutely right." "You really want to make me feel like a princess, don't you?" "At least for one evening, yes I do. It is just a one-time thing; this is all I can afford anyway." "Oh Gaston, you shouldn't." "Money spent on you is well spent Precious, besides, I owe you so much I will never be able to pay you in full." "What you think you owe me Gaston is only in your mind." "Oh, I know that nobody can prove it, but you and I know the truth and this is the ideas for the book and the songs came in my life when you did. This makes me more than happy to be able to give you a little back, so just accept it please. In my case at least it is very true that there is more pleasure to give than to receive." "Gaston, you seem to read me wrong sometime. Any woman would love what you're doing, it is just that I don't think I deserve all this and I don't want you to get any ideas either." "I always have ideas no matter what and I have one right now." "Oh, oh, this might be scary." "Don't be stupid, you are perfectly safe anywhere you are with me." "What's the idea then?" "I have the idea we're getting close to the restaurant." "Well, I don't think this is the best you ever had, but I appreciate it, because I'm hungry." "Good, because I don't like wasting."

"Thanks John, this was a smooth ride." "You're welcome sir." John retorted while opening the door.

"I'm glad you liked it."

"Gaston, I think we should take a cab later on. What do you think?" "I've got a package deal and besides, I don't want your neighbours to think you were worth a fortune before dinner and not more than a cab after."

She smiled saying I had a point and when she smiles, I can't say it better, I'm in heaven. Then the least I can do in a moment like this and it is so little, this is to thank the Lord for his goodness.

Dana looked at the spotless white and long car as if she wanted to memorize it forever.

"He'll pick us up in a few hours Dana. I'm glad you too enjoyed the ride." "I did too. Oh Gaston!" She start saying with tears in her eyes and then I stepped forward to hug her and I said:

"It is your birthday sweetie, so please don't cry, ok?" "I'll be ok, thank you."

At the same time a young couple came out of the restaurant and stood beside each of us to escort us inside. As we walked in the doors the music began. Sacks and trumpets, fiddles and guitars in harmony playing, 'Long Live The Princess.' I felt Dana's arm shaking under mine, so I put my hand on it to steady her and right away, I sensed she would be alright.

Not daring to look at her at this moment, I was a little bit afraid of her reaction. This wasn't quite the time and neither the best place or situation to start an argument of any kind. I thought if she isn't strong enough to handle this situation, she might just run away. I think a lot of women could've. Dana is a woman of situations. She is even stronger than she knows. I looked at her when I thought the biggest part of the emotions was over. I smiled at her and I whispered to her ear, this is my girl.

After the welcome song ended we were escorted on a four feet wide by forty feet long red carpet to our private table. On it lays a huge bouquet of red and pink roses.

"Does this mean peace and love?" "I don't know, but if you keep it up you will find neither one with me. I can assure you this much." "Peace for tonight then? I really feel extremely blessed to be seated at the same table than your Majesty Precious Princess." "You do me too much honour and you know it too." "I want this evening to be the most memorable for you and me." "Well, a person would have to lose his own mind not to remember all this." "Thanks Dana. Does it mean you're impressed?" "Impressed? Struck with amazement is more like it. You're something else Gaston and way too romantic for these days and age." "Oh no, not you too?" "What?" "Nothing, it is just someone said years ago I must be the last romantic lover. I actually wrote a song on this subject, if I remember well." "Hum, I'd like to hear it some day if you don't mind." "Not at all Precious, I don't have anything to hide from you." "You're putting a lot of trust in me, are you sure you should?" "I do and if I'm wrong, tell me seriously you're not trustworthy."

A young man came to our table and he offered the service.

"Lady and gentleman. Are you ready to order or would you like to look at the menu a little bit longer?"

Dana told the server we would be ready to order in five minutes and she asked him if he didn't mind to bring us a carafe of white wine.

When he was back forty seconds later with the wine, I decided to introduce one another.

"Mark this is Dana, Dana, Mark." "You know him? You've been here before?" "Only a couple of times!" "Alone?" "Yes, I have been for quite some time now and believe me, I rather be alone than to be with the wrong one." "I suppose so. You did get hurt badly, didn't you?" "It taught me enough to make the difference between you and them. I sure can appreciate the lesson and the difference tonight."

"I trust you now Gaston." "Thanks Dana. I think you're lucky to have learned this this young. It's not easy to trust the right person, do you know this? There are more and more con artists out there. Talking about artist, I think there is a new show on here tonight." "And you don't have anything to do with it, do you?"

The meal arrived when the question was asked.

"Do you really think I can change anything in this place Dana?" "Yes I do, the red carpet, the limousine and all these musicians, beside the concert you brought to Kelowna last week, I sure think so."

The two fillet-mignons with baked potatoes and a large salad dish were put in front of us and I asked Mark what was on for show.

"As a matter of fact sir, there is a brand new show starting here tonight and I heard it was pretty impressive too. It is called: 'The Masked Defender.' Some Aikido expert I think." "Thank you Mark." "Oh welcome sir and bon appétit, miss, sir."

"I don't think I want to watch this Gaston, I don't like violence." "Sometime it takes violence to stop violence Dana, but I don't think there is any violence in it. I don't think it would be tolerated and accepted in a place like this one either." "Ok, I'll trust your judgment, I know now you're clever." "Are you flattering me Dana?" "It is not my style at all. By the look of what I got here tonight with you, why would I need to flatter anyone?" "I'm touched again bright thing, you too amaze me more than I ever been by a woman before."

On this note we were ready for dessert.

"I'm so full, I can't swallow another bite." "One or two more pounds wouldn't hurt you a bit good looking, not like me." "Your little belly is suiting you very well Gaston, don't you be ashamed of it for a minute." "It wouldn't help me at all if I had to run to save somebody's life or mine though." "Maybe, but how many times did you have to run?" "None lately, but things are changing, you know? I'm a man of eventualities; I like to be ready for them at any time." "I suppose this is being wise." "So, no dessert then. Would you like some more wine then or something else?" "Not for now, thank you. This was very good"

A busboy came to clean the table for us. The M.C. got on the stage's corner and when he began his announcement I quickly excused myself to Dana, because my stomach was telling me I was invited to the washroom.

'This must be my nerves, I can't help it.'

So I got on my way almost precipitately. I was gone for almost ten minutes and during this time Mark came to chat with Precious.

'The pretty lady is all by herself?' Mark asked Dana, but not in a flirtatious way.

"Gaston shouldn't be too long. Have you known him for a long time?" "Not very long no, but I owe him my job and I don't know anyone else like him. He is one of a kind this man. I'm sure glad he found a nice lady." "Oh we're just friends, didn't he tell you this?" "He never say anything much about his private life, he's a man of a different class." "And what class is he in? Can you tell me?" "Well, one time we were left without a cook on a busy suppertime and Gaston took his jacket off, rolled up his sleeves and he cooked for two hours until our chef got back in. The chef's wife had a baby who decided to face the world at that time and at first we thought we would have to close the place down and to cancel all the reservations. Gaston saved this place a lot of troubles. Another time it was so busy that we were running out of dishes. Again he rolled up his sleeves and he helped us out with this too. Would you know any other company head presidents who would do something like this, tell me?" "No, I have to admit, I don't."

Then the show was starting and Dana felt sorry for me to miss any of it. When I came back to our table I found Dana anxious and I worried for a few seconds.

"Oh Gaston, I wished you've seen this." "You mean the violence? Do you mean it is all over already, this soon?" "Yes, it only lasted three or four minutes." "A four minutes show, I couldn't have missed a heck of a lot." "How come you were so long? You weren't cooking, were you?" "No, no, I wasn't, but you have been talking to Mark I can tell or to the owner?" "Mark was very nice to fill up the time so it didn't seem like an eternity waiting for you to come back." "Am I this easy to replace?" "No, but if it is as he said, you are irreplaceable and you can replace just about anybody. He's got a very high opinion of you, do you know this?" "What about you Dana?" "Climbing Gaston, climbing." "This is nice to hear. What were you saying about the show?"

The M.C. was saying the attackers were unknown to the Defender and vice-versa. They were paid $10.00 each for the scene and a bonus of $100.00 would have been paid to the one who could take the purse away from the lady. As it is while he was opening the purse in front of everybody, showing the hundred dollar bill, he asked the public if the Defender deserve this money. Everybody stood up clapping their hands and screaming: 'yes, yes, yes.'

"You should have seen this little guy Gaston. I think he is even smaller than you are. I'm sure he is and he's wearing a complete outfit including a mask à la Zorro, if you know what I mean?" "I got it and?" "Well, there is a lady with her two daughters walking down the street when a gang of seven or eight robbers attacked them. It happened so fast I couldn't count them all." "Take the time to breathe Dana, there is no rush and it is so wonderful to be here with you that I'm not in a hurry to leave the place. So there were three women and a gang and?" "They tried to steal the mother's purse and this little guy put them all out in no time, he put them all out. The tricks he used are something I have never seen before. At work I've seen the boys taking out a lot of undesirables as they are called and there are also a lot of fights, but I'm telling you, I think this guy here can put all the boys out and all at once." "Well, I'd like to believe you Dana, but I think you are exaggerating a bit, no offence." "Well, I'm telling you the way I saw it. I guess you'll have to come back and see it for yourself." "Oh, I believe you, but it really seems to be a bit much. I've seen these guys where you work too and I don't think that only one guy could put all four or five of them out at once like you said." "After what I've just seen from this guy here tonight, I would bet you he could. A woman should feel quite safe with a guy like this."

In hearing this I looked down on the table. Dana looked at me with sad eyes and she said:

"I'm so sorry Gaston, I didn't mean to offend you and I'm sure you can protect your woman too in your own way." "Oh, I'm not offended at all Dana, I was just thinking of how I wish for you to find your protector too, someone who wouldn't hesitate at all to give his own life to save yours. This I think is something you deserve." "Thanks Gaston. You're too kind." "Nobody can be too kind for you Dana, nobody, believe me I know."

On this note, notes start to fill up the air. Eight fiddlers began to play along with three guitarists and a pianist and the voice of the M.C. called for mister James Prince to come forward to sing a new song called: For Better or Worse dedicated to his Precious Princess.

I then got up and I took Dana hands in mine and I said: 'Happy birthday Precious.' And I gave her a tender kiss. Those beautiful blue eyes looked at me in a way I wasn't too sure if they were sad or happy. Then she said:

"No Gaston, please? Don't leave me alone now." "Do you want to come up there with me?" "Oh God, no!"

Then I looked around and I saw a woman alone sitting next table who seemed to be nice enough, so I asked her if she would be kind enough to come and sit with Dana for the time of the song. She agreed right away and to the stage I went.

There must have been one hundred and fifty to two hundred people in the place or more. I felt like my legs won't support me any longer, but as soon as I picked up the microphone, I made a short prayer, I thought about Dana and then I felt as strong as a lion.

"For you Precious Princess.

For better or worse

For better or worse always and forever
That's what my love is for you.
For ever are yours my whole heart and my soul.
My love will always be true.

The kind that does come from above, Compassion and fidelity, cleaner and purer than a dove, I'll love you through eternity.

2
For all of my life, all my days and my nights, for you I'll always be right. Through good and bad times, through the storms and sunshine
Always you'll see my love shine.

The kind that does come from above
Compassion and fidelity, cleaner and purer than a dove, I'll love you through eternity.

3
When this life's over, when I've done what I could I'll go to a better world. There I will enter where there is no suffer, a home made for me by the Lord.

In this home I will reach above, awesome gift from Fidelity, the One who is nothing but love, Master of the eternity.

4
For better or worse, always and forever, his love for all of us too. Forever are yours all his grace and his peace. His love will always be true.

The King who did come from above, compassion and fidelity. So clean and so pure is his love with us for the eternity.

5
For better or worse. Always and forever.
That's what his love is for you. Forever are yours.
my whole heart and my soul. My love will always be true.

The kind that does come from above
Compassion and fidelity, cleaner and purer than a dove, I'll love you through eternity."

There was a standing ovation someone told me, but I didn't hear much of it. Having my mind strictly set on Dana and how she was handling things. When it was quiet again, I thanked the people and I gave back the microphone to the M.C. I asked him to wait a couple of minutes before the happy birthday song and I went back to my seat. Dana was crying and I couldn't help holding my tears either. She said:

"I treated you as if you were a rapist and all of this time all you were doing is loving me to death." "How could you believe such an old fool like me?"

I put a finger on her lips and drew a hanky out of my pocket and I dried out her eyes. I told her there was nothing to be ashamed of, nothing to regret, that everything was necessary and fine.

"Only you coming to my life could create this song too, so thanks to you."

When I was sitting down the M.C. announced the dance will begin in approximately three minutes.

'But before we get ready for the dance people, would you like to join me in a singing. We are celebrating here tonight the birthday of a young princess. Her name is Dana and she just turned twenty-seven. Happy birthday to you, happy birthday to you. Happy birthday dear Dana, happy birthday to you.'

I stood up too with all the others, I stretched my arms calling for Precious hands which she gave me with shakiness. Still while holding her hand, I pulled out of my side pocket of my jacket a small box that I handed out to her.

"No Gaston, truly this is already too much." "Nothing is too much for you Precious and besides, they wouldn't take it back. On top of everything, I know I will never have anyone else to give it to. So just be gracious as you naturally are and accept this modest present, no strings attached from a humble heart, ok?"

She opened the little box and when she saw what was in it, she actually screamed:

"Oh my God, this is absolutely gorgeous. This must be worth thousands of dollars? I can't take this, this is just too much." "Dana, you did very well in your role as a princess so far tonight, please don't quit now. I'll make a deal with you, if you don't mind?" "I'm scared to ask." "No point being scared and you know it." "What then?" "I'll put it on your wrist and if it doesn't suit you, I'll keep it, is this fair?" "No, it isn't." "Why?" "Because you know perfectly well it is perfect and it matches the rest perfectly. A gold bracelet with three rows of diamonds and two rows of rubies, twenty-six, no twenty-seven rubies! Oh Gaston it must have cost you a fortune? It's a good thing I'm not fifty after all." "Shtt, this is your first princess' mistake. I might tell you just before I die how much it cost."

So, I took the bracelet and I attached it around her wrist and I repeated happy birthday Precious Princess while putting a kiss on her cheek.

'What's this?'

She pulled me towards her, she hugged me and she gave me a warm kiss on the mouth. This, I don't have to explain, I'm sure everybody will understand how I felt.

People were standing all around us and we were so caught up within ourselves that we didn't notice some people were waiting in line to shake Dana's hand and to wish her a happy birthday as well.

It took me a lot of strength not to burst out laughing when some guys paid their reverences. One guy actually kneeled down right to the floor, bowed down and kissed her hand as if she was Queen Elizabeth. Some women came up also, but I detected a little bit of spying in the air. They more or less wanted to see Dana's jewels for themselves and compare theirs. Others gave her some money and there were also a few little gifts.

Finally I was more than happy to hear the dance was about to begin. So, a little bit like they do in wedding ceremonies, the M.C. asked:

'Would please Princess Dana and her escort Mr. James Prince do us the honour to open the dance.'

Dana cried out while putting both of her hands on her mouth:

"Oh my God, I don't know how to dance one bit." "Do you know how to walk?" "You know I do." "Well, the foxtrot they are playing right now is just like walking, only you do it with the beat of the music." "No, no, no, Gaston, you won't get me into this one." "You saw me dancing a lot of times, didn't you?" "Yes, but." "There is no but. Did you ever see a woman embarrassed with me on the dance floor?" "No, I didn't." "Yet, I danced a lot of times with women who didn't know how to dance at all." "But, they looked good." "And you'll look better yet. You told me earlier you were trusting me and besides, I wouldn't lie to you even to save my life, so trust me on this one too. Give me your hand, relax, come on the floor and let me lead you to the end of this piece of music." "You want me to do this in front of everybody?" "You'll have to ignore them for now. Now when you talk, you do it low, so only you and I can hear each other, Ok?" "Ok!" "It is a four-beat, so if you know how to count up to four, you'll know how do dance this too." "This simple, hey?" "Yes, I told you." "You're incredible Gaston, do you know this?" "Yes, I do." "Vanity!" "I rather have this name than to be called perfection. So let's go, your right leg goes back first and all the other steps follow. If you relax you'll feel all I want to do with you or almost. One, two, three, four behind. One, two, three, four forward." "Is that all?" "Yes." "This easy?" "I told you." "It's hard to believe." "Who, me?" "No, that I can dance so quickly." "You just don't know it yet, but you're what we call a natural." "Me a natural, in what?" "In a lot of things. For now I'd say in dancing and in a role of a princess."

On this note the music ended to a standing ovation. I saw Dana's cheeks getting red by the seconds. It has been a long, long time since I was this proud of someone. It took her a lot of courage and a lot of faith to do what she did. We saluted, thanked everybody and we walked back slowly to our table. It was quite an experience for Dana, because it was the first time she ever danced on this type of music. For me, because it was the first time ever I danced with the love of my life. This was something I hoped to do for so long. Holding her like this is something I'd love to do until I can no longer stand on my legs.

"I should've taken you on when you offered to teach me how to dance." "You just did." "I meant before tonight." "Everybody thinks you've been dancing for years." "You think so?" "I sure do. You watch some guys will come and ask you." "Oh my God, what I'm I going to tell him?" "You tell him exactly what you want to tell."

Less than a minute later a man in is early thirties came to asked her and she was too embarrassed to say no after the exhibition she performed earlier, so up she went. The band was playing another foxtrot and now she had some experience at least. They weren't gone very long before they both came back. Dana looked frustrated and the gentleman very apologetic.

"I don't understand, I know you are a good dancer, I've seen you dance earlier." "Earlier I danced with someone who can lead and this is something I really need to enjoy dancing. Thanks just the same sir and don't you worry, this is something that happened to many other people before you." "Miss, sir."

This was the second time of the evening I could hardly hold myself back from a big laugh.

"I can't believe this Gaston, it was so easy dancing with you." "There are a lot of people who know how to dance only with someone who knows how. This man is one of them and you are one of them too, for now anyway." "Do you mean you still want to teach me?" "I never changed my mind about this. The offer is still on. There is still only one thing which is bothering me about it though." "And what is this?" "I got to find some tricks to slow you down from learning too quick. I'd like to enjoy teaching you for a long, long time." "Oh, I'm sure there are some dances that will take more than five minutes to learn." "With a student who learns as quick as you do, it will be like a beautiful dream gone too soon." "Maybe it is not that I learn quickly as much as you teach properly and efficiently." "Let just say we are both good at it, you in learning and me at teaching. And yes some dances are harder than others to learn, but you Precious can learn them all without exception and fairly quick too."

Then what I was expecting to happen happened. A pretty woman came and she asked me if I cared to dance. I didn't really want to, but Dana out of her kind heart pushed me into doing it to please the pretty lady.

'You love this kind of dance and I love watching you dance, so you go.'

So I got up and I followed the person to the dance floor and this more or less to please Dana. The band was playing one of my favourites: 'The In The Mood.' It was.

"You're a good dancer." "Likewise." She returned when the last note ended. I motioned in a way that I wanted to go back to my table and I said: 'I thank you.'

She held me back against my will to a slow dance, a rumba, the kind of dance that belongs to the romantic lovers I think or to the professional dancers for exhibitions. I felt a bit victim of the circumstances and I put up with it until she pressed herself onto me saying:

'There is something else I'm good at.'

I pushed her back telling her that when I'll have sex, I'll choose and the partner and the place. I left her there on the floor by herself and I returned to my table. I normally don't like this kind of scene, but a man has to do what he has to do sometimes.

"What is wrong Gaston, you look upset?" "Nothing that is very serious Precious, it is just I was in the right place, but with the wrong person, that's all." "What happened?" "She tried to force herself on me, taking what belongs to you and I didn't allow it." "She is a good dancer." "Yes and she is a number one candidate to win the fornication race too." "This is pretty rash, don't you think?" "Maybe so, but it is also true. One of these days the Lord will clean up the earth of all this pollution." "Maybe you're right Gaston and I know that if all men were like you, we wouldn't see women like her." "What about a last dance with the right one this time before we go?" "Are you sure this is a good idea, mister Prince?" "Yes, I do. Since we had this first dance together I'm dying to hold you in my arms again."

It was just a slow waltz and I didn't care about the steps or anything else but holding Precious as if it was the last time I was going to do this. She left herself being carried by the music in my arms where she seemed the feel secured and relaxed. To my surprise she pressed her body against mine gently and firmly.

"You're taking me to Wonderland Precious, is this you or the wine?" "The wine or the music has nothing to do with the way I feel right this minute M. Prince."

I kept quiet until the music ended leaving our bodies speak for themselves since they had a lot to communicate.

'May you feel this way for the rest of your life Precious!'

When the music ended I led Dana to our table and then a young punk chewing his gum like a cow came and asked her if her dad would let her dance with him.

"My dad is almost two thousands miles away and this gentleman here with me is my escort, the one man who gave me the very best evening of my whole life. We are about to leave so, if you want to excuse us young man, I'll say good night." "This is not your papa? I could've sworn he was."

"Young man, did you watch the show here tonight?" "Yes, why?" "Well, you see the Masked Defender is my very best friend and right at this minute he is watching us." "Oh yea!"

The punk retrieved his hands from our table and while straightening up he looked all around and started to walk away with tight butts as if he needed the washroom as I did earlier.

'This is a big guy, do you know this?' Dana said laughing?

"He didn't scare you, so why should I worry?" "This was a super good trick you used to get rid of him though." "What if he didn't believe you Gaston? This guy was here for troubles, you know?" "Yes I know, he was in trouble for himself, believe me Dana." "What do you mean? This guy is over six foot tall and he weight over two hundred pounds." "No Dana, he is only five-eleven, one hundred and ninety pounds at the most." "I thought you never lie Gaston, though I think it couldn't have been a better time to do it." "I didn't lie sweetie." "Now, now, how in the world are you going to pull this one from under my feet without tripping me Gaston? You didn't even see the show." "I could hold you in my arms. Ah, ah! I didn't lie because you see, who ever is helping the needy, defender or rescuer, who ever helps the poor and the weak and who ever looks for and forces on justice is on my side and he is by the same fact my best friend." "Wow Gaston, I am impressed, truly I am. Did you ever think of going into politics?" "I did, but you see, I hate injustice and corruption way too much to be manipulated by anyone. Shall we go?" "Thanks Gaston for this wonderful dinner and a wonderful evening all together." "It was my pleasure Dana, believe me it was. I will never forget the most wonderful time I had with the most Precious."

The limo was at the door as requested at eleven o'clock sharp since we both had to work the next day. The drive to her apartment was quiet and so were we as if enough was said for one day. For me it was as if I was afraid to say something which might spoil this wonderful evening, for her it was a time to taste the rest of a remarkable, unique, memorable and wonderful happy time. When a person is speaking too much, he ends up saying stupid things. This is something I noticed even from great speakers, even Prime Ministers. To be seated beside her in a car which I didn't have to drive was something I was contemplating to the fullest. It seems that everything I do with Precious is as if it was the last thing I'm ever going to do and each time I see her as if it was the last time. No wonder I call her Precious.

Dana broke the silence first.

"You were right about telling my children, it would be a very nice story to tell them if I ever have any. I never thought it could be possible to have the most beautiful evening of my life and this with a man who is old enough to be my father, no offence." "Do you mean that young men don't know how to entertain you?" "I'd say they mainly know how they want me to pay for it." "Now, tell me why such of a beautiful young woman like you wouldn't have children?" "Oh, I think I can have children alright, but it would have to be only with the right man, you see?" "I can see this would be a very good thing to pray for." "Do you always have your prayers answered Gaston?" "Well, I prayed for your protection and you seem to be doing fine to me. If what I pray for is the will of God and I ask Him in the name of Jesus, his son, you can be sure it will be answered. Now, I think it is his will for you to have and children and the right man. Don't you think so too?" "I hope you're right. I don't think I have your kind of faith Gaston though and I don't really know how to pray." "You told me once Denise was your best friend." "Yes, but what's this has to do with our conversation?" "Everything!" "Everything? I don't understand." "You will in a minute. Now, if it is true that she is your best friend then you're not afraid to ask her for a favour?" "No, I'm not." "Now, if you ask her for a favour, it's because you know and you believe she can and will help you out." "Anything, she'll do anything for me." "Are you sure about this?" "Absolutely, I am." "Then she'll give her life for you?" "Well, I wouldn't ask her this much." "I'm sure you wouldn't. I don't doubt your friend's friendship either. But then, if the two of you were in a position where only one could come out alive, which one of you do you think would choose to live and let the other one die?" "This is irrational." "You're telling me this because you don't know." "You're right; I don't know what she would do or what I would do." "Dana, I don't know your friend and I don't doubt her friendship for you either, but I know you enough to say you would let your friend live." "I never thought of it this way before." "This is the kind of questions a person should ask when choosing a friend. I know Jesus did lay his life for you, for me and for all of us and I also know there is no better friend than him. So, this means I can ask him anything I want that would be also the will of God. I know too I would lay my life down for him or for you Precious Princess." "You better watch what you're saying Gaston, I might just get used to this title, you know? Because of you I might just believe I am a princess one day" "Do Precious do, because this is who you are for me and this is who you're going to be to me for as long as I live."

She looked at me intensively for a long moment and I remembered that it is not easy to let somebody love us. For thirty years long I refused my Saviour's love, choosing to go my own way. How many times I hit my head against the wall though? For one thing every time I tried to reach the top I was thrown down like an apple and like an apple falling down from the tree I got myself a few wounds. Now that I gave everything I own to the Lord, I got everything I need, love included. I have so much love that I am overflowed. I give love to everyone, including my enemies and I receive love from everywhere. I've got the largest collection of hubcap in the country which is worth $5.5 millions and I have no money. It didn't come to me because I was smarter or wiser either, because I'm not. At least I wasn't. It did come to me because I had faith. I believed in them when most people didn't. I was nine years of age when I found my first hubcap and I got ten dollars for it. This was two dollars more than my dad made in those days in eight hours work. I think it was then the idea was set in my mind, that there was something to be made with hubcaps. It was a fifty-three Cadillac hubcap and even today you can see a set of those rare hubcaps on one of my walls.

You make money and the government comes to get a big chunk of it. You pick up hubcaps and they don't bother you. I should keep my fingers crossed though, because who knows what the government will do when this book of mine is out on the market?

Too early too soon we got to Dana's place and both of us I think with nostalgia as if it was the end of everything.

"Do you want to come up for a coffee? I don't want to say good night just yet." "Do you really thing this is a good idea Dana? Personally I think we are both emotionally affected tonight and if I have a coffee, I won't be able to sleep at all. It will be hard enough as it is. But, I'll have a cup of tea, if you have some and then you can say good morning in a half an hour or so, if it's ok with you." "It's wonderful, come on up."

We both said good night to John and I told him I will take a cab back to my car. 'I can come back to get you.' He said spontaneously.

"No charge." "Now, why would you want to do something like this?" "I enjoyed myself more than I did in a very long time." "Better not, your car is too obvious in the middle of the night." "I'll come to get you with yours then if you like it better." "You wouldn't mind driving my old beater?" "It will help me appreciate this one better." "Ok then, here are my keys. One o'clock then." "At one o'clock I'll be here waiting for you and don't rush for me either." "Thanks John, you're a good man, bye."

Up we went and I hate to admit it, but I was shaking inwardly to the point I was afraid it shows on the outside. I wasn't scared of her, but of myself.

It was the first time since I became a disciple I was maybe in a position to say no and to say no to Precious would be harder than anything, I thought. To say no to sex is one hard thing to do, but to say no to sex and to Precious at the same time would be martyrdom. I knew it then and it was something I didn't think about until then. It was just too late and it was the wrong place and time to be a coward. I felt I would need more strength and wisdom now than I ever did. But then, I thought too the Lord is with me in all occasions and everywhere. Now is time He's with me more than ever. I know too He is faithful and He is with me in every possible situation.

Once inside a cosy two-bedroom suite Dana went to the kitchen and she put the kettle on.

"Do you want to put some music on Gaston?" "I'd love to."

Oh, oh I thought, here comes the perfect scene.

"I'm afraid I don't have much of your kind of music though." "Do you have something from Garth Brooks?" "Who doesn't?" "Sure, I have three of them. Witch one do you want?" "the one with: 'Two Pina Coladas.'" "You do like this kind of music, don't you?" "It is a nice cha cha cha and I like the lyric." "You do know your music, don't you?" "A little, I love it." "I could tell." "I wouldn't mind learning some of what you like though, just to be fair to you." "Thanks the same Gaston, but there is no need for it. I don't think I would like it if you go spoil yourself for me this way either. There are a lot of guys out there who play this kind of stuff. Besides, you want to make sure you don't steal the show all the time." "You got a point there my dear." "Hey, don't talk to me as if we were an old couple already." "I'll try to remember this dear sweetie." "This is better. What do you put in your tea?" "One sugar only, thanks."

The music was on when Dana brought me the tea and she said:

"Here Gaston, I hope you'll like it, because it is the only one I've got." "It will be fine, thanks Dana." "So Gaston, are you going to tell me what you are expecting from me?" "Well, I didn't expect this question, this is for sure. What do you mean by this? Do you mean for tonight or for the future?" "I'd like to know for both if this is possible." "Well, for tonight I'd like to have a peaceful short time we have left. Next time we'll go out, God willing, I'll tell you all about what I want for the future." "I can't wait." "I'm afraid you will have to wait anyway sweetie, because there is no way I would have the time to tell you all of it before I fall asleep." "Getting old Gaston?" "I'll outrun you anytime, but not in the middle of the night, night bird." "I was just teasing you." "I know, but I think we both need to get a good rest." "You're right, there is no point in abusing a good thing and I got to repeat myself, I had the most beautiful evening, one I couldn't even dream of. But Gaston, you have to promise me something." "What is it?" "You have to promise me not to do something this extravagant again, promise." "Ok, I promise you that for the next five years or so I won't spend an excessive amount of money to please you and I believe this is the first time I promised something to someone in twenty years." "Not that it is my business, but do you mind telling me what did you promise and to whom?" "Not at all, I have no secret for you Precious." "I like this name, it makes me feel very important." "Well, you are very important, you are very precious, you are a beautiful young princess and if I'm allowed to, I will spend the rest of my life proving it to you." "Nobody has ever told me something this nice. You're not saying those things just to seduce me, are you?" "Seduction comes from evil. Many are seduced and when they wake up, it hurts. I show myself as I am. I promised myself twenty years ago when I quit smoking that if I take a cigarette again, I'll never quit anymore until I die and I never smoked since." "How big of a smoker were you?" "One of the biggest I think, I smoked three large king size a day and this for twenty-two years." "Wow, this is being a man of his word." "You bet it is and I'm very proud of it too." "Well, you should be." "Oh my gosh, it is one fifteen already. I have to run, John is waiting." "But Gaston, I have many more questions to ask you to which I need answers." "It will have to be another time sweetie, not that I'm bored, but you know what it is?" "No, I don't." "The etiquette?" "What this means?" "This means it wouldn't be proper to spend the whole night together on our first date." "Old fashioned." "Oh, I know we live in a world nowadays where everything is permitted, but it is not right for everybody, you see?" "I know you're right mister Prince and I think you're very special too." "Thanks Dana, I have to go now and thanks for the tea and also thanks for the beautiful time your young majesty allowed me to live through tonight." "Good night Gaston."

She said with a long kiss and a strong hug which took me to Wonderland one more time. I opened the door and I left quickly with tears in my eyes as if it was to be the last of it. As if I was lacking faith. I just knew that if I had looked back, I would have been in trouble. I quickly walked to my car leaving I knew for sure half of myself behind. John was waiting outside of it.

"Here's your set of keys Gaston. How are you?" "I couldn't be better John. I couldn't be better. It was our first date, you know?" "It must have cost you a fortune?" "It was all worth it and I'm not talking about sex either, in fact there was none of it." "She is precious isn't she?"

I looked at him a little puzzled and I told him:

"You couldn't have picked up a better word than this John." "I know what you mean." "Do you really? I doubt this somehow." "She's someone for whom you would give your life for without any hesitation?" "So you know then." "This only happens once in a lifetime." "When did it happen to you?" "Long time ago, I never got over it." "What happened?"

He was quiet for the longest time.

"You don't want to talk about it?" "I never did." "It's up to you, but if you do, just know your secret is safe with me."

Again it was a long time before he spoke.

"She was raped by who was supposed to be my best friend." "This is shit, excuse my language, would you? And?" "I beat him up badly." "Well, I think I would have too. You didn't kill him, did you?" "No, maybe I should have." "I don't think so, but what happened to her? Nothing would stop me from loving my princess." "Same here, but she felt dirty and she didn't want to see me again." "Was he convicted?" "He got two years for rape and I got seven years for attempt murder, not counting all of the other troubles." "Like?" "Try to find a job was the very worst. Not fair, isn't it?" "Not fair. Oh, I know there is no justice in this world, but where I'm going there is nothing but justice." "Where is this and who told you this?" "My Lord did." "Oh, you're one of these." "Yes, I'm one of these who are going in a world of justice, the wonderful paradise. This is where there is no pain, no sufferings of any kinds. Where there is nothing but happiness." "Sounds pretty nice." "It is offered to you too." "What do I have to do?" "Nothing but accepting it. It is already all done. Where is she now?" "In Toronto I think." "How long ago did this happen?" "Seventeen years." "You don't think she'll be willing to get back to you now?" "She is probably married now." "Are you afraid to find out? What about you? Are you married?" "I couldn't marry anyone but her." "Maybe she felt the same way as you and she wondered what took you so long to come back. Some women need to be asked a couple of times before it starts sinking in." "Do you really think so?" "She might have changed her mind since and felt rejected since you didn't try to get back to her." "You know what? You might just be right Gaston. I'm going to give it some thoughts." "Don't forget John that faith moves mountains and I have seen a couple of them moved out of the way myself." "Here we are now, but I'd like to talk to you some more about this faith you're talking about Gaston. Some other time maybe, I know you're tired and you're not home yet." "You'll have to get a copy of my book John." "You're writing a book?" "Yes, mostly about faith." "Interesting!" "I owe you a copy of it for your kindness." "I'm sure glad I went to pick you up Gaston, good night." "Good night John."

I went home tired but extremely satisfied. I thanked the Lord for the wonderful time I had and the opportunity to talk to John about faith, which might just be what he needs to turn his life around. I have seen the loneliness in this man's eyes. One could tell he suffered a lot and this for a long, long time. One could feel it in his voice too. I couldn't help asking the Lord to comfort him.

I was amazed by the entire blessing that comes my way and I prayed the Lord to keep me under his wing forever.

Once you've known how it's like, his love, his peace, his blessing, you don't want to go to hell anymore.

I went to bed that night and I dreamed almost word for word the rest of this book. When I laid my head on my pillow it was full of Precious, full of thanks to the Lord and this is how I fell asleep. If someone is going to fill your head with something might as well be the Lord, this way you'll come up with something good. How Great Thou Art forever and ever Amen.

Chapter 5

August 10 1998

The next morning Precious called me and she was crying over the phone.

"Gaston, I don't know how to tell you this, but I'm in lo-o-ove with someone and I don't know how to handle it." "Well, this is good news. I didn't think the Lord would have answered our prayer this soon. Who's the lucky man Dana? Are you sure he is the right guy?" "This is something I don't want to tell you over the phone." "I understand." I said shakily, trying the impossible not to choke or to cry too.

"Can you come to see me? I have two more hours free before school." "I'll do what I can to find someone to watch the place and I will be right over."

I thought if this is the will of God, I'll suffer through it. Not wasting a single minute I jumped in my car and I went as if it was an emergency. The traffic was so heavy that I wanted to run on the side of the road instead, thinking it might just be faster, but thirty minutes later I was at her side. When Dana opened the door she was still crying and to me tears in her eyes are just like a knife through my heart. It hurts so badly and there is no remedy for it. This is a lie, there is only one remedy, her smiles.

'Come here Precious.' And I held her tight in my arms for a long time.

"Love is good news, something to be happy about not to cry. Besides, this is killing me to see you crying like this, do you know this?" "If you want to be my friend Gaston, you better get used to it, because women always cry and I'm one of them too."

When she said this I wondered why she didn't call her best friend Denise instead.

"I'll get used to it maybe, but I know it will always hurt. Why do you act like you have to get married tomorrow?" "Becaaaause." "You don't want to tell me?" "This, not yet." "What ever you do with whoever, just don't rush anything. Don't you do something you might live to regret." "Gaston, you've been here only for a few minutes and I feel altogether so much better." "Thanks Dana, but most of the time things are not as bad as they look. It doesn't matter how you feel and with whom, just take your time, that's all." "You are a wonderful man, do you know this?" "No but, I'll make an effort to believe you." "So you don't think I should tell him just yet?" "Are you sure you just didn't dream you were in love? If it is as I think it is you just have discovered the fact and you might feel different next week. I myself love a woman very much and if she tells me she loves me and then changes her mind, I think this would kill me. This is the kind of things you just don't play with. Until you love someone enough that you would give your life for this person, it is best you don't say anything about it, especially to this person." "You said you love someone?" "Yes, I said it and yes I do love this person immensely, but until she loves me too, I wouldn't make any official declaration to her anyway." "I think you're right Gaston, I'll wait a little bit longer." "That's my girl. When you are absolutely sure, then tell him, love him and make him happy for as long as he lives and beyond." "What do you mean, beyond?" "Well, you see, I never read anywhere in the Bible where God said we are to love or be married until death separate us. I am told the two become one, I am told: 'May men don't separate what God has united.' Now, if God asked us not to separate what He has united, why then would He separates us? This is why I wrote in my song, the one I sang for you last night; I'll love you through eternity. I don't think it would be paradise to me if half of me is burning while I am in heaven. You see the real marriage the way God made it is the two become one, we are not two anymore but one. This one I think will either go to hell or to heaven. I know I'm going to heaven and I'm taking my other half with me." "I never thought of it this way Gaston, are you sure you're not a preacher?" "If I am, I'm not paid for it and this is great, because I received freely and I give freely. I'm sure of one other thing too and this is that Adam and Eve were one and still are, so are Noah, Abram, Isaac, Jacob, Joseph, Moses and many others with their other half. Also it was said that a woman was a suitable partner for a man. God gave Eve to Adam, not Steve." "Do you know what Gaston, now that I think of it, it does really make sense?" "Thanks Precious, I appreciate your comment. Don't you have to go to school now?" "Oh my God, I'm late." "I'm glad to see you smile again sweetheart. You go to your class and I'll go home and think about where I'll take you next time, ok?" "You're an angel mister Prince and I'm very happy you could come this morning. And thank you so very much." "You are more than welcome Precious anytime, anywhere." "I know this Gaston and just understand I appreciate it way more than I can tell. No more extravaganza though." "No, I promised you last night, remember?" "Yes I do. I'm glad you remember it too. I better let you go. Phone me soon, will you?" "I will sweetheart."

I kissed, hugged her and I wished her a good day.

'I already have.' She said with her most beautiful smile and home I went. All of that day I was nervous and a bit jealous of the man who Dana is in love with. Be happy for her and hope she is in love with a good man is about all I can do at this point; that she's in love with a man who is willing to give his life for his family. Almost everyone now can't go through a little marriage scene, nevermind going through the pre-tribulation or the believers' hunt. I do trust Dana though to know what is best for her. She is probably much smarter this way than I ever was. Besides, I just know the Lord will protect her as He protects all of his angels.

So faithfully I quitted worrying and I went on with my life as it was before the news. One question went through my mind though and this was: How come I don't have bugs in my arms and anxiety in my heart as it usually is when there is a bad news in the air?' The future will tell, I told myself.

In the evening of that day, I couldn't help calling Precious. I needed to know how she was feeling and if she was still in her smiling mood.

"Hi Precious, how is your day?" "Am I?" "What?" "Precious?" "I can't find a better word to tell you what you mean to me." "You really mean this, don't you?" "I sure do Precious, but why all those questions sweetie?" "Oh, I was just wondering." "We'll have to talk about this some more on Sunday night Princess." "What do we have on Sunday night Gaston?" "If it's alright with you sweetheart, I'd love to take you to a dinner type of evening, one where we can relax, talk and rest." "Not like the one last night, we won't." "No Precious, I promised you, I won't do this again for at least five years." "Good, because I couldn't, I can guarantee you this." "I don't think I could either Dana, but I'd sure like to see this show you seem to be so excited about." "Somebody told me it was out of town already Gaston. I'm so sorry you missed it." "It's ok sweetie, it might come back some day, who knows?" "I wish I knew whom the Defender is, I always been interested in this kind of men." "He could very well be a woman and you wouldn't know." "This is true too, I never thought of this, but he or she isn't a very big person and I still like to know who this is. So where are we going Sunday night?" "Can I keep the secret until then Princess?" "You are preparing something big again, aren't you?" "No sweetheart, something different maybe, but not big." "I guess I can only trust you, can't I?" "You sure can and if you need anything you call anytime, ok?" "What I need this week is thinking and I need a lot of it too." "Don't make yourself sick over whoever or he'll have to bring you some flowers in the hospital." "Don't worry Gaston, I'll be careful." "Good, this is what I like to hear." "Besides, remember one thing, I think flowers are something that goes to waste. One is enough to tell me how someone feels." "I'm glad you're feeling better, take good care of yourself sweetie and I'll talk to you soon, bye."

The rest of the week went on as usual. I kept writing the book and playing my music when suddenly another beautiful tune came to my mind and one more. I can hardly believe what's happening. This was on June the 25th 1998.

You know what they say; that seeing is believing and hearing is believing too? Now what about seeing, hearing and doing it all within five minutes? What it seems to be a heavenly piece of music as someone said when hearing it. 'It touches the soul.' I recorded it and the next day while listening to it again the words came to me as if they were already written. Almost each and every note was telling me the word that goes with it. This one I called it: The Final Warning.

Everyone who is not sure of his salvation must hear this one, because it might just be his last chance, his last warning. I have good confidence my book will be published, but one can never tell for sure, because only God knows. My inspiration is not only this song is the last warning, but also this book is. Something gigantic is coming for sure. God always been the same and I know He can't put up with this world the way it is for much longer. He always warns his people also about what He's going to do. See Amos 3, 7. 'Surely the Sovereign Lord does nothing without revealing his plan to his servants the prophets.'

The Final Warning

Listen to this one great news sent to you today.
To me it's the greatest; the Lord is on his way.
He has made the universe, the earth and heavens.
And all that you can see has been made by his hands.
'Many times I have showed you the mighty power.
I have flooded the earth, but I have saved Noah.
When Abram the good man had pleaded for his friends.
They got out of the towns Sodom and Gomorrah.

2
Do you remember Joseph I sent to exile?
He was sold by his brothers, he was put in jail
He was to save my people from the starvation
Of a deadly famine seven years duration.
And what to say of Moses drew out of water?
To guide you through the crises and lots of danger.
I told him all I wanted as for you to know
He carried all my commands down to you below.

3
The wisdom of Solomon, the strength of Samson.
Can just not save your soul from the lake of fire.
Only Jesus the Saviour with his compassion
Left his beautiful home, they took him for ransom.
I sent you my beloved Son for the sacrifice.
He has done nothing wrong yet he has paid the price.
Now if you are telling Me, this is not for you.
Just one more thing to say, I've done all I can do.
Instrumental

4
Now you are out of time and I am out of blood.
Too many of my children have died for their God.
Many of Jesus' good friends and his apostles.
And so many others died as his disciples.
Now it is time to crown My Own Beloved Son.
He's going back to run everything that I've done.
Will you be lost forever or will you be saved?
This is what you should know before you hit the grave!'

5
Listen to this one great news sent to you today.
To me it's the greatest the Lord is on his way.
He has made the universe, the earth and heavens
And all that you can see has been made by his hands.
And all that you can see has been made by his hands.

The last generation

Here are some signs of the end time and that we are the last generation of this actual world.

1- The fornication is so great I wonder how the prostitutes can survive. It is the first generation which sees this on such of a large scale since Noah.

2- We are the first generation since Sodom and Gomorrah which allows gays and lesbians to parade freely in our streets in front of our children and it seems there is nothing we can do about it. We all know what happened then.

3- We are the first generation where the divorce rate reaches sixty-five per cent since Noah. Never before we heard so much about single parents and families with multiple fathers and multiple mothers.

4- We are the first generation who has abolished the Lord's day, which is the day of rest, the Sabbath day. Just about everything is open on Sundays or Saturdays now just like every other day of the week. Although, it is truly one of the principals commandments.

5- It is the first generation where men and women are afraid of each other and they have reasons to be.

6- It is the first generation where God was categorically put out of the schools. A teacher could be fired for giving a Bible to a student during the school's hours.

7- First generation where the kids are allowed to tell their parents: 'You can't spank me and if you do I'll send you to jail.' And yet be right about it. If I'd tell my father this I wouldn't be here today to write about this subject in this book.

8- First generation who allows gangs to be called hell's angels and have cops come on the air and say they are afraid of them. They had much more pride than this in my dad's generation.

9- First generation where the thieves seem to have more rights than you on your own property. Less than one hundred years ago they were hanged on the spot when they were caught. They kind of stopped their damage then.

10-It is the first and believe me it is the last generation who allows the murders of millions of babies through abortions.

I could go on like this for another one half hour and you too already have noticed a few of those on your own. The point is we are the first generation in a lot of things, but mainly the last generation before the second coming of Jesus-Christ my Lord. When all the Jews and the believers in God are being persecuted and killed, the Lord will have no more reason to wait any longer and every reason to come back sooner and this is soon. Only this time he is not coming like a gentile lamb, but rather like the King of kings and this will be with authority.

16/08/98

Sunday, another beautiful day the Lord has made and allowed me to live through it. Worshipping my God, this is something I do every day and may He forgive me if I miss.

It is also a day I will be with Precious again and what a blessing this is. I have been a little nervous all morning and I wondered if she's going to tell me who she's in love with. I know she's not the type of person to change her mind easily.

All week I was hoping she would call, but I thought it was best I didn't influence her anymore in any way. Some decisions are best been taken in a quiet environment, especially if they are the ones which concern a lifetime. I have to admit too; I am afraid to ask and I respect her decision to tell me on her own willingness and time.

I went to pick her up at six o'clock and when she opened the door I almost fell backward astonished by the beauty that stood in front of me. She was wearing a beautiful long white dress with gold buttons and a gold belt. No one in the whole world could wear it more perfectly than she does. The gold, diamonds, rubies suit so beautifully to her beauty that I thought I'm glad my Lord is not like the kings of this world, because I would surely lose my Precious Princess to Him.

"Is there something wrong Gaston?" "I'll be fine sweetie as soon as I can breathe again. You don't want me to do something big, but look at you. Can you and your dress stand a hug?" "I don't know about the dress, but I sure can use one myself and I waited long enough." "Oh Precious, you are so beautiful that I wonder what I'm doing here." "You are looking pretty good yourself M. Prince." "My look beside yours beautiful Majesty is something we don't want to talk about. But I still have to tell you Princess though, that what attracted me to you the most is your kindness, your heart and soul. This is something you'd still have even if you were old, fat and ugly." "Are you telling me I couldn't attract you with my baby face and my young body?" "I'm telling you Dana there are a lot of pretty girls out there, but you are the only one I know with your kind of heart and if you didn't have it, I wouldn't be here, truly.

Now I think the supper might be getting cold and we should be on our way? I washed my old car, I hope you won't get any dirt on your dress." "We can use mine if you don't mind." "Not at all, it is a bit newer." "Here are my keys Gaston." "No Dana, you can drive, it is your car." "And have you to watch me all the way to-o-o. Where are we going anyway?" "It is called the Princess Restaurant." "And I suppose you don't own it and you don't have anything to do with it? It's my turn to watch you M. Prince, so I'll sit in the passenger side for a change and watch you drive." "If you insist Princess, I'll sacrifice myself." "Not that it's bothering me Gaston, but why don't you have a newer car? I'm sure you can afford it." "Maybe so, but I do have much more important things to do with the money, besides, I think new and expensive cars attract gold diggers." "I see they got you a few times." "Too many times yes. Here we are sweetie." "It's seems to be absolutely packed." "Don't you worry Precious, we have a reserved table." "I can tell that you went out before Gaston." "Oh sure, once or twice, but never with such a beautiful princess, except once." "Who was she?" "You, last week." "I'm touched. I recognise a few cars, quite a few of my friends are here." "I'm not surprised, I think it is a good place. I heard they serve very good food, the prices are good too and your friends must have heard of it also." "They never told me anything about it." "Now give me a chance to be a gentleman and wait for me to open your door, would you? This way you can watch for your beautiful dress to make it too." "M. Prince, men like you are getting to be so rare, that we women don't know how to react to this kind of things anymore. Thanks for telling me." "I'm touched too. Let's go in and let's have a good time and don't think you have to stay with me every minute even if it is what I wish the most. There might be some friends of yours who would like to steal you from me, I will understand." "You're just a sweetheart M. Prince." "Do you mean this Dana?" "I told you before Gaston, I mostly say what I mean to say." "So do I Precious and you're magnificent."

As we walked in Dana was amazed to see so many friends of hers were dining in the same place.

"You must be behind this again Gaston? I can't see any other explanation." "No sweetheart, my word, all I did is telling one of your co-workers about this place." "And they all came here tonight, all of them in the same evening?" "Maybe they have decided to celebrate your birthday too and make me feel guilty for having you all to

myself last week. Nobody can make me regret it though."
"It was wonderful Gaston, I'll never forget it for as long
as I live." "Neither will I Dana. We'll find out soon sweetie
about what they are up to and if there is anything."

Each and everyone of them praised Dana for her
dress and all of them wanted to see her jewels very
closely, telling her how lucky she was. I thought to myself,
if you guys knew how much I fought to get her to accept
anything from me, you would say I am the lucky one. I felt
I was envied by most men in the restaurant, young and
older for being with her. With such of a beautiful princess
as her a man doesn't need hundreds like King Solomon
did. Dana fills my heart so graciously and astonishingly
that I'm concern about its condition. I don't think my age
has anything to do with it either.

"I think you're right sweetheart, there are too many of
your friends here to be coincidental, but it is too late now
to go anywhere else. Who knows, you might just going
to enjoy it. Let's have our supper and relax for now, shall
we?" "You're right as usual Gaston." "Yes, but you're right
too Precious, there is enough going on here to question
yourself. They must be up to something, but I have no
idea what it is and it has nothing to do with me. In fact
I thought we were having a very relaxing tête-à-tête,
just the two of us. When I'm with you Precious the time
is so precious that I want to be very selfish and keep
you to myself every second, every minute." "What are
you telling me exactly Gaston?" "Always the same thing
Dana, as I did the first minute I met you, that you are
extremely precious sweet Precious." "It is true that you
did Gaston, but you see, hundreds of guys do and then
they turn around and tell other girls the same thing again
and again." "Huh, huh, not me, I couldn't." "I know this
now M. Prince, I know you are different. You said you
would tell me sometime tonight, what you expect from

me." "Do you want me to expect something Dana?" "Hum, maybe!" "Can I repeat the same question I asked you last week?" "You'll have to, because I don't remember it." "Do you want me to tell you what I expect from you for tonight or forever after?" "This is right too, you did and I told you I want you to tell me both." "What do you want to know first?" "The simpler order, for tonight first." "Ok, but then I'll tell you the second one only after supper." "Fair enough, so shoot." "For tonight I want at least one dance with you and maybe if I can ask, I want you to tell me a few secrets you keep behind those beautiful blue eyes of yours." "What do you mean?" "Well, maybe I too want to know what you expect from me." "I'm touched again."

Pretty soon the supper was over and I was thinking of how I will tell Dana about what I have in mind for the future. I thought tonight either I will win her heart for ever or scare her for life. Since we didn't have a too big of a meal this time we had room for dessert. For me it was as if I wanted to stretch things a little bit longer. We were later than everybody else and also we knew nothing about what was going on. So there was no rush for neither of us.

Then suddenly all the others began removing their tables and chairs all around us. We were the only two in the place who didn't know what was happening. The M.C. came up with a microphone in his hand and he said:

'. . . Ladies and gentlemen, friends and others, we're having here tonight a very unusual kind of party . . . .'

"You have nothing to do with this Gaston?" "My word, I don't."

'. . . We don't have a red carpet and neither limousines or a big band . . . .'

"All women cry and talk Dana. Maybe you have something to do with this?" "None that I know anything about Gaston." "So much for the quiet evening I anticipated with you sweetie. Nevertheless, I am delighted to be here with you Precious Princess." "Do you mean this M. Prince?" "This is not a thing to lie about Precious. Excuse me Dana, but I think we should get out of the spotlight."

'. . . We have found out Dana was pretty good in opening the dances and she has experience in doing so . . . .'

A young man came by and he asked Dana for the dance.

'No thanks Don, but I'll have this dance with this gentleman here, if it's ok with him?'

"History repeats itself sweetie and I would be very honoured to do so. Do you still remember how?" "I lived it in my mind over and over since M. Prince. I think I would know it even without counting on you or on my fingers." "I'm sure of this too beautiful. Let's go and thanks for choosing me Precious." "Forgive Don, would you? This was being pretty ignorant from him." "You are so beautiful sweetie, anyone can understand his behaviour."

'We'll do a foxtrot sir.'

"He only risked a slap and he got it, but now that I know you better I would risk my life. In fact I did." "When?" "Two weeks ago." "You didn't risk your life." "I thought I did." "This is true too. Are you going to tell me now what you are expecting from me?" "I could, but I'm afraid if I do now, I'll have to carry you all the way to our table." "This bad, hey?" "No, this good."

By the time the dance was over there were people all around us and the M.C. thanked Dana for complying. She was warmly applauded and congratulated all the way to our table.

"I didn't know you could do this kind of dances." "I didn't know either."

As soon as we reached our table Dana said:

"Gaston, now it's time, I want to know. Tell me!" "I want four children, two boys and two girls." "What?" "I told you, I want two boys and two girls, this is what I want from you."

She put one hand to her mouth and with the other one she grabbed a napkin and hid her eyes with it. Two of her friends must have been watching us, because they came right away and they accused me of being heartless for making her cry on her birthday party.

'Leave him alone.' She cried out right away. 'He makes me cry of happiness.'

'What?' This was my turn to ask.

"Do you remember Monday morning?" "How can I forget?" "I told you I was in love with someone." "I do remember." "This someone is."

'. . . Ladies and gentlemen, the party is on and all of you make sure you are here to have fun. This is what Dana's friends have paid me for. They have decided it was better late than never to give this young celebrity a party she won't forget too soon . . .'

The music was pretty loud and so was the M.C. When he was done talking, everybody in the place could hear it.

'It's you I'm in love with Gaston.'

Do I have to tell you what happened in the following few minutes? I'll tell you anyway. It was my turn to put a hand to my mouth and a napkin to my eyes. I cried longer and louder than Precious did. Another miracle I thought and this one is the greatest yet. The incredible just happened right in front of my own eyes. A huge mountain has been removed. I know who is the Lord of lords and the King of kings.

"I thought for sure that because of your age you wouldn't want anymore children. I tortured myself all week because of it. Our God must know what He is doing Gaston." "Better than we do Precious Princess." I said through my sobbing.

'. . . Would everyone join me now in this birthday song? . . .'

'Happy birthday to you, happy birthday to you, happy birthday dear Dana, happy birthday to you.'

At this precise moment, I was holding Dana so tight, everyone could tell that I didn't care for her dress anymore and once more we were under the spotlight. Then all of them began to clap their hands. They have started slowly and went on with more and more intensity, shouting:

'We want Dana to give us a speech, a speech, a speech, a speech.'

She looked me straight in the eyes and she said: 'You come with me.'

I followed her to the stage not daring blinking an eye. She picked up the microphone and she started.

'Thanks everybody, thanks to all my friends. Thank you so very much for everything. I have a very special announcement to make.'

You could at this moment hear a fly in the place so much no one wanted to miss a word.

'I found the love of my life or rather, the love of my life found me. Let me introduce to you my future husband, M. James Prince here by my side.'

We could hear some muttering and grumbling, but nevertheless they started applauding first with hesitation and then louder.

'If I could make a wish for my birthday as it is the custom, it would be that all the princesses of this world could find their princes as I did.'

She looked at me and she continued.

'If you ever see him with tears in his eyes, don't you think he is a wimp, because he's not. He is though the most sensitive human being I know and I'll be very proud to be his bride.'

Following this she passed me the microphone.

'I won't keep you long. Doesn't she look like the most beautiful bride on earth tonight?'

This was followed by a standing ovation and I held her so tight, I thought I could break her back.

'Someone said this about me once, I was a blind man with a large vision. Thank you very much.'

I gave the microphone back to the M.C. and I walked Precious to our table holding her so tight that we could hardly walk, as if we were drunk. I think we were mad with joy.

"Sweet revenge Dana?" "Very sweet Gaston!"

Once at our table a tall man in his mid thirties came to asked Dana if he could have a talk with her. She apologised to me and the two of them went towards the back of the restaurant. When ten minutes was gone I began to worry thinking Dana won't do this if she could help it. So I decided to go to the washroom which is in the same direction they have taken.

Sure enough, this man was holding her by her arms in a forcing way and she had tears in her eyes asking him to leave her alone. I walked slowly towards them and I asked the young man to let her go. He looked at me with a nasty smile and he asked:

"What are you going to do about it if I don't shorty old man?" "Are you sure you want to know?" "I'd love to." He said laughing nastily.

'Let her go and I'll show you a good trick, maybe two.'

"No Gaston, he's too big." "A jerk like this who forces himself on women is not a man and he's never too big for me."

He burst out laughing and he pushed Dana away. This was an answered prayer. I slowly walked towards him and I heard Precious crying out:

'No Gaston, he's not worth it.'

When I was close enough I gave him my arm to grab as I do with a vicious dog and he did. A dog would have had his bottom jaw broken, but this animal here might straighten up with a good lesson. As soon as he had my arm in his hand in less than two seconds he was on his knees making all kind of faces.

"Don't break my arm." "Why not? You didn't care of how much you were hurting her. You better start praying for it, because this is exactly what I'd like to do with it, big turd."

By then Dana was back with three of the boys she works with and a number of other friends.

'You apologise to this lady and I might let you go without any fracture.'

'Who did you say needed our help Dana?'

I could almost laugh when I saw her beautiful blue eyes watching with astonishment and stupefaction.

The jerk was escorted by Dana's kind of bodyguards to the exit after his apology was accepted.

"Wow Gaston! How in the world did you manage this? I saw this guy fight before and he does it like a vicious dog." "I raise and train dogs, didn't you know this? It is a very simple trick and I'll have to show it to you so, if it happens again I wouldn't have to wait for you anymore than one or two minutes." "You mean that if I knew how, I could have done this myself?" "Yes, but you don't like violence." "True, but I hate abuse even more." "If this is the case then, I'll show you a few tricks." "I can hardly believe you Gaston, you seem to know something about everything." "Well, I faced a few challenges through my life so far." "Since you seem to know something about everything, you must know in what you are getting into with me?" "My sweet darling, it is what I would have to do with the rest of my life without you I was concerned about. As it is now, I'm in heaven already.

Tonight I am the happiest man on earth and it is absolutely impossible to make me happier." "I am the happiest woman too and all of this because of you." "Before I forget Precious, I want to thank you for coming to my rescue." "You didn't need any help. I did though, thanks to you, you did rescue me." "As if I did it for myself my sweet half." "I like this. The idiot told me you were twice my age as if I didn't know. He got really mad when I told him you were worth many like him. He didn't have to wait too long to find out how right I was." "You were wrong." "What do you mean?" "You do this again when there is no help around and you might get hurt badly or worse. Life without you would be hell, besides, I was lucky." "To put a big guy like this on his knees and to force him to apologise. Luck M. Prince, I don't think so. I would call this skills. The whole town will be talking about this." "I wish no one would." "Why?" "Because I want to love you and to raise our children in peace and in happiness for the rest of my life. I don't want to be answering some risky challenges unnecessarily." "Man you are a wise man, I still have a lot to learn from you." "See Dana, this guy is the kind of men who will sell his kids for a case of beer or for a few joints. The girls who get caught with this type of persons will cry bitterly. Can I have another dance with you Precious?" "Nothing fancy." "No, I just want to hold you in my arms again." "You do this forever Gaston." "You look concerned. Are you already thinking about our children's names?" "I never thought I could find a man who would want four." "Is this too many?" "Not for me, it isn't." "One at a time and then, we'll see how you handle them. Your health comes first." "Fair enough my love, I'll go for this."

I took her to the dance floor and the two of us made one, not physically, but emotionally and spiritually I know we did. One we are and one will stay, because no one can separate what God has united.

As soon as the dance was over more announcement came through.

'. . . Attention ladies and gentlemen, it is time now to let go the presents to the beautiful young lady. Dana, would you come up here please? This moment has been waited for now by a number of people impatiently and they told me now it's the time . . .'

"Gaston, you come with me." "It's your birthday sweetheart." "Gaston, please?" "You just know I can't say no to you, don't you?" "I sure hope so my love." "I'll come up so you're not alone and to help with the presents and also to be with you." "I knew I could count on you." "Yes, one, two, three." "Very funny, come on."

I have thought of a lot of things since I met Dana, but never once it has crossed my mind she would walk with me with so much pride, as if I was a young prince.

The gifts came out and her best friend, Denise was chosen to do the talking. Just about all of the gifts were more or less jokes like condoms, theatre's tickets, wineglasses, bus return tickets, etc. Then suddenly the big surprise came up.

"Now my very good friend Dana, everybody put into this one. To make this more interesting we want you to make three guesses before you open this last box." "It is a watch? Tickets for two to Hawaii? Five days for two at the West Edmonton Mall?" "I'm afraid you have failed, but I have to admit, it is not easy. I'll give you one more chance to guess after this one last tip. We have found out lately that you are a princess and we have decided it was time for us to treat you like one as well."

Precious looked at me, she smiled and she said:

"A five-dollar tip!" "Good guess, but you're wrong again."

Dana proceeded to open the box. I was standing just behind her and it was a good thing I did, because I don't think she was far away from falling backward.

'Your Majesty Princess Dana; it is an over due time to crown you. I know you are a princess to M. Prince here, but you are a princess to most of us too.'

The incredible beautiful crown she got out of the box was really impressive. It is made out of gold, loaded with diamonds, pearls and a large ruby in the middle of it. My experience tells me it is worth thousands of dollars. For almost two minutes Precious couldn't take her eyes off it. Then she turned around, looked at me and she said:

"You put it on my head Gaston." "I symbolically did a year ago." "I know, now you do it so everybody can see, including me." "I will need your help Denise." "With tears in my eyes I screamed out: 'My Precious Princess of Wonderland.'

Then Denise asked the crowd: 'Should we ask M. Prince to say something more?'

I didn't really want to, but since they have insisted, I picked up the microphone and I went on.

'Almost a year ago I met Dana for the very first time. This was on August 30th 1997. I saw her again the next day, the 31st. This was the day Princess Diana died.'

People started humming in the crowd.

'Don't be sad. I'm sure that by now Diana has found peace and love she could not find down here even though she had a lot of money. As you all know I'm pretty sure she had to hide to love and to be loved. On this day the whole world lost the Queen of Heart, a precious princess

to many, many people. On this very same day, I met my
Precious Princess. I fell in love with her immediately. A few
days later I started a book called: The Precious Princess
of Wonderland. It should be out very soon. Please watch
for it, if you want to know the rest of this endless story.
Thank you very much.'

Dana came and she hugged me so intensively that
Denise asked her three times to let go before she did.
From this moment on I knew for sure my love was
returned for the very first time in my life. I don't know two
words to describe how it feels and the only one I know is
wonderful.

"Sweetie you are the most beautiful princess on the
face of the earth, not only on the outside, but also in
the inside. May God bless you always!" "Because of you
Gaston, I know I will be. Where do we go from here?"
"Let's go home and talk it over."

By that time most everyone had tasted the cake, said
good night and left. The ride home was quick and quiet.
We walked into her apartment and I did just what I was
dying to do for months. This was to hug and kiss her until
I was completely out of breath.

"What is your plan Gaston?" "My plan is to work out
something which will be suitable for both of us. I never
rush anything unless I have to. How much schooling do
you have left?" "Six months if I graduate." "I know you
will. Then you'll be ready to get on your own." "Thanks
to you M. Prince." "Oh, I just helped a little. I just know
sweetheart there will be very many princes and princesses
coming out of your place, because of your touch." "You
do love my touch, don't you?" "I infinitely love everything
about you tease." "A new title again?" "You deserved this
one too." "How do you see life from now on?" "I have
to finish the book and get it published and if they don't
publish it, I will need to cross the country and try to get

in every church I possibly can to promote and the book and the songs." "What about your business?" "I have six months to get everything organised."

"Oh Gaston, I hope it would be published, because I don't like the idea of you leaving for who knows how long." "I don't want to be apart from you period sweetie and this will be the last resource. On the other hand, I'd like to give you more time. You have to study and I don't want to be in your way or to be the reason for you to fail. It would be nice if we could do it all in the same period of time." "What do you mean?"

"In six months I could get my business operational on its own. I mean without me being there all the time. You could finish your schooling and get your office's building ready to operate. I can help you with this. Get the book published.

Then I could retire, stay home, love you and raise our children, play music and compose more songs and music, start another book maybe. I already have another idea for one more, one which will be called: The True Face of The Antichrist. Then I could study more Aikido and be happy forever after. Oh and I was forgetting, I could also teach you a few tricks for self defence, dancing and send you to work while I am enjoying life." "Do you know what Gaston? I couldn't even dream of a better plan. Did you dream all this too?" "I have been dreaming all this for almost a year now and it is wonderful to see it coming to reality." "What a guy you are, never in my whole life I have experienced as much pride as I have tonight with you." "Same here sweetie."

"What's the date Gaston?" "I'll tell you in six months, if you didn't change your mind." "I would never change my mind for as long as I live Gaston. Now can you believe this?" "Yes darling, I can, but I still want to give you a chance to sink it in, otherwise I wouldn't feel honest."

"What do we do in the meantime?" "What's wrong with what we have done tonight and last week Precious?" "Oh, this is absolutely wonderful Gaston, but we can't do this all the time. We cannot exhibit ourselves like this every week." "I don't see why not. All it cost tonight is a two plate's supper. We can do this probably the rest of our lives." "What about love? I want you." "I want you too my Precious darling more than anything in the world, but I also want all the blessing that comes with the things done right for you and I and for the children to come." "Aren't you a wonderful man?" "The Lord is with me, this makes the difference.

Sweetie, if you ever come to a more critical point, promise me you will let me know." "What would you do then?" "It was said; 'it was better to marry than to burn with passion.' I won't let you burn if I can help it." "Oh Gaston, I'm burning, I'm burning." "Tease, this is serious." "Gaston, I promise you I would never go anywhere else ever." "This is not what I meant sweetheart, but if your pro-o-o-blem gets worse, I want to know. I might have the same problem too, you know? Help me then if you can." "I will." "Tease!"

The following fifteen minutes were just between her, the Lord and me. She cried and so did I, but those were some repentant and healthy for the soul kind of tears.

"I better go now and give you a chance to get some sleep, otherwise you wouldn't be able to do anything good tomorrow. Phone me Tuesday night sweetie if you finish your studying early enough." "Can you not be so reasonable sometime Gaston?" "I sure can, but let's pick a night when neither of us has to work the next day." "This will never happen Gaston, you work all the time." "Oh, I take time off too now that my son is around. I'll tell you what Precious, you pick a time and I'll be here." "Now!" "Yes, you pick a time now." "This is the time I picked, now."

"Aren't you too tired and too emotional now?" "I'll always be emotional with you Gaston, you're nothing but love." "And you're nothing but lovely, Precious." "I want to know more about how you see life for us in the future." "Do you really think I can tell you all about our future Dana?" "No, but you can tell me how you think we are going to live our life or try to." "Ok, I told you before, I want to stay home and send you to work." "I'm not the type of women to go to work and feed a man at home doing nothing, you must know this." "Well, I'm glad you're not. I am ready to retire next year and I want to stay home and do all the housework. This means fixing the bed, doing the dishes and the laundry, cleaning the house in and out, do all the repairs, learning how to sew and everything else that concerns the house, the children and a wife. I will enjoy bringing up the children. This is something I really missed once and I'm thankful for having a second chance." "What else Gaston?" "I'll try to get some time to write and play my music and I already have an idea for another book. Then, I'll be happy if I can find the time to write it. I'll love every minute of the day doing this and I hope you'll come home as soon as you can every night for supper. If you're not home you'll be missing your favourite meal, because I intend to cook what you like the best all the time." "I'll get fat." "I'll love you anyway and if I have to, I'll make you a diet. If this is not enough, then you can exercise with me." "You don't mind all this?" "Not at all! Hey, I worked more than forty years doing men's hard labour, it is more than due time now for me to take it easy." "Easy?" "You seem to be very serious too." "You bet I am." "I'll support the family." "No thanks, I have more income than I need. The book should bring more of it too. You keep what you make and do what ever you want with it. Maybe once in a while you can spoil us and take us all out on a holiday. There is one thing though I really insist on." "What is it?" "I still want to be the man of the house. I will never quit wearing my pants." "It's all yours M. Prince, you deserve the title.

Now the money situation is settled, what about religion?" "Well, you already know I am a child of God and that I am very close to my Father. I know you are one too, but you don't know this yet. I'll never push it on you though, this is the Lord's duty. I want to raise the children in the Lord's way, so they too can be princes and princesses. This way they will all come to join us in Wonderland on Jesus' day." "You do have a lot of faith, don't you?" "The joy of knowing is incredible. I feel sorry for anyone who doesn't have this peace I'm talking about." "Some other time Gaston you'll have to talk to me about God and his love." "It's the greatest Dana." "I think yours is." "My sweet Precious, mine is only a particle of it as little as a star in the universe."

"Wherever you go Gaston, I want to be with you."

"As soon as you sincerely give your heart to the Lord sweetie, you'll be assured a place in heaven too." "My heart I gave it to you." "Put Him first and He'll give you everything. Give Him everything and He'll give you everything you need." "You're a good person Gaston." "Maybe so, but you are a better one yet." "How can you say this Gaston, I don't know anyone as good as you?" "No sweetie, there are a lot of good people out there, much better than I am, but if they think they are good enough not to need Jesus the Saviour, I'm afraid they are like Lucifer and they will end up in the same place." "This is sad." "This is why it is important to accept the Lord's gift." "Do you mean that God loves better a bad person who comes to Him than a good one who doesn't?" "Yes, hey you catch on quickly." "Maybe so, but I am still confused." "If I have a good dog who listens to himself or to my enemy or to my neighbour and not to me when I call him, how good is it for me?" "Not much, you're right." "You see, I would rather have a bad dog who listens to me, this way I would have a chance to train it. God's concept is very simple, but men have twisted things around and this is the work of the devil. When you welcome Jesus and his teaching in your life, all the confusion goes away and then, you can be very happy." "I know you're a happy man." "I was happy even in the saddest days, because God carries my cross for me when I couldn't do it anymore." "It is four o'clock already. Gaston, the time is flying so fast when you're with me, I won't see my life going by." "Having second thoughts already sweetheart?" "Never, never Gaston, I am with you forever." "I appreciate what you're saying Precious, but I would like it better if you would wait a bit longer before you make any kind of commitments." "Ok, I know I will die loving you Gaston, there are not two ways about it." "You don't know everything about me yet." "I know what I need to know." "Maybe so, maybe not, will see." "Now you are scaring me Gaston, what should I know?" "I wish I could spare you this sweetie, but it is impossible." "It is too late to get into it tonight, but next time we'll get together, I'll have to tell you something that might be a shock to you." "You didn't kill anybody, did you?" No, don't be ridicules; it is nothing I'm ashamed of." "Can't be this bad then?" "I better go now. I hate to leave you this way, but it would take way too much time to go over it tonight, I mean this morning. As it is you won't have much sleep and I shouldn't have stayed this long." "It has been wonderful Gaston, I'm in another world right now." "Wonderland?" "Something like this, yes. I don't think you should go home now, I think you're too tired." "I'm ok." "No you're not, you're exhausted. You take my bed and I'll sleep on the couch." "No sweetie, if I stay I'll take the couch, but I don't think I should."

"Yes, you do." "Bossy." "I want to see you alive again, so be reasonable and stay. A tired and sleepy driver is just as dangerous as a drunken one. You can leave when I do. Here are some blankets, good night my love." "Good night darling."

When I woke up, Dana was already gone and I found a note on her coffee table saying:

'Sorry I kept you so late. You were sleeping so well if I'd wake you up, I would have had remorse. Have a wonderful day and I'll phone you soon my love. Kisses and hugs as strong as you are, bye, Dana.'

It was ten o'clock then and I could already hear my son say:

'You had a good night dad?' And this with a smile on his face.

"Lot of talking." "Sure, I'll buy this." "You can buy what you want, but I'm telling you the truth." "Too bad." "How do you know? Short nights sleep have never made me the most patient person son and you already know this, so please don't tease me anymore, would you? You're doing alright here. I think I'm going to lay down for a couple of hours." "Maybe she's too young for you dad?" "No more teasing I asked you and for what you are suggesting remember one thing; a thing which hasn't been abused lasts much longer than an abused one. You will probably run out of ink before I do. Go to work and come and get me only if it is necessary." "Sleep well and have sweet dreams." He said laughing.

"Keep this for yourself too." "Oh sure, you can tell the world through your book, but I can't tell my friends, right?" "Right, this is my story. Besides, I might be eighty when the book gets out." "Hey dad, where is your faith?" "Right, go away, this is enough talking for me."

At six o'clock the phone rang and I answered it to the tired but beautiful voice of my angel.

"Hi my love, how are you?" "A little sleepy still, but ok. You sound pretty tired yourself Precious, are you alright?" "I'm tired and I'll go to bed early tonight, but I miss you Gaston." "Oh sweetheart, I miss you very much too." "Gaston, I never felt this way before, what is it with you?" "Maybe you just have discovered what real love is all about." "I thought I was in love one time before, but it was nothing like this, I just can't get enough of you." "I just hope you never will sweetie." "Can we get an earlier date?" "How's your schedule for tomorrow night?" "I don't know yet." "If you finish early enough, we'll get together and we'll talk about it, if you can wait till then." "Can't you tell me anything now?" "Yes, but not about our future over the phone." "Why?" "When I do Precious, I want to look into the beautiful eyes of yours. Get a good night's sleep sweetie and we'll try to get together tomorrow night and don't worry, everything will be fine, trust me." "I trust you Gaston, I never trusted a man like this before." "Believe me Dana, give it some time and you won't be sorry." "Ok my love, you have a good night, love you." "Take my lips to your dream sweetie." "I will, kiss you, bye."

From this goodbye kiss until I met Dana the next day I prayed God for the right words to tell her about the nightmare of my life. I sure hope she loves me enough to overcome this obstacle and there is only one way to find out.

I'm not afraid of suffering myself, but oh my God knows I would hate to cause her any pain. Hey, every good musician has to face the music and the crowd. I'll have to do just this too.

Tuesday evening, the music sheet is in front of me and I hope I can play it without any mistakes, because I have the most important audience of all my life. She is one for whom I want to play for over and over for the rest of my days.

"Hi Dana, how are you?" "Nervous." "Why? I'm the one who has to play." "What do you mean Gaston? I'm not Precious tonight?" "Dana, you will always be my Precious Princess no matter what. I was just lost in my thought, that's all." "What do you mean, you have to play?" "I was thinking I have to face the music with you." "This bad, huh?" "It is just a nightmare." "Don't you worry Gaston, I'm a counsellor, not a judge. Sit down and I'll make you a cup of tea, so you can relax over it. You just take your time and tell me what you want." "You wouldn't happen to have some rye by any chance?" "I know it is your favourite drink and I was just wondering how long it would take before you ask for it." "I don't really need it, but I have the taste for it." "Sure. I wish you had the taste for me." "Oh, I'm so sorry sweetie, come here, I want to kiss you too so bad. What preoccupation can do to you! I better get rid of this nightmare quick, because I wouldn't want to miss another kiss from you ever.

Might as well start from the beginning. Eight years ago, I was basically put out of business by the maintenance enforcement of Alberta. My children's mother had decided to take a year off work to stay with my handicapped daughter, but she neglected to mention we had an agreement between us. So the enforcement came after me after she told them I had several businesses and then I took arrangement with them. Everything was fine until one day the service manager of the bank where I had my saving and business accounts decided they wouldn't go automatically to the saving or the business account to cover the other one anymore. Only one thing though, they didn't bother telling me.

So I found out the hard way when all four of my bank accounts were emptied by the law enforcement. They basically put me out of business by leaving me with less than $20.00 to operate.

At that time I was running three construction companies and my D.J service. I also had my school dance which was more or less a hobby.

"Why so many Gaston?" "I was mostly contracting in small construction jobs, building garages, decks, fences and retaining walls. One day I realised the cement contractors were the first ones to be contacted and they were pulling away from me a lot of garages' jobs. So the only thing to do wasn't to cry out, but to start my own cement company too, which I did. Concretition Construction can compete anybody, can concrete everybody's garage, sidewalk, retaining walls etc. This is how it was advertised." "This is funny Gaston; it must have worked for you." "I was doing not to bad until." "The seizure?" "Right." "You had two more?" "Yes, Fencenation construction and Deckoration construction." "Where did you get those clever names?" "I created them. I'm a composer, remember?" "I can see this. Bravo!" "Thank you."

"Would you like another drink?" "Later on maybe, thanks.

I had up to twenty jobs at the time and I had to turn some down." "You must have been doing pretty good?" "I would've, but I didn't have enough of good employees." "What happened?" "I was making money on half of the projects and loosing on the other half." "Too bad!" "No sweetie!" "What do you mean no? I think this was too bad." "I know you do Precious, but you see; it took every single thing that happened to me in my life and in your life to get us here together tonight and there is no where else I would want to be." "Oh Gaston, what a treasure you are. Let me thank the Lord for us." "You're sweet."

"In the long weekend of thanksgiving of 1989 I came to B.C. for the first time. When driving down the valley I spotted the place where the hubcap collection is sitting now and I told the girlfriend of the time this would be the perfect emplacement for them. It is just a beautiful corner on the highway near Westbank with hundreds of large Ponderosa pine trees. Not even a little one of them needed to be put down.

There is a natural clearance where the hubcaps are sitting now on the side of the road lit up by two huge streetlights, one on each side. Everybody who drives by can see it just as good at night as in the daytime. It is one of the best spot in the whole Okanagan valley." "How clever of you!" "No Sweetheart, I'm not. I think I'm there more or less by miracle." "Gaston, it doesn't take a miracle to get a nice spot in B.C. What happened to your girlfriend?" "She didn't believe in the hubcaps business too much and she also had a good position near Calgary, so she left me." "Were you hurt?" "Only my pride, really! The miracle I'm talking about is the piece of land where the hubcaps are is on the Indian reserve and it is worth millions of dollars. Here I was totally broke sitting on a multi-millions dollars piece of property which no white man can buy and on top of everything, it was leased to me by someone who didn't own it and he had no rights to do so." "Wow! But Gaston, let's go back to the law enforcement, would you? What happened after this?" "They were questioning a little bit too much about my girlfriend, so I moved out of our apartment and I went to stay into my shop fearing they could go after her money as well." "Now, this was clever." "Thanks sweetie. Then I started thinking that if they can go into my bank accounts they might also be capable of coming after my hubcap collection and it was then I decided to move to B.C. My lawyer said afterward it was the best thing I could have done. What it did is giving me enough time to get a lawyer to fight back. This is what I did with success too. But they don't reimburse any money to anyone, as far as I know.

I first moved at a flea market on July first 1990 and then in October of the same year I moved where I am now. It took me five days and five nights in a row to do most of the moving, but I did it. I was stolen from both places, because I couldn't afford someone to watch on either place so, I decided to leave behind in Calgary over forty thousands dollars worth of material of all kind." "I guess Gaston this is what they call a little man with a big heart." "I couldn't get my first meal until I had my first sale. I had to sleep in my van on top of the hubcaps for two months before I could rent a very old trailer. There was not even a spot on the campground across the road from the hubcaps.

I had to go back to Calgary to finish some jobs people had already given me the money for. One of them had already called the police thinking I took off with the money he had given me for the material.

I told the police officer when he came to ask me the government has the money, not me. After a short investigation the officer went to reassure my customer who bought the material and allowed me to finish the job.

I had a man selling hubcaps here in Westbank and in the same period of time two thousands of them got stolen. I don't think he has anything to do with the stealing though.

Many, many times and many things have been stolen from me and I don't know by whom, but the Lord knows and who ever did it, he won't escape God's power.

As far as I am concerned I forgave them all and I forgot all about it, it is in the Lord's hands." "What a story Gaston, but this wasn't the nightmare you were talking about, was it?" "No Darling, the nightmare came later, but now that I am a little more relaxed, I wouldn't mind a cup of tea." "I'm sorry my love, I was so involved in your story that I forgot all about my manners." "I'm sure glad you're interested." "So much happened to you that you could write a series called: Gaston's Adventures." "If I was sure to have listeners like you, I would."

"Tea will be ready in two minutes." "Do you want to listen to the rest of the story tonight or some other time?" "Now, if it's alright with you?" "I'm ok now sweetie. The music wasn't easy to play, but the audience is absolutely marvellous." "Oh, you're so wonderful." "There was this old trailer I still owned by the way. It is a real antiquity. It's not this great, but it was a roof over my head. My neighbour, the same guy who leased me the property offered to rent it to me for $100.00 a month. This was on the 15th of September. On October first he was leasing me two acres for two hundred and fifty dollars a month. Only one thing though, he didn't own it." "How did you manage to stay there Gaston? This is incredible." "Maybe so, but it's true. This guy who I'm talking about sold the same horse to two different people the same day. He delivered it to one of them and got the money, he stole the same horse that night and he delivered it to the other man in the morning and he got the money again and he let the second man being charged for stealing the horse." "What a crook." "As far as I know he is still in the valley. Surprisingly no one kills this kind. He also stole his best friend's horse that was boarding at his place and it is worth thirty thousands dollars and he sold it without the owner's permission. The owner had to fight in court to get his horse back. The strangest thing of all is I got this place through the most dishonest man I know, but I just cannot be grateful to him for it.

The Landlord, an Indian who was drinking heavily at the time showed up there for the first time screaming and swearing as big as my belly."

'This is my land here.' He yielded. 'Who the hell gave you the permission to put anything on it?'

I could have told him it was the devil himself, but he wasn't in a laughing mood.

"Whoa, whoa I said, Jerk did and he told me he talked to you about this whole thing." "No, no, he didn't." "Ok then, let's go see him right away."

We walked the three hundred feet that separated us from Jerk's place. When we were beside Jerk I said:

'Jerk, you told me you talked to this man about me being there on his land and he's saying you didn't.'

'Yes Alan, remember? I told you that if you needed hubcaps we have thousands of them.'

The poor man didn't even have a car or driver's licence at the time.

'This is my land.' Alan was mumbling when walking back to my hubcaps' place. I told him this was his land and I would be more than happy to pay him the rent that belongs to him.

'I'll see.' He said and then he left leaving me in a very uncertain position. I couldn't afford by then to move ten feet away, nevermind moving out of there completely. He came back to see me with a temporary month to month lease in his hand two days later.

Jerk also sold me this trailer of 1964, size 10 feet by 32 I talked about earlier for $500.00 at $100.00 a month, but when it was time for the last payment I couldn't find the guy. I went to his place three times. I went there with witnesses the last two times and I left my business card on his door. I just couldn't find the man; he could just not be found anywhere. Two weeks later, he was at my place with somebody else and he wanted to repossess the trailer.

'Over my dead body.' I told them and someone called the police saying there is going to be a blood shed if they don't come quickly. There is when the last payment and the final receipt were made in front of a police officer. I gave them a severe warning also in front of the officer, not to ever come on this parcel of land, that I would use the necessary force to clear them out of it. The officer asked them if they heard me alright and he insisted for an answer. They both answered in an affirmative way. Jerk is an ex football player.

The trailer is only a piece of garbage that was cheep enough, it is for the principle I fought. I had to live in this trailer though and I did it for fifteen months.

Someone told me that in the valley winters were very mild and I wouldn't likely need a stove. What a lie this was. One night close to Christmas my son and I would have died with frozen brains if we went to sleep. It was minus 37 outside and minus 36 inside. We both spent the whole night turning around the little propane heater I had. The next day I had to pound my beautiful compound bow and arrows to get enough money to buy a stove and the necessary stove pipes and I gathered all the fire wood that was there on the property. I also had to pound my VCR to get some food. Sales were just dead by then.

Welfare won't help white men with this many hubcaps on the reserve and the Indian band would have kicked me out of it before they helped. It was just me the Lord and I, but I wasn't a born again man at that time, so for me then, I was alone in this part of the country, because my son had left by then. I was living with hundred of mice and not a spare dollar to buy a mouse trap either." "Gaston, you're going to make me cry, this is too sad." "We need a break then, don't we? It's getting late too. I should tell you the rest of my story another time." "No, I want to know all of it tonight." "I'm warning you, the worst is coming." "I'll be strong Gaston, I only have to listen to it, but you had to live through it." "It's life and this is what builds us up. The tougher it is the stronger we get.

Then Christmas came and I guess I was quite vulnerable, because I fell in the worse trap I could have. I met a woman who is a social worker and who was on sick leave. She wanted to give me the world as she said and she seemed to know a lot about what is going on around here. She said: 'You are going to lose everything you owned to the Indians.' By this time I heard a lot of stories from other people as well about the Indian Band. She really went out of her way to help me out and this is something I'm not used to. Normally I'm the one who helps others. I have poor eyes and she called a bunch of universities around the world to find out what was the best thing that could be done for them. She said she would mortgage her house and buy me a shop to put my hubcaps in to secure them all. I hired a man to sell hubcaps and I went back to work on construction as a carpenter to bring a better income. She couldn't believe it, within twenty minutes I found a job and I was on it the next morning.

In my spare time I started to work on her property, fixing everything that needed to be fixed and painting everything that needed to be painted. Within a month her house and garage were worth twenty thousand dollars more than when I started.

One night she got home with a pair of wedding rings, a five hundred-dollar man's clothing certificate and a marriage contract which was fair for both of us. She has been so wonderful for three months that I thought there is no way a person could be this good and then be bad. Now I know how the devil can make himself look like angels to get what he wants. I found this out too, but it was a little too late. She is an atheist who told me she wanted to learn about the Bible.

I knew a bit about the Lord then, but I hadn't accepted Jesus as my Saviour yet, or I would've known maybe. She also knew a lot too, because her children, her parents and her ex-husband are Christians.

She told me her ex-husband forced her to get baptised, because he wanted to become a deacon. She said: 'I almost died from drowning.'

This was why she had left and she refused to come to the Lord. Her parents were ex-communists and they became very good Christians, this I knew and I think this is what fooled me the most.

The Bible teaches us that a man who marries a repudiated woman commits adultery. Oh, how I wish I knew this then. It took me a very long time to understand why it is true for men and not for women. It is very simple and yet so hard to understand. Jesus is talking to his disciples. Now a disciple is not to commit adultery if he follows Jesus and he is not allowed to repudiate his wife unless she commits adultery. If she commits adultery and he sends her away, no other man can marry her without committing adultery." "No wonder now you want to take your time with me." "Sweetie, I want you to have the chance I didn't have.

One night at one fifty in the morning I woke up and she was holding a .38 pistol fully loaded on my head. I didn't really like facing the barrel, but I calmly pushed her shaking hand away and I asked her what was wrong.

She was in a kind of a trance, her whole body was trembling. A kind of white foam was leaking out of her mouth as you have probably seen in some exorcist movie (Fiddle attraction).

I thought then it was a miracle if I was still alive, now I know it was one." "Now Gaston, tell me why all of this was necessary?" "Because I was stubborn and I refused to come to the Lord and He wanted me. God brought me so close to hell that I could only want to go to heaven.

I took her to the hospital that night and I was very fortunate, because our family doctor was on guard and he could finally see for himself exactly the way she was. She had done few other things before and he didn't want to believe me when I told him about it. He actually thought I was the bad guy, a man who was not deserving of her. He knew her for over three years for working together on some child abuse's cases. That night he hit his head saying: 'I treated her three years long for physical and now I'm finding out it is in her head.' He made her promise to stay in the hospital until some deeper examinations were done, but the staff called me at five o'clock that morning saying she left. This was in Penticton. I brought her back and she asked to be transferred to Kelowna's hospital. Before all this she asked me to never take her to the Kelowna's hospital because she said she was mistreated over there. She was in there for two weeks and the staff told me I should make a life for myself, she won't get any better. The day before they released her she broke into the emergency drug cabinet to get stronger drugs. Twice they had to call the police, because of her. Her daughter also told me later on that her problem was the drug. Before this happened she had mortgaged her property and bought a shop in Sicamous. I got her back home and one day when I walked in she got absolutely hysterical and she asked me for her keys. She didn't recognise me when I opened the door and I thought if she had a gun then in her hands, she would have shot me thinking I was a rapist or something like this. She was just out of the bathroom and she kept looking at her rifle which was lying against the couch about ten feet in front of her, a 303 fully loaded. She could get away with murder too and she knew it.

I told her I will give her the keys in the weekend. I took my things out day after day until there was nothing left of mine and I moved back to my mice box. Two weeks later I had a phone call from her daughter in Edmonton asking me if I knew where her mom was.

"Actually my dear, I really don't." "I think Gaston it is time for me to speak up. Mom is in Alberta with someone else and if I were you, I would move the hubcaps out of the shop." "Thank you so very much girl, I got the message."

Right away I went to see a lawyer who advised me to get the hubcaps out of this shop and get them out quick.

This is what I did. I left for Sicamous at five o'clock p.m and I got there at seven. I loaded the truck until three in the morning, got back in Westbank at five and I went to sleep for three hours. I did the same thing for three days in a row. When she came back from Alberta with her accomplice the shop was empty and the twelve thousand hubcaps were back where they belonged in Westbank. It was so bad I started to have some nightmares. It was during one of them that I bit my upper mouth with the bottom part. A year later I was losing my upper front tooth and this was followed by the bottom one a few months later. I would have enough stories to tell you about her to make another book, but I rather talk about you Precious Princess."

"No wonder now you want to take your time. I don't blame you one bit." "Precious, if I'd married you then I would probably have been the one who wasn't good enough for you.

The lawyer told me I would have my divorce in one year and one day. I fought for two years in court and then I gave it up. Eight years later I am still waiting. Maybe someday she would need and want it. 'Wait till then.' This was the lawyer's last advice.

I know now though how to get her to let go and it is her greed that will do it. I should have known about this, because I was warned the first time I came to Kelowna about the gold diggers who live in the Valley. I guess most of us think we are smart enough not to listen to others. At least I didn't and I should have. Here I am with you fighting to make you accept something from me." "I'm taking you Gaston, but I also giving you my whole being. I never ever want to belong to anyone but you and to the Lord. Is this what you were afraid of when you came here tonight?" "You are more important to me than my own life sweetie and so is your happiness. Sure, I'll always be afraid to hurt you in anyway, shape or form. Now at least you know why I want you to take your time, besides, what we have is just wonderful, so there is no point rushing anything." "Do you know what Gaston? You are absolutely right. What we have is wonderful and I want to taste every minute of it.

Do you want to hug and kiss me now?" "No point asking for what is all yours Precious, just take it." "Hum, I am. Do you think it will take long before you get your divorce now?" "It is in the hands of the Lord, but I know now it is his will to set me free from any devil." "What a man you are and what a life you've had." "I often asked myself too why so many things happened to me and the only answer I got is the Lord moulds me the way He wants to. I guess He wanted me to be ready for you Precious Princess and here I am ready to build a family with you." "I'm glad the Lord wasn't so hard on me." "He didn't have to." "How come?" "Because you are much easier to tame than I ever was." "How fortunate you are to understand all those things Gaston." "I believe God does this to who needs it. If you don't come to Him after all He has done, He leaves you on your own and then you might be lost forever. I'm sure God gives each and everyone of us all the possible chances there are." "So we can get married as soon as we get your divorce?" "If you still want to sweetie." "Gaston, I'll never change my mind." "Do you know what Precious? I believe you." "Well, it is about time, because I didn't know what to do or to say anymore for you to believe me." "Oh, don't cry sweetie, I know you are sincere." "I'm sincere, I'm frank, I'm faithful, I love you and I'm yours. What more do you want?" "This is more than I deserve." "Oh no, not you too?" "Who else?" "Me, how many times I told you I didn't deserve this or that?" "Here comes the daylight again sweetie. I don't think my son will believe me again when I tell him all we did is talked." "Oh, he'll believe what he wants no matter what you say Gaston, just let him think.

Let's go to sleep, we know what we're doing and we're not doing anything wrong. Do you want me to wake you up when I go?" "No!" "Why?" "Because I want you to wake me up before Princess, so I can make you breakfast and kiss you good bye before you go." "Oh Gaston, how can you have such a thought when you are so tired?" "I'm sleepier than tired Precious. Sleep well and have nice dreams."

Chapter 6

Shortly after that night I finished the book. The last ten days I was writing twelve to sixteen hours a day. It seemed to me there was no end to it that I could go on over and over with it, that every single minute I was doing this; I was spending time with Precious. I simply didn't want to see my dream ended. Once the book was completed, I thought it was too important, that it contained too many good messages to keep it for myself. I didn't want to wait for the publisher to get back to me. I just hit the road and churches' doors right away.

One night when I called Precious she said:

"Gaston, you have to come back right away." "Sweetheart my schedule is full. I'm so busy, everybody wants to hear me and they can't make the cassettes fast enough. I miss you so bad; do you think you can join me soon?" "Gaston you have to come back, because I'm dying here without you and the publisher has decided to make you an offer on your book." "What about you Precious, did you read it." "Not all of it Gaston, I didn't want to know all of my future ahead of time, I was too scared." "I can see that your faith has improved. You believe now, praise the Lord." "I want Him to bring you back my love and I don't want to be without you any longer." "How's the building coming? Is there some walls up yet?" "I was told today I would see them grow from tomorrow on." "It's too late for me to cancel this Sunday's meeting, but I'll fly back Monday. Can you wait till then?" "No." "Me neither sweetie! I was going to be in Thunderbay in two weeks and I was looking forward to meet your parents." "Just as you often say Gaston, I guess it wasn't meant to be just yet. Besides, I want to be with you when you meet them." "I understand. Are you afraid they wouldn't accept me?" "I love them very much, but this is going to be their problem if they don't and so is everybody else, because you'll be my husband and you'll father my children. Nothing else really matters." "Aren't you the Precious of my heart? You make it harder for me to wait. I better go now sweetheart and I'll see you Monday night. It might be late though." "Anytime, I'm waiting. I love you." "Love you too, bye."

On the way back there was a violent storm and the plane was shaking to a very critical point. We were all told to fasten our belt, but when I saw and I heard people screaming and scared for their life, I got up and I started telling them we will all be fine.

'How can you tell?' I heard someone shout.

'Because, I know I will live until I'm at least eighty-four.'

'Go sit down sir.' The flight attendant ordered.

"Do you rather have a panic on the plane?" "This is my job sir, let me do it." "It seemed to me you have your hands full, so don't mind me, would you?"

Shortly after this everything went calm again and I went to sit down. When the plane arrived many people came to shake my hand and they thanked me for the good words.

'Thank the Lord.' I told them.

'I thought we were all going to die.' One said.

'Maybe you should get ready for this.'

The ride to Dana's place was just endless. I was looking at my watch every thirty seconds or so. I was gone for a whole month and I missed her every minute of it. My business is self-functioning now and the building is well on its way. It is time now for me to take care of the wedding preparations. I got good news from my lawyer. He said the divorce is almost there now. There are only a few formalities left and I wouldn't even have to go to court. All I'll have to do is to sign some documents and pay him. I brought him an idea he welcomed with a smile. My almost over nightmare was saying all over the places she was still my wife. She owns three houses, so I asked the lawyer to get me one, since she's saying she's still my wife and I have to live in a shack with no power, no water and no sewer. Once you get the house, I told him, give it back to her in exchange for the divorce.

'This should be easy enough.' He said. It must have worked since he said he has good news.

I paid for the cab and I just ran from it to Dana's door. No answer. I rang the bell again, nothing. I wondered what could've happened. Should I go home or should I sit in the stairs and wait? I shut my eyes and I prayed for an answer and the answer was to wait till she comes back. Ten minutes later I saw her little car pulled in front of her place.

"I drove all the way up to the airport to pick you up and here you are waiting for me." "I flew all the way from Thunderbay to see you and you're not home to open the door for me. Oh how I missed you, how I missed you. I never want to go away from you anymore." "Good because I don't want you to leave me anymore either."

Once all the tears were swept away we walked in and there is when I told my Precious we should be married within a couple of months.

"Is this true Gaston?" "You know I wouldn't lie sweetie." "Oh Gaston, this is the best news I heard in months. I guess it wouldn't be too long before you meet my parents after all." "I just wish I could meet them before the marriage, that's all." "I'll ask them to come a week before the wedding, so you'll have time to know them, how's this?" "Splendid! Did they tell you when the building would be finished?" "There are eighty to ninety days to go." "This is perfect." "Why?" "Because, you could open your office at the same time we're getting married. This way we can get married in the building and have the house opening at the same time. Garth said he will come for the opening. What a surprise he'll get when he finds out about our wedding. Did you have a chance to think about what kind of ceremony you want?" "You're the man of the house, so you decide Gaston and I'm following you all the way to heaven." "This is almost the best thing I ever heard from you sweetheart. Don't forget to tell the pastor this." "What is the best?" "The very first time I heard you say, you love me. I thought I was going to faint so much it went to my head." "The day I'll see you faint Gaston, I'll faint too." "I just hope then there will be somebody around to pick us up." "Ah, ah, very funny. This is a marvellous idea about the wedding and the opening together in the building my love and I hope everything goes well and the building will be ready on time." "I have an old friend who is a pastor and he is very close to our God. His name is Arnold and I'd like you to meet him soon, if you don't mind." "Everything you do is alright with me Gaston." "On our wedding day Precious, I want us to do something different than everybody else do. And this is to marry you the same way Isaac married Rebekah." "And how is this?" "This is something I wouldn't tell you my sweetheart. You'll have to do the same thing than all my readers. This is to take the Bible and find out for yourself. When you do, let me know what you think of it." "I will. How soon do you have to know?" "As soon as you're ready to let me know sweetheart, before the wedding preferably." "I love the way you never put pressure on me my love." "If I ever do, just remember it's because I have no other choice. I mean it would have to be life threatening or something. Tomorrow my sweetheart I'll try to meet with the publisher." "Oh, I hope it works Gaston, because I don't want you to go away anymore." "This is something I was afraid of." "What do you mean?" "Well, because you don't want me to go and because I don't want to go, I'm losing some negotiating power." "Maybe so my love, but they don't know this." "Ok smart thing; I'll just have to hide my love for you. This is not going to be easy." "What do you mean?" "This is mostly what the book is talking about, my loving you." "This is right too, what are you going to do?" "I will negotiate with the Lord by my side as my lawyer." "Then you'll come out of it as a winner M. Prince." "Did you finish reading it sweetie?" "No! I don't want to know it all anymore, especially how we're going to die." "This is understandable." "You don't mind?" "No, I never thought about this part. How far did you read?" "I quitted at the beginning of the believers' hunt. I liked what you said about the Masked Defender. He's a good man, isn't he?" "He is one of the best. The world needs a lot more men like him." "I had good vibrations about him." "Are you trying to make me jealous sweetie?" "No, but I wanted to tell you this for some time now. The night you celebrated my birthday, I had strange vibrations, good feelings for you Gaston and also for the Defender." "Now I feel like I have a very strong rival." "You're being stupid Gaston, I've been honest by telling you my feelings and now I feel punished. Besides, I would never cheat on you for as long as I live neither with the Defender or anyone else." "Forgive me sweetheart, I was just telling you my feelings too. I lied in a way though, because it has never crossed my mind you could cheat either me or anybody. You are just too honest for this sort of things and I know it."

The next day I went to meet with the publisher editor and he offered me a lump sum of money for my story, something I refused as quickly as it was offered.

"I'll give you the right to publish it if I agree to your conditions. I also have to tell you that I sent a copy of it to eight other publishing companies and I will wait for every offer to come in before making any decision." "You will receive ours too within five days M. Prince. Thanks for coming over." "You're welcome sir, good bye."

Three weeks later I had received seven offers out of eight and three of them were just good for the garbage can. I kept two of them as serious enough to make appointments. One is from Surrey B.C. and the other one is from New York.

The latter one won the price and so did I. I think it's a shame though that our country loses business this way, but considering the money exchange and everything else, the last offer was worth 60 per cent more than the one from Canada. The way I look at it the Surrey publisher could get the book from me, sell it to the New York's publisher and make more money with it than me who spent almost a year on it and all of this in less than one hour deal.

The day for the building to be completed has finally arrived. Hundreds of people were invited. If Dana always dreamed of a small wedding, she will be disappointed.

'Whatever you do Gaston it will be alright with me.' She said. Well, my sweetheart darling you're going to have your money's worth and this will be free. Personally, I like this kind of deals.

The Mayor was invited for the inauguration. My friend Garth said he wouldn't miss the opening for the world and it was advertised this way both the opening and the wedding for the fourth Saturday of May 1999.

Grand Opening
Visiting of the building from 10 a.m. until 5:00 p.m. except during the wedding's ceremony and from 2:00 to 4:00 p.m. on the forth floor.
Lunch 12-1 at your convenience.
The inauguration and the cutting of the ribbon by the Mayor are at 1.05 p.m.
The wedding ceremony from 1:30 till 2:15 p.m.
Bride and groom privacy from 2:30 till 3:30 p.m.
The Isaac Tent was installed on the fourth and top floor, which will be closed to the public from 2:00 until 4 p.m. The buffet will be served from three till five.
Live band and a special invited guest, a popular singer-imitator will be with us from seven until midnight. After this, we're gone.
Advertised as
Very special event

Come to see the unique Royal-like wedding ceremony of Precious Princess Dana and of M. James Prince of Kelowna. This marriage is the first of its nature in millennia. The two become one to stay and are not eligible for divorce ever. The same thing goes for any couple who wants to get married the same way. Who ever marries and lies in the Isaac Tent can't divorce or remarry ever under the only Jesus valid marriage Law of God. See Matthew 19, 6: 'So they are no longer two, but one flesh. What therefore God has joined together, let no man separate.' You better know whom you're marrying. It is the cheapest since God is not interested in money.

The cost for the night of a unique peaceful time in the Tent is $100.00 plus the government exaggerated taxes. The only other cost is the fees of the godly man who marries you. Come and visit the Princess' Children Care Centre and the Tent for a couple of twonies per person to help financing Princess Dana's project. The tent size is 16' x 20 feet and content a large 8' x10' x 8 inches comfortable mat, a complete bathroom and a Jacuzzi. If you want to be in heaven for a couple of hours there is no radio, no television and no telephone.

I phoned my place that evening and this was one week before the wedding. I was told I had a phone call from Toronto. Somebody by the name of John had called for me and he insisted I phone back as soon as possible.

Who this could be? I don't know anybody at all in Toronto. With the time difference it was just too late to call then and if I call before eight in the morning it would be cheaper and a decent time down East.

"Allô! May I speak to John please?" "Maybe, who's calling?" "My name is Gaston and I'm calling from Kelowna." "Just a minute please." "Gaston, this is John." "John who?" "Did you already forget the ride in this limousine of mine?" "Oh, this is you the John I was wondering what happened to. I often think of you. How are you doing buddy?" "I'm just doing marvellously Gaston. I found my Madeleina again." "Did you really? I'm so happy for you. Did you thank the Lord who allowed this to happen?" "My Madeleina made me." "Good for her." "She's very thankful to you too and she said she will always love you for giving me the idea." "Did you see John what faith could do?" "I am very grateful too Gaston and I will never forget my ride with you." "It was my pleasure John. I got good news for you too." "Tell me quick." "Dana and I are getting married in a week." "In a week, this soon?" "It seems like an eternity to us." "Do you know what Gaston? I knew it. Did you hire a limo already?" "No, we are marrying and sleeping in her building." "This is fine, but you're not having your honeymoon in there too, are you?" "No, we're going to Whistler." "This ride is on me. My Madeleina and I are coming and who knows we might just get married too." "I know a place where you can marry only once and never have the right to divorce." "I never heard of this, but it sounds good to us too." "Then you can watch our marriage and see." "What is it called?" "It's called: The Isaac Tent. Open a Bible and find this out for yourself John." "I will and I'll see you Wednesday night, so long."

I went to the mailbox right after this phone call to find a letter from New York which I opened in a hurry. I found a cheque from the publisher. I never held this much money at once in my hands in my whole life. The biggest sum I've held before was eighty thousand dollars. I've got to think quickly and smartly here I told myself right away.

Oh my God, You know so much about timing? Thanks to You. Do I tell Dana or do I surprise her the way I like to do it? My vote went for the surprise and if all of you want to know, you'll have to come to the wedding.

Since the event will attract thousands of people and the building can only contain one thousand people at the time and only five hundreds on one floor at the same time, I had to make some decisions.

There will be one hundred guests on my tab. Four hundred tickets will be sold for the ceremony at $20.00, this includes a video of the event. Videos sold for $15.00 a piece.

Thirty-minutes visit of the entire building for $4.00 without assisting to the ceremony. Be aware though, there will be a line-up. I put the advertisement in all

Kelowna papers and also in the Province, newspaper of Vancouver.

When John came to see me on Wednesday night after he introduced his beautiful Madeleina, I arranged with him the final technicalities. After we were done I asked John:

"Did you ever think of coming to the Lord John?" "In a matter of fact I did, but I don't really know how to do this." "How did you get here tonight John?" "I had your address." "Jesus' address is everywhere you are. Right here now, walking down the stairs or in your car going home. All you have to do is telling Him you want Him to take over your life from now on. Tell Him you are sorry for all the sins of your past and you need his help for the future not to sin anymore." "I don't need a priest or a pastor?" "Only if you believe they can do better than Jesus, the Lord. You needed to see me tonight, where did you go?" "I came directly to you and no one else could have been as efficient as you are for what ever concerned us anyway." "You got it John. It is a sure thing that if you went to ask my mom instead, you would have had a hard time to come back here in time for my wedding. She spent half of her life cooking in hotels and restaurants, but this doesn't make me a cook for all this. Now if you are sincere you can get baptised anytime before the wedding and be my best man." "Gaston, I want to." "Let me call Pastor Arnold and see if he can do it soon enough. Tomorrow afternoon at the lake and don't worry he's a big guy." "Oh, I know how to swim anyway." "Do you want me to come along or you prefer not?" "I want you to be my witness Gaston."

'You're a born again man John.' I told him when he was coming out of the water still a bit cold.

'Jesus said: 'Unless you are, you can't see the kingdom of heaven.' See Matthew 7, 21. 'Not everyone who says to me; 'Lord, Lord will enter the kingdom of heaven, but he who does the will of my Father in heaven will enter.'

Welcome to his beautiful peace John. I'll have to talk to you about his soldiers next or you can find out from my book.'

Then I went to call my Precious for there is so much to look at right now.

"Hi sweetheart, are you still nervous?" "Oh Gaston, I can hardly believe it's happening." "Is Denise organised yet? I'll have to talk to her about the synchronism. I have to meet with her as soon as possible. Can you arrange a time for us?" "I'll see what I can do." "Oh Dana, we have to go over the old time waltz one more time and the only time left is tonight. Would you ask Denise to meet me tomorrow at the building, let's see, at ten o'clock?" "I will. Bye." "Big kisses to you, see you later on tonight at around eight."

I don't know about everybody else, but for myself I speak now. So great is the blessing which comes my way I can hardly stand it. It is so overwhelming it's hard not to cry of joy, which is something I do every once in a while.

I saw Dana just for a short time this Thursday night and we practised the dance for half an hour. She was doing beautifully and she seemed to relax in spite of all the excitements.

So I let her go to her things with the girls while I contacted the chef of the crew who was working on the furnishing and the preparations of the building.

When I met Denise Friday morning she couldn't believe what she was seeing.

"Gaston, this is a miracle. How in the world did you manage to do all this in such of a short time?" "I used to be a general contractor, so I know a little bit about how to get things done." "This is absolutely incredible." "Now

Denise, this has to be a surprise to Dana. In under no circumstance she can see this before Saturday morning. You have to do anything in your power to keep her out of this place." "I told her I had everything under control." "Wait to see the inside." "Oh Gaston, this is the most incredible thing I ever saw in my entire life. Every single thing is signed with love." "Do you thing she'll like it?" "You just try to find someone who doesn't." "There is room for about 500 people here on the first floor. We're going to have the ceremony down here." "You just make me envy her." "Now, now, this is not nice." "Can I marry here too later on?" "This is something you'll have to ask Dana, it is her building. Here's what I thought, tell me what you think. The ceremony will be right in the middle so people can see us from all around." "This is absolutely perfect and original Gaston; I don't know anybody who could do any better." "On the second floor we will have the buffet and the dance. I'll put the stage over there in the centre against the wall. All the chairs and the tables are coming at 7:00 o'clock tomorrow morning." "Now I can see why Dana loves you so much. You are very special and I'm happy for her now. I'm sure glad you invited me in here this morning, because until a few minutes ago, I wasn't feeling too good about this marriage. Now I just know she'll be happy with you." "Thanks Denise, this is very encouraging coming from her best friend. I was hoping to meet her parents before tomorrow as well." "Dana told me you're going to meet them tonight, but don't you worry, they'll like you." "Parents are protective, you know? When one of my mommy dogs has puppies you have to see her, she doesn't like anybody, not even me anymore." "I'm very protective of Dana too and I know now she'll be happy with you." "I want her to have nothing but the best." "Just don't spoil her too much, it's not better." "Oh, just a little."

"Yes, I can see this." "She deserves every bit of it. Let's go on the third floor now." "Gaston, this is an absolute paradise for children. Every possible thing a child could dream of is here." "I want them to dream too Denise." "This must have cost you hundreds of thousands of dollars. How did you manage? Dana said the finances were low. You didn't get into debts, did you?" "No, the book came through for us, but this too has to stay a secret for the time being." "You can trust me Gaston." "I know this Denise, otherwise you wouldn't be here. As it is now Dana can begin as soon as we come back from our honeymoon or whenever she wants to. The fourth and last floor is the one I like the best." "I wonder why." "You didn't see the advertisement in the papers then?" "No, we have been too busy to see anything else than the preparations." "Here's a copy of it." "Let's climb the stairs and see what is there. What in the world is this?" "This, my dear Denise is a tent made in Jerusalem and it came directly from Israel and it is called: The Isaac Tent. Take a look inside of it." "It is absolutely marvellous. But my God Gaston, you are a genius." "No Denise, you just got all your words mixed up. What you should say is: Gaston, my God is a genius. Do you think Dana will like it?" "Absolutely, I am. Let me read this here a bit. What an idea Gaston, but you're going to make thousands of dollars tomorrow." "Not me, Dana will. I just want to make her day, that's all. She neither knows nor expects any of this? All she knows is she is marrying a Prince." "Yes M. Prince, incredible." "So, now you know the layout Denise, we should be on our way. There is a lot to do yet." "I have the feeling thousands of people will know before Dana what's happening here tomorrow." "The limo picks us up at 9.30. Tell Dana I'll meet her parents at eight tonight."

I feared the worst with Dana's parents, especially her father, but my only concern was for Dana, because I didn't want anything to spoil her day. I thought I would find out soon if her father loves and trusts her as much as I do.

When I walked in her apartment, I hugged and kissed my bride-to-be and then I said hello to her parents.

"Gaston, dad would like to see the building tonight. Do you think you can take us all out there?" "I would love to have a private talk with your dad sweetheart, do you mind if I go with him alone? Besides, you better be resting and chat with your mom, since you're having a tremendous day tomorrow. We'll be back shortly Dana, you just relax, ok?

"Gaston, my name is Bill." "Nice to meet you Bill. I was hoping to meet you sooner." "Is this your car?" "Yes! I'd rather put money on something more important like what you're about to see. Dana doesn't know half of it though, so I have to ask you not to say anything to her tonight." "I can manage this." "Good, because I went out of my way to do this." "My goodness, this is not the building she has described to me." "She doesn't know I spent $250 000.00 on it this week." "She said right now you had a shortage of money." "Well, the book paid me some, this was unexpected and I have decided to surprise her with all of this." "This is unreal." "Oh no, on the contrary! This is very real and so is my love for her." "She is crazy about you and this is what scared me, because I never saw her this way before. She normally has her head solid on her shoulders." "As it is now she is set for life, I don't think this is too bad either. Let's walk inside quickly, because I don't want her to worry and to come after us. I just want her to get the surprise tomorrow morning, not before." "My God, this is a palace worthy of the queen." "It is all hers and I don't even have a share in it. She has a loan I intend to pay off with my next income from the book." "I just can see now why she loves you so much. You give everything you have to others and you live like a poor man." "I've had everything in life but love, a loving wife and a solid family, now I'd give everything I have to get just this." "I see that you are rich but poor and poor but rich. I admire you Gaston." "Thanks Bill, I can see that you are a sensible man. Can I count on you to talk to your wife?" "She loves you already like a son and you are five years older than her." "Real love has no age, no race and if it has a colour, it has to be blue like the skies." "I already know she loves you. I also know you love her too so, I can only say; be happy both of you." "We will papa."

We shook hands and I knew I had an ally in this man for as long as Dana would be happy with me, so this is for life. I drove back pretty fast knowing very well Dana would be impatient and worried.

"You don't have to rush Gaston, I told Dana I wanted this talk with you and I didn't want to be disturbed." "Does she always listen to you?" "She always did." "Tomorrow she'll cut the umbilical cord for good; you don't mind this, do you?" "This is something I'll have to get used to."

I wanted to have a talk with this man too, but right then I was dying for a hug from my sweetie. This is what I did as soon as I walked inside the apartment. This being done I hugged another one too and I called her young mama, which gave her a good laugh.

After this I phoned all the concerned people and I was pleased to find out that according to everyone everything was under control.

'Lord Almighty, You are an awesome God to allow me to do all of this and give me so much. Thanks a million times for Dana, the angel You have chosen for me.'

The big and wonderful day finally arrived. John was there just on time at 9:30 as a professional he is and Dana said as soon as she saw the limousine:

"Gaston, you've promised me you wouldn't do this again." "Shtt sweetheart, this is John's wedding gift to us. He got baptised on Thursday and he is my best man."

As we arrived near the building Dana said:

"There must be something wrong here Gaston, look at all the police officers and the crowd." "Nothing is wrong my darling sweetheart, they too came to see your building."

'John!' She yelled. 'Stop this car right now.'

Dana began to cry and I thought for sure the whole thing was a mistake. The sun was shining on the large letters of the name on her building. Two feet high in gold colour she could read: Princess Children's Care Centre and above the building the biggest crown you've ever seen. Fourteen feet wide and ten feet high, all in gold colour with what looks like an enormous ruby in the middle of it.

'Gaston!' She said crying. "I don't think I can survive this much joy." "I think you are better sweetie, because this is only the beginning."

Two police officers came and escorted us to the building.

"Gaston, there must be two thousand people out there." "They all are waiting to visit your building sweetheart. Let's go open the doors." "Gaston, how did you manage all this?" "The Lord helped me." "I'll say so too, this is a miracle." "It is the miracle of faith Dana." "You're right this is miraculous, praise the Lord." "Come my sweetheart, come to see what's inside." "Gaston, I'll never be able to pay for all of this." "It's all paid for already, this is my wedding gift to you." "You didn't have to do this." "I know it; this is why it's more fun." "But, you don't have any money." "Now I don't, but the book paid me some." "And you gave it all to me." "Almost." "Gaston, this is all Louis sixteen." "No! It's Louis fourteen." "It is absolutely beautiful, but how did you know I like this style?" "I didn't, but I know you are a princess. Let's go sweetie, the doors will open at ten to the public. They are going to pay a part of your building too." "Right, wise man!"

On the second floor there was all the serving crew, so we went to the third floor where she cried out again.

"This is a children's heaven Gaston. Look at this nursery and the playroom. Look at all those toys." "There is a crew coming in for the afternoon and also another one for the evening, all with a very good reputation." "Where in the world did you get the time to do all this Gaston?" "I just got the right contacts. Did you find out how Isaac married Rebekah?" "I did, but Gaston; you don't want to do this over here, do you?" "Come to see what I call, the bride's room sweetie. This is my reward Dana. You are becoming my beautiful wife in the eyes of God and of the whole world." "You're my Prince M. Prince, forever." "Come on." "What a beautiful thing this is Gaston." "Look inside." "No snakes in there?" "Nothing is bad in there and here is where I am going to marry you, my Precious Princess later on today." "I could marry you right now Gaston." "Tease!" "I mean it." "I know, I could too, but I want everything to be perfect. Besides, the floor will be packed in five minutes and I hate to rush anything, especially this." "I'll always love you my love." "I suppose Denise told you about the layout for the day." "There is only one problem Gaston." "What is it?" "I won't be here." "This is not something to joke about Dana." "I'm in another world my love and I don't know when I'll be back on earth." "Let me kiss you quickly. This way you'll know everything is real." "I still don't know, kiss me again." "I'm afraid if I do, I might send you farther yet.

Maybe I should pinch you instead." "No, I hate pinches." "Now I can see you're back." "What did you think of my parents?" "They're wonderful." "My dad wasn't too hard on you, was he?" "The only one who is too hard on me sometimes sweetie is me. Let's go welcome our guests Princess of my heart."

At noon when most of the guests where through Dana asked me:

"How come we didn't see Garth yet?" "He was one of the first guests to come in sweetie." "Why didn't you tell me?" "He didn't want to steal your show and I appreciate it. He might come out of his cover just before midnight and maybe not. I think if he does, we would have a riot on our hands." "You're something else my husband to be."

There was a drum sealed with a slot on the top of it for letters and cards. It was decorated with little kids and little angels who play together and it was installed for comments and donations as well. There was also a square fenced area which was installed for the gifts. Both were under continuous surveillance.

Then it was the time to cut the ribbon, which was done by the Mayor of the town to a very loud acclamation. Following this, Dana and I didn't have much time to change our clothes, but the necessary help was with each of us and neither of us wanted to be late to this.

Did you ever see a groom cry? I thought she was the prettiest bride on earth the night she said she loves me. She told me with her mouth then, now she's telling me with her whole being. So much beauty I thought, it must be because God is getting me ready to enter the heavens.

The cameras were flashing from all over. Not only she's the most beautiful bride, but she's also the most beautiful princess of all times.

Never in my whole life I have seen a woman, princess or not wearing a dress so graciously. She was carrying the rubies I gave her, the crown which was given to her by her friends and a necklace made of white pearls. I don't think death threats could've made my legs shake as much as her at this moment. The guest singer-imitator was introduced then.

"M. Lorne Winfield will sing for us one of Gaston's last songs in an imitation of Garth Brooks and it is called: For Better or Worse. Ladies and gentlemen please welcome Lorne Winfield."

'For better or worse

For better or worse always and forever
That's what my love is for you.
For ever are yours my whole heart and my soul.
My love will always be true.

The kind that does come from above, Compassion and fidelity, cleaner and purer than a dove, I'll love you through eternity.

2
For all of my life, all my days and my nights, for you I'll always be right. Through good and bad times, through the storms and sunshine
Always you'll see my love shine.

The kind that does come from above
Compassion and fidelity, cleaner and purer than a dove, I'll love you through eternity.

3
When this life's over, when I've done what I could I'll go to a better world. There I will enter where there is no suffer, a home made for me by the Lord.

In this home I will reach above, awesome gift from Fidelity, the One who is nothing but love, Master of the eternity.

4
For better or worse, always and forever, his love for all of us too. Forever are yours all his grace and his peace. His love will always be true.

The King who did come from above, compassion and fidelity. So clean and so pure is his love
With us for the eternity.

5
For better or worse. Always and forever.
That's what his love is for you. Forever are yours
my whole heart and my soul. My love will always be true.

The kind that does come from above
Compassion and fidelity, cleaner and purer than a dove, I'll love you through eternity."

He was applauded to the point where we had to ask for silence. We could hear people whispering in the assembly.

'He's very good. He's just like Garth.'

I smiled at Dana who understood better then the secrecy. After this we heard another nice voice.

'The great moment is here.' Said the pastor.

'I don't know why I charged Gaston for doing this, because this is a wonderful pleasure for me to be here. Him and his princess are two of the greatest people I know.'

'One moment Pastor Arnold.' I gave him an envelope which contained my divorce papers and the liberation from my nightmare.

"I have in my hands at this moment the official proof Gaston has obtained the legal documentation for his divorce in this country and I personally know this was an eight years long battle. Praise the Lord. Who gives this woman to Gaston?" "I am Bill, the father, happy to do so."

"Who gives this man to Dana?" "Me John, I'm the happy guy."

This brought a laugh and released the tension that was in the air at the same time.

'Husband, you may kiss your bride and princess now.'

This was followed by many minutes of applause, but I couldn't keep kissing her this long in public without getting into trouble anyway.

'I now pronounce you husband and wife.' Said Pastor Arnold. 'Huh, huh!' I said. 'It has to be consumed first. This is something we're going to do right away, if you don't mind.'

Someone asked: "Isn't done yet?" "I will answer you with a question too. You would have spoiled a beautiful thing like this, wouldn't you?"

Then I took my beautiful wife in my arms and up the stairs we went to the approval of the mass.

'Let's take the elevator.' Dana said when we were up two stories. "Keep your breath for me." "Don't you worry sweetie, I'll manage anyway."

People could see us getting into the Tent, but this is as far as they could go. There is only one thing I would say about the following hour and this is sex just doesn't measure up to it. When your heart, body, soul and mind are involved, nothing else compares. I could just tell Dana told her friends something similar, just by the way they looked at me and smiled later on that evening. It was the kind of look which says; congratulation, you made her happy, if you know what I mean.

The buffet was quickly served and then came the eternal line up where a lot of people lie through their teeth and you can tell who's sincere and who's not.

I am so straight forward that those situations are scaring me and I feel tied up by my manners.

Then seven o'clock finally came and the band started playing. This was more of my cup of tea. As it is often done in weddings we were asked to open the dance. We had both by that time changed our clothes to something a little bit lighter and we promised to come back by 10:30 with the wedding dress for the cutting of the cake and for the cameras.

We opened the dance to a beautiful old time waltz I composed called; Returned For You and Dana did it beautifully. It was wonderful to have the whole band and the whole floor to ourselves with the flashes of the cameras acting as fireworks. Then it was every woman wants to dance with me and every man wants to dance with her. This was something neither of us was crazy about. I guess this is where starts the; I'll do everything to separate you. Don't you know people we just got married because we want to be together?

This went on until 10:15 when Lorne came on for another song. He sang; Everything's Yours Oh Lord and another song from Garth Brooks this time called; Fit for A King. He was very warmly applauded through a standing ovation. Many people said he was incredibly just like Garth.

When the midnight bell tolls it was also time for me to take my beautiful Precious wife away from the partying jungle. To tell you the truth, I was dying to take her back to the Tent again.

This is what I did as soon as I could after talking to Garth and a few others. My Precious Dana didn't complaint about this one either.

This was an exhausting sixteen hours day. At around 2.30 a.m. while sitting in the Jacuzzi I mentioned the barrel.

"I wonder what we're going to find in there." "And the gifts Gaston, do you think we could slip down there for a while and take a look?" "We can't stay too long though; we have a long ride this morning. It's all yours, you can do what you want sweetheart." "Gaston it's ours, not mine." "You're right, but I'm all yours." "But I'm all yours too, don't you know this?" "I sure do my Precious love and you're right, we are one now. I better get used to this idea, but give me some time to adjust, this just happened today.

We should dress just in case there is still somebody down there." "Let's look at the gifts first." "Then we can roll the barrel to the elevator and take it up there by the Tent. It looks like we're going to have a garage's sale darling. There are about twenty toasters in there. I can see five ironing boards also. Sweetie they want to keep me busy." "No one knows about our arrangement Gaston, not even my friends yet." "They'll laugh soon enough Precious, don't worry, but I don't care about anything but your happiness." "You're a darling my husband." "Doesn't this sound a little old-fashioned sweetheart?" "Sweet revenge my love?" "Sweet revenge sweetie. I wished there was a better way to tell you how much I love you Precious. It seems to me I can't show you enough how much I love you and what I feel inside." "After all you have done Gaston; you want to find a better way to show me your love." "You'll have to get used to it sweetie, because my inexhaustible love fountain will be overflowing forever."

After a long kiss and a hug we took the barrel up to the top floor and we put it out of sight. We went through it fairly quickly and we only opened the letters and cards which caught our eyes the most. There were some from my family, one from her parents, but the one which intrigued me the most was the one from Garth. Here what it said:

'I have been just about everywhere in the world my friends. I have been in so many different places that you can't even start to imagine. But I've never been amazed as I was today by this marriage of yours. The only regret I had today is to come here without my wife. Please take this gift from me and send me a book of yours Gaston. Both of you be happy always, Garth.'

'Dana!' I yelled. "Take a look and read this."

"A $100000.00 cheque. Oh my God, Gaston, this can't be true." "It's there in front of you." "I know he's got lots of money, but nevertheless, this is a lot." "Your building will be paid in no time sweetie." "No Gaston, this is yours."

I looked at her for a long time without a word and she said:

"And you are mine." "Why do you always understand things so quickly bright Precious?" "Because it is late and we need to go to sleep." "Do you mean you're tired already?"

This was almost our last words before the nap at 4:30 a.m.

We woke up to some bang, bang on the door at ten o'clock. Denise was all upset with something and Dana went to open the door for her.

"Dana, we have to call the police, because the barrel has been stolen." "No my good friend; we were too curious and we took it up here earlier." "Oh thanks goodness, I really got scared. Dana, we had a full house yesterday, this is incredible, but you got thousands of dollars out of it." "What do you mean, I got thousands?" "Just what I said, you made a fortune out of Gaston's idea. Four hundred people paid $20.00 to see the ceremony and seventeen hundred and sixty-two bought the video of your marriage. Besides, twenty-seven hundred and forty-four visited the building at $4.00 a piece. On top of all this, one hundred and fifty-two have booked for a marriage like the one you just had. This totals $ 60606.00 besides the gifts and the donations. Your husband is a genius Dana, do you know this?" "Denise, Garth Brinks was here yesterday." "Oh, I could have just bet this was him. Why did he hide?" "He wanted it this way probably to enjoy himself. He gave us a $100000.00 cheque." "What?" "He did. It is just like a fairy tale. Maybe you should pinch me to make sure I'm real. I know Gaston is unreal. When I think I almost turned him down." "Oh sweetheart, don't cry, you didn't and be happy for it." "He is the most wonderful man there is." "Then love him and love him strongly forever." "I will."

After this little chat Dana came to tell me about the good news of the previous day and we barely got ready on time for the honeymoon ride. It was nice for a change not to have anything else to think about than my lovely wife. What a honeymoon this was. Here's what Dana said about it:

'If heaven is better than this, I want to make sure I go there.'

The car the cop said was falling apart

The family dog that will save your life more than once

The car the cop couldn't reach

Cabine in progress

Chapter 7

On the 28th of June, three days after I composed the Final Warning song I had another dream, the most revealing one a person could get. God revealed to me who's the Antichrist is. So I started writing another book called: The True Face of The Antichrist. I mentioned my discovery to Pastor Arnold when he came to visit with me one sunny Sunday afternoon. He first congratulated me for the four songs I composed, telling me they were very good. Those are: Everything's Yours Ho Lord, The Precious Princess of Wonderland, For better or Worst and The Last warning. Although, after I told him about my new book, he told me my book wouldn't go anywhere. We'll see if he's a true or a false prophet like Agabus. Arnold said if there was an apostle like whom he would want to be like, this would be like Paul. I told him that Paul continuously fought against Jesus' apostles.

Arnold is close to eighty years old, but he's still very alert. He's been preaching for more than sixty years. I told him then I would want to be like Peter and we will be like them. Peter and Paul were like water and fire to each other, just like the truth is to the lie. He got up then and he said:

'I'll talk to the others about this.' Meaning: We'll see what we can do to stop you. I told him maybe they could stop me, but they can't stop God. God woke up another spokesman like Louis Riel to bring the truth to people and if I don't do it someone else will.

I let Pastor Keith read the manuscript also and he returned it to me saying he and his wife didn't like it.

'Not even 50 per cent of it?' He said none.

I also left the manuscript with Pastor Lyndon of Westside. I could never get it back and believe me, it is not because he likes it too much either. Aren't they supposed to be honest these people?

My hunting companion is an ex pastor who returned to the preaching since and he also visited me. When I mentioned to him that most of the truth was in Matthew, he asked me who Matthew was. He said:

'Matthew was a sinner, a rich educated Publican who collected the money for the Romans and for the Pharisees.' I told him:

'Yes, you too would be quick to tarnish the reputation of a man who left everything behind to follow Jesus. Yet, all he had to do is sit down and take people's money to make a living and to get rich. Although, among all of the Jesus' apostles there was none like him who had a lot to lose and he left everything behind with joy. He knew then he had just found a fine pearl of great value, the word of God, the kingdom of heaven. Paul, who was he? How many people did he kill? How many Jesus' disciples did he kill? Look for yourselves. He was chasing the true disciples to the foreign countries to kill them, who knows after how much torture?

I call Pastor Tony, a man with whom I prayed, but he had no time for me. I thought they all learned from Paul who said:

See 1 Corinthians 5, 11. 'Have no relation with the sinners, don't even eat with them.'

And we all have sin, as they say.

Although, my only wrong doing in all of this, if it is wrong is telling the truth according to the Bible. Paul in this verse says exactly the opposite of Jesus in Matthew 9, 12 - 13. Now, what ever is contrary to Jesus' teaching, the Christ I think is Antichrist.

I talked to my sisters about this too. One of them brought the subject to her Baptist church's pastor and she was kicked out of it. What a blessing this was to her. See Matthew 5, 11 - 12.

'Blessed are you when people insult you, persecute you and falsely say all kinds of evil against you because of me. (the word of God) Rejoice and be glad, because great is your reward in heaven.'

I should have opened my eyes longtime ago, because there are things which happened that should have told me.

I was at my niece fifty thousands dollars wedding once at a Baptist's church and I went outside to have a cigarette. I was at the limit of the church's property when one of their members came to tell me to get out of the property completely to smoke. I was only two feet away from the city sidewalk.

Now I know these same people would tell Jesus to go wash his feet and his hands, shave and get a hair cut before he could walk into their church, to assist at their assembly or to speak about His Father.

A very good friend of mine who was brought up hearing about Jesus only around Easter and Christmas time told me a bit about her story. When her kids were still young she decided to joint a Christian church. She didn't really know any so she picked one out of the phone book.

Because she didn't drive at the time and her husband would have nothing to do with her new religion, someone would come and pick them up, but he wouldn't quit yelling at them. Her husband was brought up Catholic, which meant to him any other religion is no good. He was right in one way, but he didn't know his religion wasn't any better or yet it is worse.

She found the rules a bit strange at first not knowing any better. She didn't have the right to cut her hair anymore and she couldn't wear anything but a dress either. But here comes the worse because of the time consuming for having three young kids. She had to get down on her knees to pray for two hours every day. She got in trouble for this one, because she just couldn't find the time.

As far as I know Jesus never kneeled. Besides, he taught us everything, where, when, who to pray, but he never said we have to kneel to do it. Jesus told us not to be like pagans, who keep babbling many words thinking they are going to be heard because of it. 'God the Father already knows what we need.' See Matthew 6, 7 - 8. Also I don't see the point of kneeling either, because it was said in the Bible that God doesn't like sacrifice.

She was baptized at age twenty-two. She got into trouble again, because she didn't want to let her kids be baptized. She argued no one should make this decision for them. She was given a good living Bible by a very close friend, but, they wouldn't let her take it to the church and they would void everything which comes from a King James version.

Pretty soon there will be a Bible for each Christian denomination. There are more than twenty-five hundreds of them in North America.

Finally she got tired of their rules and being told she was nothing but a sinner. So she decided not to go back anymore. The pastor got very mad and he phoned her saying that because of her decision she will burn in hell and so will her family. She told him she was willing to take those risks.

I'd say it is better to be in hell maybe sometime than to be in hell now.

She was the only attendant left and he scared her away. Blessings come in many different ways.

She didn't think God wanted her to be afraid of him. She never really attended another church after this.

God loved her so much He prevented her to be brain washed, so today when she hears the truth from Jesus, she can receive it. She really loves God with all of her heart and she's thankful for all of the blessing which comes her way and to her family. She misses singing those beautiful songs, but she realizes now she doesn't need a church to sing or to pray in.

Maybe one day she will sing my songs of praises to the whole world to please God. Singing in group at church is a very attractive thing. We have to be careful it doesn't become a trap, a sort of golden calf to seduce you. Also when they're looking for a pastor today, they don't especially look for a man who loves God, but rather for one who is capable to preach good and loud and possibly a good singer to attract the clientele just like a good hotel manager.

'God is everywhere.' She insisted. Alleluia. It was a small church with only a dozen people when she got in and there was no more than five when she left. The number of people in the pastor's family is five.

Persecution

What I'm about to say here is not easy to believe or to understand for most people. Only these who know God and have knowledge about the end time will. Only these who have faith in God and what He has told us will understand. If I could put a name on this chapter I would call it; God's people or if you like it better, the believers' hunt. These people who believe the truth.

The Holy Bible tells us through Jesus all about what will happen. Nothing until then is equal. Nothing has been as bad from the beginning of the world until this time.

Can you imagine something worse than the killing of the Jews from 1939 till 1945? Six millions Jews were sent to the gas chambers and tortured until death. A lot of people still alive today don't have to imagine this, because they can still remember. They pulled their teeth out from them while they were still alive to get the gold. Fifty millions died during this war alone and the worst is yet to come. They hanged the believers with their head down and they burned them alive in the time of Caesar, because they say they were the light of the world. Can you imaging the soldiers or police officers coming to your house and ask you to tell where is your son, daughter, your sister, your brother, mother or father or your loving wife and have your life depending on your answer?

This will be something else, isn't it? When your idols like champion boxers, wrestlers and marshal artists of all kinds come to get you by the throat. If you don't tell, you're against the beast and if you tell you're against God. At that time it looks like the beast is in control of the whole world.

In the same family of five, three will be against two and two against three. Don't forget what the main message is; the one who wants to save his life will lose it and the one who loses it for the Lord or others will gain it. See Matthew 10, 39. This doesn't look too good for the cowards on the beast's side. Even though you think you're not too courageous, if you love the Lord and his word more than yourselves, He'll give you all the strength and the courage you need to face the enemy or even death when the time comes. I too don't want to die and who does?

But just like Moses and King David at the time the enemy (the devil and his followers) was killing the Lord's children, my hope is I will be God's right arm and be able to help as many people as possible to survive, to escape and mainly to turn them to the real God.

In 1996 I was assaulted three times physically and many more times verbally. This is what triggered me to take some Aikido lessons. At first I went to a studio in town and I watched for a couple of times. I noticed they were saluting or bowing to each other and kneeling to a picture on the wall. I didn't like this idea very much.

I asked if this was an obligation. Yes, I was told so this was out of the question for me. I don't bow down to any other god than my God. Next thing I could do is to order some videos on the art and this is what I did. This way the teacher is always on the shelf when I need it.

They can bow down all they want as long as I don't have to. Since I hate to hit anybody even though they deserve it, this is why karate wasn't for me. I also knew I didn't have many years before I was to need it. So I took lessons in the evenings and I practised during the nights. Strength and speed were natural in me. Like everything else I do I learn quickly. Quickly I learned and soon I was ready to battle two, three, four and up to eight guys at once. As I often say there is time to run and there is time to fight. You can run against the guns, but away from the bullets would be rather wise. Wise and wiser than your opponents is what you need the most. Don't you ever forget that only three attackers can touch you at one time, so if you are in good shape enough and if you can beat three men, you can also beat many more.

Since I got a strong message from the Lord about how soon the end will be here, how bad it's going to be and how much I will be needed, I knew then I had not a minute to waste. Finish the book in French and in English is the most important since it will warn I hope millions of people in a short time. Secondly, I have to try to get it into a movie if it's possible and the sooner the better. This way I might just trigger more good men to follow the example of the Masked Defender. Wouldn't this be wonderful if this book could help to create thousands of these guys like the one Dana admired. It would be wonderful if this story could create men of justice who are against bad cops, bad governments and against the beast. To create defenders of the little ones, defenders of the oppressed, defenders of the weak like old people, women and kids. These defenders who are ready to sacrifice their own live for others. Wouldn't this be exactly the kind of soldiers Jesus is looking for now and for the end time? This is exactly how the Lord will be like. When he came two thousand years ago, he came like a lamb, but when he'll come next he will be the avenger.

Now I know this is an answered prayer I'm living through since I asked God to mould me as He wants me to be. I just realised it for the first time though, but I praise Him for it.

I just had someone in my office a few minutes ago, who had a speed ticket for driving too slow. He was crossing the Kelowna floating bridge at forty-five Km.p.h, nobody ahead of him and nobody behind. He got stop and he got a ticket fine of $125.00. Really this is too much. They scare you with their radar and when you slow down they get you again. I suggested he goes to court to dispute the matter since there is no minimum speed posted. He said: 'Ah no, somebody has to support them.' He told me before he was an atheist so I couldn't help telling him he was faithful to his master. He looked at me with a crooked smile on his face knowing exactly I knew who he was.

"I couldn't hold your hand on my propane burner for ten seconds without having you crying out to the devil and yet, you're ready to burn for the eternity." "I won't burn." "You're kidding yourself. Outside the walls of heaven there is nothing but fire. This fire is nothing but suffering from not having what God's people will have. Since the demons are jealous and envious, they will live a burning pain worse than heartburn for the eternity. God's children will be happy and blessed for having done His will. God told us Himself, His prophets told us and His Own Beloved Son, (Jesus) who received his words directly from God told us too.

Also let me tell you that you have more faith than you are willing to admit. Take it right now if you believe you would get killed by crossing the road, you would stay right here.

We all have the same chance to be saved though, only the devils will reject it and then you and they can only blame yourselves for it. Your weeping and your gnashing of teeth will be like being in a lake of fire and well deserved. You are faithful to your master, the beast, taker of blood and money. We all have the same chance to be saved and to be with God, only the demons will reject it."

As we are approaching the year 2033, which is approximately two thousand years after the death of Jesus, I can see a great accumulation of fornication. More and more priests and ministers are marrying gays to gays and lesbians to lesbians in what is supposed to be the Holy Places. Wouldn't this be the abomination that causes desolation in the Holy Place? See Matthew 24, 15.

This I'm sure will contribute for a large part in causing straight people to pull away from the sacrament of marriage. They can adopt more and more kids and this easier than the straight couples used to. These poor little children, how in the world would they have a chance to know any better and to find out the truth. Most of them have been either abandoned by their parents or else their parents were forced to let them go.

Others were stolen and sold to the best offer. Married and straight people are looked as the dirt of the world and they are mistreated.

Russia and a lot of Islamic countries are preparing to attack Israel, the people of God. All the governments are in confusion to the point they don't know what to do to help the needy. All welfare and old age pensions have been abolished. Many people are trying to escape to other countries, but all of the borders are the most watched. It is not any better anywhere else anyway. The world dictator, the Antichrist has already shut down the business market. For days at the time you can't get any food from the food store and if you try to, you get beaten up and you could get killed. More than one half of the world is doing business through the Internet and when the Antichrist decides to strike, all the computers shut down. Many businesses can't survive it and neither a lot of individuals. The bankruptcy act doesn't exist anymore either. So your creditor comes and takes everything you own with the authorities and if you say or do anything, you're a dead person. It is a real fish game. The biggest eats the smallest one, one after another. Your choices are limited.

Your money in the bank is worthless and whatever you have in a can or in a shoebox isn't worth anything anywhere either. The beast is forcing his way on the world population and this is it. Slowly but surely he gets to where he wanted, which is to control everything and everybody. Rich and poor weak and strong, it does not matter to the beast. His plan is to force you to reject the true God and to take his satanic number, the six, six, six.

Shortly after the last world war he knew then why his father Hitler failed. People in general loved each other too much then and families were too strong yet to allow him to destroy the work of the Lord. Ties between members of the same family were too strong back then, which created a very strong resistance causing the government of Hitler too much in efforts, time and money. The man was satanic enough, but the timing wasn't just right then. Now is it all together different. Who cares if I'm charged wrongly? Who cares how many tickets I get whether I am guilty or not? Who cares about who dies and who doesn't?

Nobody cares anymore, so this is the right timing. The only one who seems to care is your lawyer and consider yourselves lucky if you get one who is sincere and he really tries to help you, because most of them just want to get a piece of this big pie too for what is left anyway and half of what he gets goes to the government, the beast. If you have nothing left, you simply don't get any help.

A thirty-six year old man friend of mine visited me last week almost in tears. He lost control of his vehicle last year on an icy road and the man driving another car beside him got nervous and he went down the cliff. Now he's being sued for one million dollars, but he only has half of this in insurance. All he has left from what he worked for so far is going down the drain or to somebody else. I don't think it is fair either, but this is today's society for you.

His lawyer suggested to him he takes a mortgage on his property and bring him $30000.00 for his defence. I told my friend if the other guy doesn't ruin him, his lawyer will.

The beast already has a huge list of names of Jesus' people and he is collecting more from family members, relatives, neighbours and friends. It is imperative and he knows it that they are destroyed. He sure doesn't want to make the same mistake than his dad made.

The Antichrist reign will only last a short time though, probably long enough nevertheless to show a lot of people what hell is like or close to it. He is a two-face individual, the hardest kind of person to figure out. So smooth that at first a large chunk of the population will think he is the Christ. He will be impressive and charming so much that all countries leaders will surrender to him.

Only and I repeat it again, only the ones who know the Lord Jesus, the Son of God and his teaching will be capable to tell the difference at first between the two. Understand this now and know that the only way to know the real Messiah, Jesus Christ is either by reading the Bible being inspired by the Holy One or by finding one of his disciples who teaches the Word of God brought to us by Jesus. I'm telling you that half of a line a week that you hear from most of the priests in Catholic churches, which is only twenty-six lines a year and this is not much wouldn't change a lot in your life. This might and yet it might not tell you how to recognise the Lord and tell you how He is coming back and what for. I'm begging you to grab the holy book while you still can and don't waste any time before you start reading it. This is much more than some churches are doing for you. Find someone who really loves Jesus to help you with it and I guarantee you, you will find the Lord's peace He has promised us.

Not that I want to compare myself to and far away is this idea from my mind, but as Noah was warned about the flood I am warned about the end time. So is everybody if they listen to the word of God. See Matthew 24, 37.

So as Noah did I get to do different things which will get me going until the second coming of the Lord. When God the Father said to Adam and Eve not to touch the central tree, the devil came and seduced them and they were lost. We are still paying for this mistake. When through Noah God warned the population about the flood, they didn't listen either. Again they were seduced by their corruption. The population of Sodom and Gomorrah was warned too by Lot. There too they ignored him. They even tried to rape him. We all know what happened then.

Many people tell me today the same thing is said for thousand of years. Are you going to be seduced too or be ready just in case? Most of you are more careful with and for your money than you are with and for your soul.

I got myself a piece of crown land on a different name in the middle of nowhere, a place which is not too easy to access, a place which is known from nobody but myself in the middle of the forest. There is a fairly good-size lake nearby so plenty of fish to feed a small group for a long time.

So, I stoked hundreds of little propane cylinders, a dozen of five hundred litres for heat, thousands of bullets, three different rifles, three bows and hundreds of arrows.

I also stoked a dozen fishing rods, reels and hundreds of lures plus two Bibles, one is French and the other one is English.

With this equipment my family and I can survive I'm sure for twenty years. Many times during the past ten years I questioned myself about my ways of living and so did many other people. Up until I married Dana I lived in a 16'X24 feet shack built out of insulated doors cut-outs. This stuff has an R. 16 factor of insulation. The cost of the material for the shack was only $1000.00. I had no power, no water, no sewer and basically no bills. I can say that for the time I was by myself, I didn't miss any of them either.

I liked the idea of not feeding the system which would sooner or later turn on me and get everything I own. As it is, I gave it all to the Lord so when the time comes, He can use the one million hubcaps I own and play Frisbee with them. I can imagine the one million disks into one million devils' heads with the six, six, six number on their forehead. I know He can bull's-eye them all too. I'm sure I couldn't find a better way to use them all either. Everything comes from the Lord and everything goes back to Him, this is fair and what ever He is going to do with whatever, this is his own business.

We are told that in the future world a person will get exactly what he works for or what he deserves. As for this world I worked and earned at least twenty to thirty times my living or more. In fact it is pretty hard to calculate. At times I thought I earned it more than one hundred times.

I don't mind giving to anyone I choose to, but when it is basically stolen from me before I could even touch it, I think it is a crapulous crime worthy of the beast. I don't understand why so many people are afraid of a godly world of fairness. Personally I can't wait for this to happen.

As I was saying, I stocked enough of those insulation boards to build many camps. Most of those boards are 20" inches by 64" by 2". I also took rolls of greenish glued paper for disguise in the summer. Those camps are white as snow and this is good for the winter. I also stocked three wood stoves since they can be used until the very critical time in a place where there is more firewood than I can ever use. Don't you ever forget too that smoke can and will give you away, therefore the propane and the propane heaters. Each and every camp is built with two getaway exits. Everyone of them has a false wall with a separation of two feet. Under each floor there is an underground cave and a tunnel with air vents also stocked with gas masks, flashlights and spare batteries. Everywhere I have a stockroom there is some of imperishable can food and medicine of all kinds.

In the last twelve months I took some rescue and delivery assistant courses. Help I want to be able to provide, especially to my Precious darling and to the children. Many first aid kits were also stored up. I made a search on my last eyes prescription and I have forecasted a couple of pairs of eyeglasses knowing very well a blind or a half-blind man can't lead others very safely.

One snowmobile and many sleighs, one four-wheeler (quad) and a trailer, besides gasoline and motor oil were also put away. Many batteries, starters and alternators are essential not to survive, but to enjoy whatever is left of life.

The lake will supply the water and most of the food. I brought in the area dozens of rabbits and chickens. I hunted down or I rather say I chased away the coyotes, the wolves and the cougars to save the future food supply including the deer and the moose that graze around the property.

One thing I'm sure of is I wouldn't be able to buy or sell, because I'd rather die than to accept the number of the beast. But I might be able to trade for the others of the family once in a while wild meat or fish for a few pounds of beef.

I myself can live on wild meat and fish all year round without suffering at all. I am personally ready and I hope Dana will be too when the time comes.

Every chance I have to take her and the kids to this place I do. I need her to get used to it, but she is a town girl and she's always happy to return home. It is just the opposite for me. Every time I leave the place it seems I'm going to a very risky area where I would be helpless.

I have my good moments at home too though, taking care of my dear children, my wonderful wife, writing and playing my music, practising and learning my own songs. All those are to me a splendid retirement.

Dana is working in her office and she is as I forecasted a wonderful blessing to the homeless kids. Every now and then she brings home a little one until we can find a rare good place anymore with caring people. So far, thanks to God we have been lucky. By the time we found it we are attached to the poor little child and it is hard to let him or her go. It is only after a serious investigation we are able to do so.

Each and every one of them once they've been close, seen and touched Precious can die knowing they have met an angel. Many times a day I thank the Lord for her.

Because my business is still supporting us very well and there is no point putting money away, we don't really need Dana's income to live on. Like I told her before, she can spoil us once in a while and help others or do what ever she wants to do with it.

Besides, the income I get from my business, the book, the movie and the music allow me to help the needy as well as stocking the imperishable.

Last time Dana had a party for my birthday she had invited a fairly good number of people and one of them did make a few stupid comments about our age difference. I invited him in the kitchen aside from the others and I asked him for some explanations.

"You're too old for her you little shrimp. She should be out there having fun with all of us instead of coming home to a little retired old man who can't do anything other than babysitting a couple of little bastards." "Do you know what? I think you're right."

At that moment I stretched to give him my hand to shake. I grabbed his small finger all at once and I brought him down to his knees.

When Dana walked in and she asked what we were doing I told her that her friend was asking for my benediction. So she left us alone thinking it wasn't any of her business. Close call I thought, but a man has to do what he has to do.

"You're nothing but corruption young man and if I ever see you around my wife or my kids again, I'll cripple you in a way you'll have a very long time to repent."

It's amazing how a big boat is governed by a little rudder, how a horse is lead by the mouth, how a bull is by the nose and a big jerk by a little finder. The guy stayed a few minutes longer and he excused himself politely before he left.

I don't have much respect for these big guys who are six to twelve inches taller than me and think they can walk all over people. I'm only five foot six; same than Bruce Lee was and like he did I don't let anybody intimidate me no matter how big he is.

There were a dozen of similar scenes, but nothing would make me regret my marriage to Precious. I noticed Dana put some of these guys right at their places a few times too.

"Why are you still taking training and Aikido lessons Gaston? Don't you think it is time for you to rest and enjoy life now?" "This is just it sweetheart, I want to enjoy life many more years and I don't know any better way than to be in good shape every day. I want to be able to run right to the last of my days. I want to be a little bit like the Masked Defender and also be in the best shape as possible for everybody else and for myself, but especially for you and the children." "You can still outrun me day and night." "Yes but, if I can't protect you and the kids in every situation, I would feel like I have failed my duties. You should be in the best of shape too, do you know?" "Yes, I know I have been working too hard and I have no much time for other things." "If you make yourself sick you won't be good for anybody, you know this too, don't you? Remember that nobody can really replace you, nobody has your touch. I told you this a hundred times or more."

"I asked Rick about what you were doing in the kitchen. He said you almost convinced him to become a believer." "Did he, really?" "Oh Gaston, what did I do to deserve you and all the good things which come with my wonderful husband?" "Precious, you deserve even better." "But Gaston, you're too humble and besides, there is nothing and no one better." "Oh yes, there is."

You should have seen those beautiful blue eyes looking at me questioningly.

"Better is where we all are going soon my sweetheart. Just think of how it will be wonderful not to worry about each other and for the kids in those days. I know I shouldn't worry at all, I should have more faith in the Lord." "Gaston, I think you have the greatest faith on earth and you're telling me you're lacking it." "Peter had the greatest faith and he was told by Jesus: 'Man of little faith.' Peter also denied being Jesus' friend three times and yet, he's the one who loved the Lord the most." "But you yourself said you would give your life for the Lord." "I did and so did Peter and without having the Holy Spirit with me, I would have done the exact same thing he did. Only God through His Holy Spirit at the time of physical threats of death could give us the strength to accept the Lord and to refuse the number of the beast. Human beings are way too weak on their own including me to choose the Lord over their lives." "How do you know all those things my loved and loving husband?" "Well, you see Jesus has chosen his disciples when he came to teach. He died for us while doing this and then he rose again. This is something he never stopped doing. Back then there were people to teach and there were people to listen to them and learn. There were people to prophesize and there were others to kill them. This is still going on. We all have a job to do down here for the Lord and I think we both doing it." "Do you think I'm doing what the Lord wants me to do?" "Yes I do sweetie." "I'm not preaching to anybody like you do." "Helping the little children as you do is exactly the same type of work as I do. You add to your job a little word about the Lord to whom you think needs it and there will be no difference in our duties. Either one of us is doing what the Lord expects. We both are a light He expects to shine and light up someone else. When we do something wrong, don't you worry, either we are good or bad, God tells us through our conscience. This conscience is a very similar thing than the largest computer disk, it is known by men, but made by God and no man can change any part of it. It is probably the same box which carries the thoughts and the ideas from our birth until our death. It is also the little box which allows us to be happy or unhappy. The conscience is connected directly to our heart and our heart directly to our soul. Believers and non-believers can hear it. Some listen to the voice and follow it. Others do as I did, listen to it for years and argue with everyone who talks about the Lord refusing his grace, his blessings, mainly his protection and the wonderful interior peace. During a thirty year period I turned down his beautiful invitation as you did with me at first sweetheart. Only you are smarter than I am and not as rebellious as I was. I'm glad you didn't take thirty years to find out I was good for you. Although, I was resigned to wait for you forever, because I knew my love for you is endless." "How did you know this? You basically said you love me the first time we met. Gaston, I think this was infatuation." "Infatuation doesn't last and it is very deceitful, you know this Precious, but real love last forever. I think it was the little voice I'm talking about. I try to listen to it all the time now the Lord is with me continuously." "God knows I fought with all my strength not to love you M. Prince, even though you are perfect for me. I always wanted a real man and there is not this many around, besides, I know many young men who are physically older than you." "Aren't you a sweetheart Precious Princess and a real gift from heaven?" "So are you Gaston, so are you." "One more thing before you go to sleep sweetie." "What?" "You are due in a couple of months and I think you are working too hard. I'm worried about you and the baby." "I know you're right as usual my love. I'll try to find someone to replace me as soon as possible. It wouldn't be easy though, the office is full to the bursting point with abandoned children. It would be awesome to spend more time with you, but difficult not to worry about them." "Can I help you with anything?" "You already have your hands full." "She's going to be a Leo just like you, sharp as a whistle, I just know it." "Your little voice again?" "Exactly darling, you're too smart." "Nice dreams." "Good night."

I dreamed this night that Jonathan was agile and as fast as a cat. The girls were wiser than her parents and the little Benjamin at age ten could lift two hundred pounds off the ground without too many efforts.

The Lord told me that whenever He'll take me away from Precious for a short time this is, everything would be taken care of.

'Raise your children in the Lord's way and they will take care of their mom until I bring her back to you again. Wait until I tell you before you speak to Dana about your leaving the earth. I am pleased with what you've been doing, because you are following my voice. Your reward will be accordingly to your faith and your deeds.'

I woke up in the morning as if the night had lasted twenty seconds and yet rested, fresh and mainly reassured about the future.

'Thanks to You oh Lord for this wonderful peace You brought to my heart and mind. How Great Thou Art? Thanks to You for giving me the opportunity to share it with the rest of the world. You are an awesome God with unlimited goodness. You said your peace will return to us and your word is true. Thank You for Dana and the children, thanks to You for Guy and Marlene. Thanks to You for the entire family and friends who threw at me words from You. I know now it took every single thing and every single word to bring me where I am today. Thanks to You for forgiving me all my rotten mistakes. I am totally yours my Lord, today and forever.'

I felt like going on more with thanks, because I think this is so little in comparison of what I received. I can't count far enough for the entire blessing I received known and unknown, remembered and forgotten. What ever I give back to the Lord is nothing but bits. He is so gracious; He takes those bits and returns them to me in mountains of blessings. If the Lord can do miracles and wonders for me, a little Frenchman in the West, think of what He can do for you if you surrender to Him.

Jonathan, the first born knows many tricks already and his speed is absolutely incredible. The only way Dana can catch him is through obedience and yet he's only three. Leah, almost two now shows signs of intelligence I never have seen before. I can just feel her wisdom will get her and many with her through life no matter how it is. Jonathan is taught not to use or to show his tricks unless it is absolutely necessary.

"If you ever teach a friend some of them you have to make absolutely sure this person is from the Lord, otherwise this would turn against you. You don't show a devil how to beat you up, because he will. Your mom doesn't know much about what I can or can't do and this is good for her own protection. Same thing goes about you Jonathan. Too much confidence could cost her her life and you and I don't want this, right?" "I love mammy." "I know you do and this is why it is important you listen to what I'm teaching you. We love you too very, very much." "I know this daddy." "How many back flips can you do for me today? One, two, three, four, five. Jonathan, this is two more than the last time. Did you get your breath back yet?" "I didn't lose any." "How high can you jump now? Straight two and a half feet! Jon, this is almost your height. Pretty soon you'll be ready to beat me up." "I don't want to beat you up dad, you're my best friend." "Oh Jonathan, this is almost the nicest thing I have ever heard." "Who beats me?" "Your mom the first time she said she loves me." "I miss mommy daddy." "She'll be home soon son. You'll have to tell her this." "I know she loves you dad and you love her too." "We both love you and your little sister too, very, very much." "I know. Sometime I think I'm jealous, because you spend a lot of time with Leah." "When you were her age I was with you all the time and you had no one to share me with, but she is so lucky to have you." "This is true, I love her too daddy." "Can you promise me to always try to protect her too?" "I promise dad." "So from now on you're going to help me watch over her, ok?" "Ok!"

"Can you and I pray for her protection now?" "Yes daddy, do this." "You repeat after me, ok?" "Ok!"

"Oh my good Lord." "Oh my gooood Lord." "You have been so good." "You have been so-o-o gooood." "To give me a little sister." "To give me a lit little sister, Leah."

"Leah. I don't want to be jealous." "I don't want to, to." "To be jealous." "Be jealous." "But I want." "But I want." "To love her." "To love her." "And protect her." "And protect her." "Always." "Always." "Thank you Lord." "Thank you Lord."

So Jonathan is growing up with defensive skills, two parents' love and the knowledge of the Lord. It is a rare thing nowadays.

Denise, Dana's best friend has decided to take three months leave from her job and to come and help us out. I just can't be thankful enough for it. My sweetheart was right about her, she is a good friend. Precious and I know now everything will go smooth and this is very important for her in her condition.

"See sweetie how the Lord arranges things for you when He's pleased." "You make me see things differently than I used to Gaston, but you're right about one thing among others and this is I did worry for nothing. There is no way I could even imagine something like this would happen. Do you know I couldn't find a better person than her to take care of this place?" "I know God knows your needs and how to help you better than yourself." "We can always rely on Him, right?" "Always, don't ever forget this and everything will be fine Precious. We have a breathing lesson tonight, remember?" "We have to be there at seven. I hope the babysitter will be here on time." "She was late only once, can't you forgive her?" "This is something I've done long time ago. It is just that when something this important comes up, I want everything to be right." "It's me who needs to learn the breathing love." "Everything which touches you, touches me too sweetie." "You're too protective." "Hey, this is my job, ok?" "You're wonderful." "I like this better. It is just that if we are caught at the camp for you to delivery with no doctor around and no hospital, I want to know what to do for both you and the baby." "Oh, we'll just rely on the Lord." "This is not funny at all; besides, you should know the Lord helps the one who helps herself." "I'm sorry Gaston." "Tell the Lord this, not me." "You're right. I hope everything goes fine. Do you think He'll forgive me?" "Hey, if He asks us to forgive our brother who has repented seventy times seven the same day, how many times do you think He can forgive you if you repent?" "Just as many times as I truly repent!" "Got it Precious. Precious to me and Precious to Him too, so don't mock Him anymore, would you?"

The little Sarah came to this world with a smile on her face. She is Precious number two. She looks exactly like her mom. She has the same gorgeous smile. The doctor couldn't believe it, he slapped her twice, but she wouldn't cry. He looked at her after each time and she was smiling as if she was telling him: 'You can try all you want, you can't make me cry. I'm a happy girl and this is it.'

This was the twelfth of August, only nine days after Dana's birthday.

"Now Precious this is it for Leos, since the celebration goes on for two weeks. The next one will have to come in another month." "Yes my Prince, when are we going at it?" "It was this easy, huh?" "Gaston, you were breathing so well, I didn't feel anything." "Get out of the hospital first, ok?" "Come and kiss me. Don't worry; I'll be up and out of the hospital in no time." "You've always been beautiful sweetheart, but right this minute you are the most beautiful I've seen you. She'll be very beautiful and a happy girl too."

"You've been talking to her so many times already Gaston, she might just know what's waiting for her. How did you know she was a girl before the doctors did?" "I dreamed of a girl." "Your dreams, dreamer." "Just like you Precious, you are just a beautiful dream come true. I have to go now and let you rest, this is very important too." "A full night without you my Prince is a nightmare. I wish they could change the rules and let you stay in for the night. I feel like being punished for giving us another baby." "Just rest and you'll be out of here sooner. I'll miss you too." "You're so wonderful." "Don't cry sweetie, you break my heart when you do." "They are tears of joy my love, let me have them." "I'm going home now, but as you know, I carry you in my heart with me. Don't forget there are two at home too waiting for me and you too know how it's like." "You will never get tired to tell me how much you love me Gaston, would you?" "I just hope you will always welcome it." "I told you before my wonderful husband, forever. Good night."

On my way home that night there was a roadblock and I put my seatbelt on while I was waiting in line. As soon as I was close enough I saw there were six police cars. This must be something serious, I told myself, it looks like there are a dozen officers as well. When I was as close as the third car behind, I saw two officers dragging out of his vehicle a man whom they were mistreating. At First I thought they had their man, now they will let everybody else go. Not so and I found this out when my turn came.

"Do you carry any guns in your car?" "No."

"Do you have any Bible?" "My Bible I carry it in my heart." "Very funny! This means I'll have to get your heart out of you to get the book."

I look on the pavement and when I saw the man bleeding to death without care, I knew he was serious.

"What a man like you is going to do with a Bible anyway?" "We have to destroy them all. The law was passed at six o'clock today and it took effect immediately." "What is the penalty?" "Are you a lawyer or what? I'm the one who asks questions around here. Get out of the car and stand over there. I need your papers. Do you have any criminal record?" "No." "James Prince, just a mailbox address? A good man, huh? Where can I find you for questioning?" "Here now." "How come I can't find you?" "I live in the bush ten miles off the highway." "No home and no street address, this is very unusual?" "I'm a kind of hippie." "You don't think you're too old for this?" "No." "Where is this bush you're talking about?" "It's hard to explain, It's called; the virgin forest." "Why?" "I was the first one to get it." "I never heard of it." "This is exactly why I like it." "I'm going to lock you up. You're giving me too many suspicions. No street address, a Bible heart, a virgin forest. You're a hippie whose car is falling apart."

I looked up behind and I could tell the line-up was miles long. I looked at the bleeding man and I asked the officer why he doesn't do anything to help this man out?

'He had a gun without a permit and he carried a Bible also.'

My brain registered at a lighting speed. I knew right then my new career had already started a few minutes ago. I thought for sure I would have time to teach my children a little bit more before this happens.

"Get in there." "I got kids at home." "Sure and I have three wives." "Is this legal?"

I walked toward his car and when he put his hand behind my neck that was it for him. I was lucky we were a bit distanced from the others. He laid in the ditch with a broken leg, a broken arm and a broken jaw. I threw his gun as far as I could in the field. It was completely dark by that time. His car was still running and of course you and I are paying for this with our taxes. I got in his car and I backed it up to all of the other police's cars that were there. All the other officers seemed to be confused and watched as if this was a car show or something. They might have thought this was the other officer who was doing this.

Once all the other cars were out of driving condition having the front fenders smashed down to the front wheel blowing off their tires, I drove away towards the line-up. At about a quarter of a mile away I stopped, I got out of the car and I warned the other people about what happened.

'These officers have committed murder and you wait another twenty minutes, the highway should be cleared by then. Wait for the signal, the light will be blinking four times when it's safe.'

One car was coming at a very high speed and I hid behind another car hoping no one would give me away. The car I drove almost got rear-ended having no tail-lights anymore. I wondered if they could have given me a ticket for this.

The two cops got out with guns in hands. I thought hearing guns were illegal. Lucky for me they took different directions from one another. One was questioning passengers from a car and the other one was scrutinising the ditch. He is the one I got first. There were another broken arm and a leg. I saved his jaw, because I needed him to call for the other one. The other one came running right were I wanted him to and up went his gun and down to the ditch he went with the other one in the same condition.

I ran back to the murder scene to find a bunch of confused cops. A couple of them calling for reinforcement. I walked the field and I studied the situation knowing what is to be done has to be done fast, because if more of these cops come before I'm done, it will be my end. I could see three bodies lying on the pavement then. These must be the owner and the passenger of the car they took to come at me with. When I was close enough I made some kind of animal noises to attract one of them who might be courageous enough on his own to come my way. One did alright, but when I saw him pulling a flashlight out of his pocket, I didn't waste a second getting out of the way.

I'll have to try again but this time I'll have to come and get them, there are not two ways about it. Most of them were hiding behind their cars looking for the other two to come back, I supposed. These guys are bad news. They have killing instinct and they will kill anyone who stands in their way. Besides, they have the law on their side to do it. One thing I still don't understand is the fact they were hiding. They must have known they were in the wrong. They are the ones who have the law, the guns, the flashlights, but no more driving cars though. I always wanted to be in a demolition derby, but I never thought it would happen this way.

What a waste of people's taxes this was, but for this too they don't care. So I took them all one by one until the last one, throwing their guns as far as I could in the field. My biggest problem was that I didn't have my mask with me for the simple reason I didn't expect this to happen so soon with no warning of any kind. When I came to the last one he was so scared I thought he would do something in his pants. I disarmed him and I asked him what was wrong.

'Is your conscience bothering you?'

I dislocated one of his shoulders when he came to grab me. I put him in a car where there were three men, I gave them the cop's gun and I asked them to drop him in town with the message the Masked Defender took care of the situation.

'It is very important you don't let him go before four or five in the morning though. Good luck.'

Then I went to the first officer who wanted me and I got my papers back from his packet. I just knew it would have been much safer for me to finish him up like they do, but I just couldn't do it.

'Remember me and remember well that if I come against you one more time you might not be as lucky as you are now.'

I got in my car and I turned it around, then I gave the proper signal. I turned around again and this was twenty-one minutes after I have said it.

I went home and I drove around the block three times before I parked the car seven houses further than mine, just in case. I turned the radio on at the news time to a special news flash.

'The government is having a press conference right at this minute. The gun's deadline might be extended. Guns deadline disaster. The police is looking for your help.

Anyone who has any information about the Masked Defender is asked to contact the R.C.M.P at the closest detachment.'

I listened to the radio all of the next day and I was expecting the name Prince as well to come on the air, but it didn't happened. It could be that the cop took the message very seriously or he had decided to take the matter in his own hands. Maybe too he wasn't as rotten as the others after all, but this is something I doubt very much. It bothers me though that somebody out there knows who I am even if he has a broken arm, a broken leg and a broken jaw. On top of all he's a cop. What a beginning of the end this was.

The phone rang and I thought for sure this was it. I picked up the receiver.

"Gaston, did you hear the news?" "What news Precious?" "The Defender and the police. The Defender whom we saw this one time." "You saw him sweetie, I didn't." "Right!" "How are you this morning sweetheart?"

"I'm fine, but I'm all excited about what is going on. There are eleven cops in here this morning with broken arms and legs. The hospital is full of police officers and special agents from all of government sources." "I wonder why the Defender would do something like this sweetie. For what I heard about this guy, he is the defender of the rights and justice. I'll have to get another car sweetie, because I was told by one of these officers last night it was falling apart." "You like your old wreck Gaston, you're going to miss it." "It's got class, but hey, security is important too darling. I guess I'll get the Lincoln out and I'll take this one to the camp or to the yard." "I miss you Gaston." "I miss you too sweetie. How's my little girl?" "Nobody can believe it; she's smiling all the time. When this one cries we'll know she's in need of something. I can bet you she'll cry to have you near her as I feel right now." "She might just know she came to a beautiful loving family, besides, her mother has the most beautiful smile in the world." "Oh Gaston, you're such a love bug. I want you here with me and now the breakfast is coming." "I suppose the food is heated up three times before you get it as usual." "It is not too bad, but it is nothing like yours either my love, you beat them all by a long shot." "You're a darling love bug yourself Precious. I'll phone you later on this afternoon. Bye, kisses."

I took the two children to Denise and then I got my car to the farm to be stripped completely. Whatever is left I'll take it to the crusher as soon as possible. I know a man who operates one and he is discreet.

'Goodbye my old friend, you have given me your best, but I have to do what I have to do and I know you deserved a better ending.'

I got in the Lincoln and for a time now, I'll have to be Gaston Lapointe again. Coming down the highway 33, I decided to put the radio on again to listen to the news. I don't think I've ever been interested in the news as much as I did that day.

'The guns and the Bibles deadline have been delayed to a further date. The riots have spread out all over the country. There were exactly six hundred and sixty-six of them and the Masked Defender has been noticed in hundreds of places. The police said that either he is an angel who travels very fast or there are many of these Defenders. In every manifestation the crowd was shouting: 'People no guns, cops no guns, people no guns, cops no guns.'

I felt this was a sure victory. This was also an answer to my question in the book about the Defenders. Now I know I am not alone anymore. See how the Lord works?

'I'll give you peace and rest.' He said it and you can rely on Him. Another thing I know now too is they (servants of the beast) have started something and it is not over yet, delayed maybe, but not over. Oh my God, tell me how am I going to do with three young children at home? I picked up a newspaper and the answer was right there in front of my eyes on the first page.

'The Bibles are prohibited in all public places including schools, hotels and motels. It is allowed in your home only for yourself and in the churches. The deadline has been extended for two years for those two. All firearms are prohibited everywhere in the country. You can sign your guns out from the police stations for two weeks in the hunting seasons, if you qualify for the permit.'

Did I warn people on time about this one, I thought? Good, I told myself. I probably have another two years of peace in front of me.

I want to have a chance to see my little Sarah smile more than once. Four o'clock, I better give Precious a call before she start worrying.

"Hi sweetie, how are you?" "You got me worried Gaston, is everything alright? I phoned Denise and she told me you dropped the kids over there." "I thought it was the best thing to do. Remember I told you this morning I have to get rid of the car and it was too hot to take the children with me to the farm." "You're right; it was thirty-six degrees out there this afternoon." "Did things settled down at the hospital with the police?" "A little, I think." "I hate to do this to you sweetie, but I might be late tonight. I still have to pick up the children and feed them." "I hope you won't mind this Gaston, but I asked Denise if she could keep them for the night to give you a chance with other things. I just sensed you had your hands full for the day." "What a great idea Precious, I never thought of this or rather, I didn't dare asking. What a treasure you are." "No my love, you are the treasure." "I'll drop in to kiss them good night for you and I and I'll be with you at eight if everything goes well." "Something is wrong Gaston, I can just feel it? Something happened since you left me last night?" "Yes my sweetheart there is something. Last night the cop told me my car was falling apart. Now I am driving one for the first time today and I'm not sure how it is. It's an old 76, you know? You're in the hospital, the kids are not home and I'll be with you at around eight o'clock." "Oh, I got it now Gaston, you're afraid the car might not make it. What a man you are. I love you so much." "So do I my darling, don't worry and don't cry. I'll be there one way or the other." "I know you will, even if it would cost you your life and this is what I'm afraid of." "I'm going to live until I'm eighty-four at least." "Did you dream this too?" "Maybe. You'll have a lot of time to get tired of me anyway." "But I never will." "I Hope so darling, see you at around eight o'clock."

When I got to the hospital that evening there were just too many police officers in the lobby for me to take the risk to be recognised. So I returned to my car and I tried again twenty minutes later. Then I got in and I headed for the stairs right away. Up to Dana's room I went. It was already 8.30 p.m. and I knew she must have been worried knowing perfectly well I would be on time if everything was ok. Before I stepped in the room I took the hat and the moustache off and then I put my glasses back on. When I walked in the room Precious was in tears and I went to hug her right away.

"I was so afraid you've got into troubles Gaston." "They are questioning people in the lobby, so it takes time to get through. I have to ask you something sweetie." "What is it?" "I have to ask you not to mention the name Prince from now on, unless we are alone." "Why?" "Because of the book I wrote. Remember I wrote about the Defender? It might cause me some troubles." "Right, I didn't think of this." "I would hate to spend hours in the police office answering questions. They might think I know where to find him." "You must have been worrying all day?" "I have to admit I did a bit of it." "And worry about the car, the children and the wife. Are you sure now you don't regret it?" "I wouldn't change my life for anything else and why should I? I am the happiest man on earth. I have been so blessed with you and the children; I can't thank the Lord enough. I want to see Sarah." "The nurse will bring her here in ten minutes, can you wait this long?" "Hardly!" "You've loved her even before she was conceived. You are a strange but wonderful man Gaston. What a husband and father you are." "You all deserve better yet." "Stop this, there is nobody better and I am so happy, I never thought it could be possible to feel this way."

"Here is your smiling treasure Mrs Lapointe, she's just incredible. Tomorrow if you want to she can stay in the room with you." "Of course I want to. I'm a working mother and my time with the children has always been too short."

The nurse looked at me as if something was wrong.

'This was my choice.' Precious said.

"And they don't miss anything. My husband here is a wonderful housekeeper and the best parent you can find." "Oh, alright, if you're happy this way." "I can only wish you were as happy as I am Lynn. This is my loved and loving husband Gaston." "Hi."

I could just tell she was ready to divorce us probably just because of our age difference, but I've been over the stage of letting people affecting me with what they think. My family's happiness is way more important.

"Thanks Precious for rescuing me. You were very smooth, much more than she deserved." "You didn't need any rescuing, but people are people and until they know you, they just can't understand." "I know you're right. This gives me a lot of chances to forgive people and this is alright too." "I'll have a talk with her tomorrow and if she doesn't smarten up, then I'll ask for a different nurse, simple as this." "Not for me, you don't have to." "She did act like an ignorant and this is not right in her profession." "Oh, you noticed this too. Don't fight for me sweetheart, it's not worth it." "No Gaston, I'll do it for myself and if I want to fight for you I'll do it too. You yourself would fight the devil for us." "Yes but, I'm a fighter." "Watch me." "Isn't she gorgeous sweetheart? She's the most beautiful baby I have ever seen, do you know this? I can see traces of wisdom in her look." "How can you say this, she is too young?" "Huh, huh, the first minutes I met you I could tell." "This is right too. Gaston you must be a wizard, a psychic or something." "No sweetie, I'm only a dreamer." "Right, now how could I forget this?" "You got lots on your mind too sweetie."

'Attention visitors, you have to leave the premises within five minutes.'

"I know you need your rest sweetheart, but just know darling how much I hate this way of telling us to get out. Even if they could say ten minutes instead of five, this would be half as bad. You're saying that you have no pain? You're not lying, are you; just to spare me the worry?" "Gaston, would you lie to me for the same reason?" "No, I wouldn't lie, but I might hide something if it was the only way and necessary for your own protection." "And I trusted you." "I do my best my sweetheart." "I know you do and this is plenty. Good night my love. I'll see you tomorrow." "The house will be very empty tonight sweetie, good night."

I hugged and I kissed her, but I could hardly hide my tears. Firstly, because I had to leave her behind and secondly, because I was forced to hide something from her. I couldn't even feel guilty, because I also knew it was the best thing to do, knowing perfectly well it could safe her life.

It took me a very long time to go to sleep that night. I shouldn't though, because I know I can rely on the Lord for everything. When I thought of it, I put on one of my gospel tape and this is what put me to sleep.

We are humans and we often want to do things our own way, but this could be costly, because no matter who we are, we all are too weak on our own.

The following two years were pretty quiet and not much happened except the coming of Benjamin, the horse some friends called him. At five months old he could grab one of my fingers and hold himself to it for the longest time.

Jonathan and Leah love to sing along with me now and Sarah slaps her hands and laughs of happiness all the way to the end of every piece of music. I just can't have a better audience than this. They like my songs and they always ask for the ones made for the Lord. No wonder Jesus said:

'To see the kingdom of heaven, you'll have to be like the little children.' To me they are little angels singing praises to the Lord and I know this warms God's heart as it does mine.

Dana too now is very close to our Lord. She cried one evening while she surrendered all of her being; repenting for all she had done wrong since she could remember.

"The Lord has been so good to me. I want Him to forgive me all of my wrongdoing and especially my laughing and mocking at Him." "Welcome to this new world Precious Princess born again. You can be sure now the Lord has accepted you. Now peace, love and all of his blessing will be with you forever."

It was then I composed the welcoming song of the princes and the princesses to Wonderland.

The Precious Princess of Wonderland

This song has the same title than this book.

This is men best friend, my best friend

Resting dog after a good race

Chapter 8

A ll the soldiers, all of the police officers from all of the police's forces, all of the athletes and strong men including martial artists are in the same boat. They have to either bring their share of slaves in, meaning Jews and believers or be executed themselves. There is a big confusion at first, because all of these officers are sworn in.

Their choices are simple, either they work for the beast or they work for the Lord. See what is written in Matthew 6, 24. 'No one can serve two masters; for either he will hate the one and love the other or he will be devoted to one and despise the other.' You cannot serve God and his enemy.'

If they are working for the Lord chances are good the Lord will delivery them from the devil's hands. There is no guarantee though they won't suffer or die, but if the Lord takes you away, He'll make you much stronger then you already are to fight the battle. Just remember that even Jesus suffered and died. Take a look at Matthew 10, 39. 'He who has found his life will lose it and who has lost his life for My sake will find it.'

So this is where the war of the end time begins, the battle between good and evil, the battle between the good and the bad soldiers, the battle between the good and the bad police officers, the battle between the good and the bad athletes and all sports people. Think of King David and Samson, their enemies were falling by the thousands and the ten thousands. God will do it again and here I am for Him.

'Take me Lord and equip me with what it takes to put down your enemies.'

More than 80 per cent of all businesses in the world is computerised now. More than four billions people communicate through the Internet. The battle between the monsters of the economy was tough but decisive. The name of the beast could have been the Internet, but it isn't. It is only one of their tools. The devilish trinity is in place now. Their world-wide system governmental and religious is the beast. The world leader, Satan is sitting on his throne and the world-wide religion leader who is the false prophet whom God's prophets talked about thousands of years ago is asking all the people of the earth to adore their god who took charge of everything. There is only one currency and 90 per cent of all your earning goes to the treasury. This is exactly the opposite of what God had asked from us. Another difference is God didn't kill you if you didn't pay your 10 per cent, otherwise the world would've ended many thousands years ago. There are only ten dollars out of every hundred that goes directly to your bank account if you have one. If you don't, it is just too bad, because you get nothing and you are better being looking for a Defender.

The believers' hunt is so violent that most of God's people don't even have time to say yes or no and this is the way God has chosen for you not to suffer, just like John the Baptist was killed. God will restore your body the way you'll like it the best and if you've never liked it, He'll give you another one. These are the ones whom the Antichrist knows he can't turn around. You can find a good example of this in Acts 7, 54 - 60.

The undecided (the neither hot nor cold) will be tortured, because the beast has a chance to get them on his side. This is what he is out for. When I decided to become a disciple this was the exact question I asked myself. 'Do I want to serve God or do I want to serve the devil?' Jesus said:

'If you're not with me, you're against me.' Believe him, he knows. See Matthew 12, 30.

Dana saw enough of this dirt now to believe and to trust me that it was time to go to our refuge. It was a strong battle though, because of all the homeless children without any parents. I told Dana God was in charge.

"We'll do our share and He'll do the rest, but you and I can't save the world. How many children do you have now?" "Thirty-two." "I think we can manage to keep them all, but they can't be too fussy with the food and neither are you from now on." "I know this my man, we're so lucky to have you." "Today you have answered the very last question I had about you even though I knew the answer. God loved and blessed me today more than he ever did." "Why?"

"Because I'm taking you to the camp you don't like very much?" "I always knew Gaston you would take the children and I, but all of the other kids, I love them all too just as much as they were mine. You too have just answered my last question my loving husband." "You don't mind leaving the house and your building behind?" "The safety of these children and my family are much, much more important to me." "Don't cry Precious. I know, let me have it. I have lots of joy in my heart right now too sweetie.

Joy is something brought to our heart for being good about what you or somebody else have done, thanks to the Lord for this.

I can't take all of you at once and I can't leave the children over there by themselves either so we need somebody to watch here and somebody over there. Can you trust your helpers for a couple of days?" "I would say so." "Then you, our children and seven kids come first. Do you remember everything I told you for the safety at the campsite?" "I'll be fine Gaston and I'm sure glad now you are a dreamer. Thanks to the Lord and thanks to you, we'll be all safe." "This is the main reason why I met you." "Do you mean you never thought of me for yourself?" "Not for months, I didn't." "Oh Gaston, you really are from the Lord." "Let's go now; there is a lot to do yet before everyone is safe. Do you remember all the four trails?" "I sure do." "Then I'll leave you with the kids and I will run to get the four-wheeler and the trailer, then I will come back and get you all." "Gaston you are a gallant even in the bush, you're absolutely incredible." "Here is a little pistol just in case you need to make noise." "I don't want a gun." "There is no real bullets in there, it is just in case a cougar or a wolf come around, it is not going to kill anything or anybody, but the noise would scare them away and this could save yours and the kids' life. You just can't expect to have a Defender around every time you're in danger. It is most of the time better to stay all in a group and later on I'll show you why, but trust me for now." "Maybe you should stay with us Gaston." "To walk the whole ten miles with the kids would take hours and they would cry and they would be exhausted and give you more troubles. Listen to what I say and you'll be fine and the kids too." "I know you're right, but I'm scared." "I know, but you have to show some courage for the sake of the kids. Take the trail number 3 and I'll be with you in two hours." "How can you be back in two hours Gaston? You're not twenty anymore?" "Oh sweetheart, not you too?" "I didn't mean it this way my love." "I know, but I got to go now, we'll talk later, ok?"

I left them at 10:00 in the morning and at 12:05.

'Can you hear this mom? This is papa.' Jonathan said.

'You must have bugs in you ears.' Leah told him.

When they all stopped walking all of them could hear the machine clearly.

'I'm sorry Jonathan, you were right.'

I was back with them at 12.10 and I could not believe what I heard.

'You're late.' Dana told me with tears in her eyes. She hugged and she kissed me as if I was gone for a whole mouth.

"I told you I'd be back. This is only the beginning of your training my darling and there is a lot more to learn yet. From now on we have a new life. Thanks to the Lord who gave me those dreams, we'll be able to live it until He comes back to get us."

I took them all to the campsite. Then I kissed Dana and the kids and I rushed back to my car. I drove the seventy miles to Kelowna, loaded the car and drove back again with twelve kids. This was an old car, but strong, fast and spacious. I was sure glad I didn't just have a little four cylinders then. I packed the trunk as much as I could with Dana's and the children's things. There was not a minute to waste, because every one of them could cost a life or more. The little trailer wasn't as big though and I had to put four kids on the machine and on my laps, making the other eight jealous. I could tell these kids needed the father some of them never had.

I also knew then I would have to extend my educational skills. I can't stand jealousy. I gave orders to two kids to watch behind and see that all the kids in the trailer stay where they were. This was one of the conditions to sit with me. We are never too young to learn responsibility, not anymore anyway.

The ground is pretty well level and the ride was smooth and fast. Is there any point telling you the kids enjoyed it? The biggest problem was to get them off.

'More, more!' They all shouted and one of them was even crying so much he didn't want to let go. Now that I think of it, this will be just a heaven for these kids. Then I thought:

'My God, You are so wonderful to show me how You take care of your children.'

"Gaston, you must have been speeding to make the trip this quick." "There is no time to waste sweetie, there are lives on the line and I'm going back right away. Will you be alright with all these chicks, mother hen?" "I'll be just fine, go."

When I returned to the building I found twelve children on their own just having an absolute blast and they shouted at me:

'The two nannies are gone and they took Sylvia along with them.'

'Oh my goodness, what a mess! If you kids want to see Dana again, you'd better straighten up, because I will never put up with this kind of mess again, understood?'

This was like thunder in the ears of these poor little minds. Some of them started to cry and they said:

"We want to see Dana, pleaaase, pleaaase." "Alright but, no more of this garbage, ok?" "Ok, ok, let's go sir; we'll do what you say." "Now all of you, I want you to help me with the toys and fill up all the boxes you can find, then drag them to the elevator. Hurry up."

When the car was loaded with the kids and everything else we could put in, I drove away fearing the worst. I had a premonition something was going on. I drove around the block and I parked the car at about five hundred feet away from the Princess' Children Care Centre and I waited. Sure enough four minutes later three jeeps full of soldiers with machine guns stopped in front of the building and they shot the door wide open.

'Why are they doing this to our home sir?' One kid asked.

'Because they are bad men and they like to destroy everything, especially beautiful things.'

One of them shot down the beautiful crown on top of the building and I was happy Dana didn't see this, but I'm afraid it will be useless trying to get the kids to keep the secret. I knew then this was marking the end of all civilizations.

I made only one stop and this was to pick up a newspaper. I quickly looked at it and it seems all they have to say is about devastation, rape and murder. The paper is twice as thick as it used to be.

'Goodbye Kelowna, I don't think you're going to see the Precious Princess again.'

I quickly hit the road knowing very well they might set up a roadblock and if there was one I would not have a chance with all these kids in the car with me. If there is one I'll have to go through it as fast as I can, hoping my car is faster than theirs.

One police car followed me and I presumed it was just for a routine identification, like show me your papers sir, but I just couldn't take any risk. When he was close enough I stopped my car and he stopped behind me, but before he stepped out of his car I backed mine up into his, activating this way the air bag, keeping him prisoner of his own car. Then I just sped out of his way knowing very well he might already have my licence plate number, my name and no known address. Shoot! I'll have to get another car again. Good thing I have eighty of them. Maybe I can just change the colour of this one too. I like a lot of its qualities.

The kids are having a bigger blast now than the one they had in the building. You should have heard them telling the others. It was as if we have been to an action movie.

What a supper I'll have to cook tonight. I hope some of them like fish and too bad if they don't, because this is all they'll have tonight, fish and bread. If this was good enough for the five thousand people Jesus fed, it should be good enough for thirty-five kids. I always knew I was going to have a fairly big family, but my goodness not this big. The Lord will help me though, I'm sure of this. I just know He loves these children too.

"Are you still sure you don't regret it now my wonderful husband?" "I'll love you through eternity Precious, I meant it, I never changed my mind and I never will. Oh don't cry sweetie. Let me say it, this is joy. Come here."

Did you ever want to hug someone so hard she would just go inside of you? This is how I hugged Precious for the longest time.

"I'm hungry Dana, when do we have supper?" "You better ask Gaston, he is the cook." "What, a man cooking?"

Most of them laughed? Jonathan replied to this by saying his dad was a much better cook than his mom.

We all quickly got used to our new routine. I made a bunch of bunks with the insulation boards I had left for the camps and with some car back seats. I thought I had put enough blankets and pillows away for twenty years, but now considering everything, I know I didn't. I know too now I'll have to do a lot more of horse trading than I had anticipated.

I might be able to do some buying for a little while yet and I'll have to go and check this out. When I did

I passed by the hubcap collection and I found out no employee was there and there was not a single hubcap which didn't have a bullet hole in it. Then I thought:

'Precious, they got my crown too, but at least we had our heads out of them.' The ones who put their faith in their belonging or their belonging has become their god have a good chance to be killed for it. See in Mathew 6, 19.

The message is very clear that you'd be much better to accumulate treasures in heaven where no thieves or beasts can take them away.

There is desolation, destruction and abomination everywhere. It is a total chaos and this had to happen, because the Word of God never lied. The world has to get down to the very worst ever before Satan sits and proclaims himself to be God. When everything is absolutely out of control the most powerful man in the whole world will have a solution for everything and everybody.

'Nobody but God the Father knows the day or the time.' Jesus said it, so if anybody tells you otherwise, you'll know he is a liar.

Everywhere you'll see some individuals pretending they are the Christ. They are the deceivers we are warned about not the Defenders. If you really want to know what will happen and how the end will come, go read Matthew 13, 41 - 42. Just try to believe the One who is telling us the truth for your own sake.

By the time Christmas came that year we were pretty well set up in our little community. I managed to phone Dana's parents and members of my family a couple of times. I couldn't talk very long though, but enough to know the anarchy had spread out all over the country and possibly worldwide. All telephone conversations are listened to and if you talk too long, you would be picked up in no time, especially if they find out you are a believer in the true God. You're just good for the guillotine as far as this world is concern.

There are only a few places left where you can still buy with cash. What an inspiration I had in the last five years to buy every pair of shoes of all size and all kinds of clothes from Value Village at a dollar or two a pair. God give us some ideas sometimes which seems useless, but it is better to never underestimate them.

I really think I'm ready now for the next twenty years to come. I stocked one thousand bags of seed of all kinds and even some flowers for the Princess. Precious Princess, I'm afraid she's having a tough time adapting to the new kingdom of ours.

Life always been an everyday gift for everyone, but this is more obvious nowadays than ever. I personally think we are very blessed not to see the worst as many others do. Once in a while I bring a newspaper to Dana so she can appreciate better the security she's having. I just sense though I won't be able to rest much in the near future.

I talked to some friends who can use the building as a refuge for whatever is left of it. I also suggest to them they learn to survive in the bush somewhere, their chances to live longer would be better. One of them asked me:

"Who wants to live in this mess anyway?" "This is just it, when you don't see it, it's easier."

We have to be careful not to be seen in groups too long as well. When these groups get caught by the soldiers or the cops, their lives don't worth more than a bullet.

One of the newspapers I read today assured me the Defenders were at work all over the country and even in some isolated cases in the United States, France and also in England. They could be anybody, soldiers, police officers and martial artists or any person with skills and wisdom who loves the Lord and cares for others. If one of them happens to be a traitor there is no time to waste, one, two or even three Defenders if it's necessary have to find him and challenge him into a combat to finish. We are not going to win the war, but only some battles. The Lord Jesus will win it to God's Glory, Hallelujah.

It was a long winter and to me it was the very best, because every day and all day long I got to spend it with Precious. Most of the kids love the music and learned to pray like my family does.

"Do they have to learn this too Gaston? They're not really our kids." "Dana, if I remember well you said you love them just as much as your own children." "I do Gaston in a way." "Well Precious, if they going to be my adoptive children, they'll have to go by the same rules than my immediate family and this includes praying to the Lord every day. It won't hurt them one bit and I don't know why you're so concerned about this. Also if at any time I see our children getting spoiled by any of them, I'll find another place for him. It was said: 'Take the bad out from the middle of you.' Trust me Dana; I'll do the impossible to help each and everyone of them." "I know this my love, you already did much more than you had to." "Don't forget your dance lesson tonight sweetie." "I won't, this is one of my best moments." "Which is your best one?" "Shtt, I'll tell you tonight on the pillow, ok?" "Precious, you always have been the sweetest." "Who's the second?" "Me, of course!"

Most everyone enjoyed ice fishing, which lasted four and a half months. They enjoyed the snowmobile riding and also the dogs sleigh rides. Jonathan knows all the tricks of the trade now and the dogs love him just as much as they love me. I told Jon one day.

'The dog that loves you would do anything you ask, even to jump in the fire to please his master, but you are never, never to abuse him at all, because he will save your live more than once, I can assure you this.'

I made a garden emplacement for a dozen people. Now with all those little mouths around the four tables, I have to extend it three times. All of what is left from the fishes is the very best fertiliser there is. We also collect all the manure which is around from the wild animals especially the deer and the moose. Almost each kid has a row. The one who likes the onions the best will take care of the onion rows and on until all the rows are taken care of under supervision of course. Dana is very good in this area. If we didn't know any better we could think this was paradise.

No kid under any circumstance is allowed to fight. If they have a disagreement or any grief of any kind, they have to bring the problem to our attention. If it's a minor thing we usually can solve the problem right away. If it's more serious, we set a time for a sort of little trial where all the voices are heard and listened to. Then a decision is taken as to who is at fault and who's not.

It was very hard for Leah to apologise one time, but she complied gracefully. The way I hugged her afterward showed her how much I appreciate someone who does what he has to do no matter how hard it is. Jonathan is six now and he is following my steps every day. He also questions me a lot about the pass and the future. I just know in my heart and in my mind he is going to be a fine man. He can swim the lake back and forth without losing any breath, which is not my case anymore. I'm sixty-two now and I'm still in a very good shape, but I'm not getting any younger. So far the children know how to fish and how to snare the rabbits and the chickens.

Jonathan and Leah know how to approach the deer and the moose even to the point they can feed them from their hands, especially Leah.

'Dad, let me go by myself, I want to show you something.' She got as close as five feet from the animal.

"Always remember this Leah, because maybe one day you'll have to do it again and put it down to feed the rest of the family." "Oh dad, I could never hurt this animal." "But you would let your family starve to death?" "Noooo." "When you have no other choice, I hope you'll know what to do and how to do it." "They are so pretty dad." "What do you think of the cows?" "Oh, I don't like them." "Why?" "They are stupid and ugly."

"Jonathan, do you want to come here please. Both of you listen very carefully now. Cows give their milk all their life for you and at the end we take them to the butcher to be killed. They end up in people's plates for their food and no one thinks they deserve any better. On the other hand the deer will come to break our garden and steal everything he can of the precious food we worked very hard to get, if I don't do anything to stop it. Now are you telling me the deer deserves to live more than the cows just because it is pretty?" "I guess not dad." "The ugliest and the stupidest people want to be loved just as much as the prettiest and the most intelligent girls and the handsome and strong men and very often they deserve it much more." "I never thought of this before dad, but it makes sense."

"Leah is right dad; it never crossed my mind either to think this way." "I love the two of you very, very much and also little Sarah and Ben, but they are too young to understand all of this. Now, can I count on both of you to teach them? I like to have from you the promise you will always try to see the two sides of everything before you make any kind of judgement.

I have to warn you about something. Sometimes we don't have the time to think, but if you're trained to do it, it will come automatically." "Dad, this is almost the best lesson you've taught us." "Oh yeah and what is the best one Leah?" "Everything you said about Jesus." "Now, could the two of you help me teach the others? Jonathan has helped me with you Leah for some time now and he did a very fine job. I'm very proud of him." "You'll be proud of me too dad." "You're a sweetheart Leah. Good man Jonathan." "What did you do dad to protect the garden? I don't see anything around it." "I've done two things, but either one of them could do the trick, it depends." "What is it dad?" "Well, I put a bundle of my air at a distance from each corner of the garden, because we never know witch way the wind will blow. Now that the deer is used to you guys, it wouldn't keep him away anymore. So I had to do something else." "What's this?" "You can't tell anyone." "We won't." "Every once in a while I pee on each corner." "What?" "This repeals them and this turns them away from far. I'd say three to four hundred feet. I offer the invention of my repellent to the government, but they kind of laugh and ignore me. I wanted to save the deer from being killed by the vehicles on the road. The deer is the wild animal that kills most people. An average of one hundred and fifty people are killed each year in North America because of the deer on the roads. If someone hit a deer with a $30,000.00 car, chances are good the damage would be $5000.00 or more. Half of this money goes back in the cases of the crown in one form or the other. (Taxes and income taxes)

I also proposed a machine to the government of B.C. that would keep the road clean and dry all winter long. It would save thousands of accidents and save at least 50 per cent of the $72 millions a year they spend on broken windshields. It would also save millions and millions of the money they spend on salt and sand. But for as long as people will pay their premium they don't care.

Let's go join the others now. We've got a job to do." "Oh dad, I'm tired now." "Are you too tired to go kiss mom, Sarah and Ben?" "Is this the job you were talking about dad?" "Part of it. Later on this afternoon we are going for a swim." "The water is still too cold dad." "It will be best you get used to it Leah for when your life depends on it. Scuba diving is what we'll have. We need to find out more about this lake. We already know what kind of fish is in there and approximately how big it is. Now we need to know how deep the lake is and if there is any place to hide in it."

'I found a few good places dad.' Jonathan yelled right away.

"How deep do you think they are?" "Like the houses." "Jon, this is over sixteen feet." "Oh dad, I can go deeper than this, I turn around when my ears are making a funny sound." "Did you hear the music down there too?" "Yeah, this is funny dad, but you can play better." "Really? It wasn't Everything's Yours Oh Lord, was it?" "No!"

"Don't forget to give your heart to the Lord before you dive, both of you." "Dad, do I really have to?" "Let me ask you something Precious Leah." "Mom is your Precious." "She is and so are all of my children, don't you know this?" "Yes we do dad." "Let me ask you something. If many men come over here when I'm not around and they want to take all of you away and the only thing that could save your life would be to dive and go to the hideout in the bottom of the lake or somewhere in there, what would you do then?" "I guess I would dive then." "And where would you go?" "I don't know." "See sweetheart, I want you to know where to go. This is why we're here today. Tomorrow or another day, you can show it to somebody else and I know I can count on you. One, two, three!"

"You're funny dad." "I did this to your mom once and I knew then I could count on her and she could count on me too."

Jonathan came back from his dive at that moment and he was totally exited about something.

"Dad, dad, dad, you wouldn't believe this, but I think I found something very special." "Calm down my boy, I have no reason not to believe you at all, because I know you're not a liar. What happened Jon?" "I found a room below the lake." "What kind of room?" "I don't know, I never saw something like that." "How big?" "Liiike your bedroom." "Yes, but it was full of water?" "No dad, I could stand up in it and breathe."

'Get ready Leah, we're all going to look at it.'

"Can you remember how to get there Jonathan? Point out to me the direction, would you?" "Everything looks different from here. I think it is this way." "We'll follow you under the water; this might be easier for you." "All set?" "All set."

'Let's follow Jonathan, the explorer Leah.'

I could tell by looking in Jonathan's face that he enjoyed his new title. We had a few turns-around and hesitations here and there, but thirty-five minutes later, Leah and I could see the discovery too.

I was absolutely amazed by what I was looking at. There is a cave that must be eighteen feet in diameter and twenty feet high. I looked all around and I found out that Jonathan might have been the first man to walk in it. I was speechless for the longest time. When I opened my mouth I asked the children to come to me and I said:

"Jonathan, Leah, God showed us today the place where He is coming back for you. Try to remember to thank Him every day for this. The Almighty has all kind of ways to show us His love. This is one of them and He also uses people as young as Jonathan to do it. Explorer, the Lord loves you so much that He made you a very important man today in the history."

"What are we dad, the two first witnesses?" "You've just said it bright thing and I don't know about you Leah, but I am extremely proud of it."

I asked for Jonathan's hand and I shook it.

'Congratulation sir, not only you are a great explorer, but you are also a famous discoverer and I'll be your admirer forever.'

When I finished talking to him, Leah too went to shake Jon's hand.

"Did you find anything else even though it's not this important?" "Well, there is bigger fish than the ones we have caught already and the water is not much deeper than what we saw coming over here." "Man, this is what I call a good report. I'll have to come back another day with you Jonathan and make plans for the future and also in case of an emergency. This would be the safest place around to go. We just have to make plans to get here fast."

When I got on the pillow with Precious that night, I told her about a discovery without telling her what it was exactly.

Jonathan and Leah weren't allowed to speak of it to the other kids either, so they had to hide their excitement, especially Jonathan.

'The Lord is good.' Dana said.

"He provides us with all kind of good things Gaston and I frankly believe it's because of you." "He loves you just as much Precious Princess. How were the kids today?" "As you must know, they get to be a little bit looser when you're not around." "But you managed, didn't you?" "I'm exhausted though." "This is not an excuse, is it?" "What do you mean my husband?" "You know." "No it isn't and I'll show you. I'll love you until 3:30 in the morning. This will teach you." "Is that all? We have to make escape plans sweetie." "Not tonight though. Tonight I want to love you as I never did my love." "Sweetie, you're getting better and better all the time."

This was a short night's sleep, but it seems the older we get the less sleep we need.

'We have Granny's crepes this morning kids.' The majority of them accepted this with acclamations. This is when the two spare stoves come in action. Ninety-six crepes and each and every one of these kids want the first one.

'Get the bingo game Dana.' I shouted. 'We need winners again this morning.' Two hours later it was my turn, but I wasn't hungry anymore having tasted just about all of the ones I cooked. Leah said:

"Dad, I need to talk to you in private after breakfast if you have time." "I'll make time for you sweetie girl." "Let's go in the bunkhouse, I don't want anybody else to hear this." "This must be very serious Leah, are you ok?" "Oh yeah, it is just something I thought about." "What is it sweetie?" "Mom is your sweetie, not me." "Now, now, what is this? If I didn't know you any better, I would think you are jealous. Your mommy is always going to be my sweetie and you Leah are my little sweetie too, not in the same way but just as strong. Sarah is also my little sweetie and I love you all just as much. Let me get a pen and a piece of paper here and I'll show you something. What is this?" "Two circles." "Right. Let me make another one, ok?" "Ok. Now there are three circles." "Right again. This one was your papa before he married mommy and this one was mommy before she married daddy. Do you follow me?" "Yeah, I see the two circles are empty." "This is right again and when we got married this one and this one became only one. So, we have to get rid of one circle now. Which one do you want to eliminate, dad or mom?"

"Oh dad I love you both." "You don't have to eliminate neither one you see, because you have two parents, but we are one couple. So can you imagine I take this one and put it on top of the other one?" "Yeah, but it's still empty." "Right, but you know now there are two circles over there." "Yes, you've put mommy on top of you." "Right." "Now this circle is you and mommy." "And what do you think this circle is?" "I don't know, it's not me, because it's empty." "Mommy and I were empty too and this is when we've decided we should fill up this circle that I will call family. So, I have to ask you again to imagine this circle on top of daddy and mommy circle." "But the circle is still empty." "I think we should do something about this, don't you think?" "Yeah!" "Because mommy and daddy love each other very, very much they decided to fill up the circle. So the first quarter is Jonathan, the second is Leah." "This is me?" "This is you. The third is little Sarah and who do you think the fourth one is?" "Baby Ben." "And you are right again. Now the circle is full. We never know, God might decide to send us another one and we'll have to squeeze all of you to make room for him in the circle." "This is not a circle anymore dad, this is all of our family, all of the kids on top of you and mommy. Hi, hi, hi." "Is there anything else you wanted to talk to me about sweetheart?" "You've done all of the talking daddy. I wanted to talk to you." "This is right too. What's on your mind? I'll do my best to listen this time." "I couldn't go to sleep until late last night dad and I was thinking a lot about safety for everybody." "And you came up with a very good idea?" "I, I, I think so." "You tell me about it sweetheart." "Dad, if we could put a tunnel all the way from the lake to underneath the bunkhouse here and a lid in the floor to go in it, we could all escape in daytime or at night while they are waiting outside for us to come out." "Precious Leah, you are a genius. Let's go tell mommy."

"Are you sure it is a good idea dad? She is scared of the water and you know this. Maybe we should wait until she knows how to swim."

"You have made a beautiful discovery Leah. Do you want to thank the Lord for the idea He gave you?" "Yes dad, let's do this. Oh my second Daddy, I love You and I thank You for my papa and mommy, the whole family in the circle and for the good idea You gave me, thank You." "May God bless you sweet little Leah. I'll never stop being proud of you for as long as I live." "In those moments I need strength for not being too strong. I could just have squeezed her to death so much my love for her is great.

There was no way I could find or I could bring a big enough culvert to the campsite though, but it was easy enough to dig in this kind of soil. I still had a lot of those insulation panels in the reserve. I didn't waste any time before starting on this superb project of two hundred and fifty feet long. There was already an escape cave under the building which Leah knew nothing about yet. The biggest problem we had were the roots, because some needed to be cut and I was afraid to kill the tree which covers part of the house and hide most of it from an air view.

I have a couple of picks and lots of shovels. When we began digging we told the others this was to find worms for fishing, which was also true. For one thing this stopped everybody from questioning anymore; secondly it kept the secret safe a little bit longer.

Guess who wanted to help me the most? Leah and Jonathan were with me most of the days. They had sensed the importance of a quick getaway. And did we ever find worms. We found so many that I started to fill a plastic barrel which I set in the ground so we can get at it and get live baits even in the winter. We can raise them for fishing all year round.

The ditch went at a rate of thirty feet long a day. I dug it four and a half feet deep by three and a half feet wide. Because of the heat I began to dig a couple of hours at night and I started early in the morning. Both Dana and I didn't like the separation from the comfortable and warm nest of ours though.

Jonathan loves to work and this is another blessing to me. I know I'll be able to count on him whatever happens. A week later the tunnel was done. Jonathan was invited to go pick up the braces that was holding the walls in place until the water was let in.

Sweet precious Leah was invited to be the first one to try her splendid invention. Seeing her coming out of the tunnel and entering the lake was one of the greatest joys I've had. I told Jonathan then the idea came from her. He looked at me, smiled and he went to welcome Leah. He took her in his arms; he carried her all the way back to the bunkhouse and he asked her if they could do it together this time. I could hardly believe what I was seeing. The strength of this little boy was just astonishing. Then I remembered myself when I turned thirteen on my birthday.

I went to get a fifty-pound bag of potatoes that day at the grocery store a mile away. I carried it at home without putting it down a single time and this in three and one half feet of snow. This was the talk of the village for quite some time. I heard later on that many young men tried to do it on a clean road and they couldn't do it. I'm not too sure if I could still do it either, but just when I saw these two kids of mine together, a wonderful peace of mind got to me. I knew it was another confirmation the Lord was in charge and there was no reason for me to worry anymore for anything.

When they came out of the tunnel and they entered the lake, I just dived to join them in an extraordinary joy that is hard to describe. Jonathan took his mask off and he yelled:

"There is a big trout in there dad, we can catch fish right from inside the house." "Oh my gosh; we could be prisoners in our own getaway." "What's wrong dad?" He asked worrying.

"I'll explain it to you when you come out of the water." "What is it dad, I want to know, tell me?" "Did I ever talk to you about spawning?" "No, I don't know. What is it?" "All the mommy fish find a safe place to have their babies to protect them from the hungry daddies that care more for their stomach than for their offspring and they might just like our getaway a little bit too much."

Leah said: 'The mommies get on top of the daddies and you don't see the daddies anymore, but you can see lots of babies.'

'Thanks Leah. When they do, they are thousands of them and they would fill up the tunnel so much we wouldn't be able to get out through it.'

'So.' Leah said sadly:

"My idea wasn't this good after all." "Your idea is wonderful Leah; we just have to do some more thinking, that's all." "I know." She said all exited.

'We just have to make a grill and put it in place to stop the mommies to go in there.'

Both Jon and I gave her the high five.

'See kids, when we think positively how the Lord is giving us some good ideas. We'll have to watch for the spawning season and put the grill in place in time to stop them from blocking the way.'

Jonathan asked:

"Maybe we could make them another tunnel dad?" "This is very kind of you son, but they have their own place, it is just they could like ours better. Let's go see what mom and the others are doing. Don't tell anything to anyone yet. Later on this afternoon, we'll start to teach them how to dive too, but we'll pick another spot, because we have to keep this one here a secret for as long as possible. Even until we really need to use it will be the best thing to do." "You can count on us dad." They both said at the same time.

'I know I can.' They both smiled and I said:

'Let's go. One, two, three.'

I went to play with all the kids to give Precious an hour of rest. Pretty soon it will be time to collect the vegetables from the garden and the kids were getting pretty exited about it.

'Spaghetti and potatoes will be ready in thirty minutes.' I said when I left them to their games.

'Alright!' Most of them shouted with joy and laughter. I'm sure glad most of them like it; because I have the impression they're going to have a lot of it in the next while.

While lunch was cooking, I went to talk to Dana about the next trip I'll have to make downtown and she didn't feel too good about it.

"I feel so much better and safer Gaston when you're here." "You'll be alright too sweetie, I just know it." "Oh, I'm not worried about us my love as much that I'm worried about you." "I'll be fine too Precious. The Lord who has been with me all of this time is still there and He will bring me back to you always. Nothing will happen to me He wouldn't allow." "How do you know all of this?" "Because I know He loves you too. Excuse me, I better see to the lunch."

While I was finishing the meal Dana had set up the four tables and she called for the kids to come in. I knew then I needed to find a way to spend another hour with her and the sooner would be the better.

'Ok kids, I have a good job for you this afternoon.' You should have seen those questioning eyes that made Dana laughed.

"What?"

"what?"

"what?" "I think it is time to get some of the garden now, but I don't want any waste at all. We need to take out the radishes, the lettuce and some tomatoes for now. All of the leaves are needed to feed the worms. There are three wheelbarrows to help you with the work and you all know where the cold storage room is. I'll leave you alone for an hour or so and I don't want anyone to come in the house unless there is a death threats. Everybody got this?" "Yes!" They all shouted.

My Precious couldn't hold back laughing and when she does I don't think I could be happier.

"Before I let you go I got a question for everyone. Who is the chef out there when Dana and I are not around?" "Jonathan is." All of them agreed.

'If this is understood by everyone, then you can go.'

"Leave the dishes for now Dana, I need to talk to you." "You don't think you can talk to me while we are doing it?" "I'm sure I could, but I need you to relax and tell me what bothers you these days, you're not the same anymore." "So many children, you know? It gets to me more than I thought it would. It is one different thing to have them eight to twelve hours a day, than it is to have them around the clock." "I know you're not built for this big of a family. It is one of the reasons why I want to go to town and see if maybe I can find somebody like we used to who would take a child or two.

Another thing I meant to tell you is that Jonathan knows a lot more than you do about what is around here. So if for a reason or another I'm slow returning, just know you can rely on him. He knows the lake inside out now and he has discovered a safer place than here for us to hide if needed. But sweetie, you'll have to learn how to swim." "Gaston, this was my surprise to you, I know how." "Oh sweetheart, you have your little secrets too, haven't you?" "I knew it was important and I've been practising for almost two months now."

"I'll see if I can find a dishwasher or two." "Maybe we shouldn't Gaston. I think we should keep the fuel for something more important. We have so many hands here and if they can do the garden with so much enthusiasm, I'm sure they can do the dishes too." "My sweetie, you're absolutely right and now it is the last time you and I are doing it. We have to celebrate this. What about a glass of wine? White or red? Should I put some music on and have a few dances with the most beautiful Precious Princess of this whole world?" "Yes my love, I'll dance with you. I hope I can remember how though. I know my wonderful husband I can trust you for anything."

When one and a half hour was gone one of the kids came to the house and when hearing the music she went back to tell all of the others. They came in all surprised to see Dana and I doing the old time waltz.

"Can I learn too?"

"Can I learn too?" Most of them were asking? But Dana told them:

"If you can find daddy doing nothing one day, then you can ask him." "Ah, ah, ah, might as well forget it then."

"We never know, just keep it in mind for now, ok?" "O-o-o-ok." "I got news for you kids." "What?" "Starting tomorrow morning, four of you will do the dishes one day and four others will do it the next day. We'll go on like this every day over and over again. If one of you ever feels this is not fair, then you can come to me and we'll see what we can do. You can discuss this between yourselves and form groups. If for some reasons you can't do it, then I'll form the groups myself. You have an hour to do it while Dana and I are doing it for the last time. After that we are all going for a swim and we have to learn how to dive. Now, you may give us some applause for this decision, can't you?"

'Wow Gaston.' Dana said laughing when the kids were out of the house.

"You're a real leader, aren't you?" "They are much easier to lead than adults, simply because they are much more honest."

When we got back to them, I found out they had only one problem, one of them was alone.

'This is not a problem, who wants to be suspended from it? One, two, seventeen!' And I noticed little Sarah didn't lift her hand. All of the boys except Jonathan had their hands up.

"This is too many and I'm very disappointed in you. All of you get good meals?" "Yeah." "We're just going to suspend the youngest. Would you think this is fair?" "Yeah."

It just happened the youngest one was Sarah and I told them she is going to do it sometime with mommy or me or with both of us until the next vote. It is time to go to the lake now; we'll join you as soon as I have finished talking with Jonathan and Leah. Go get you bathing suit."

"Is there something wrong dad?" "Not at all, it is just that I told your mom a bit about your discovery Jonathan and she admitted to me having a surprise that you going to discover yourselves in a few minutes. Tonight we're going to have a talk with her and both of you can tell her then about your mutual discovery. What do you think of this?" "This is dandy dad, we'll go for that."

We all went for a swim and when Leah and Jon saw their mom they had the surprise of their life.

"Mom, you're swimming, since when?" "A couple of months now." "What a surprise and if we knew about it we would have told you something." "What is it? You can tell me now that I swim." "We can't tell you before tonight's meeting." "Oh come on now you guys, you put water to my mouth, tell me." "Mom, the lake is full of water. We can't mom, we promised dad." "Well, if you have promised, you'd better stick to it." "Mom, try this on." "What is it?" "It's scuba diving equipment. You can go almost as deep as you want with this." "Where did you get this?" "It belongs to Dad." "I got the feeling there is a lot more here than he told me."

The two kids looked at each other and they realised they have said more than they wanted to.

"It's alright kids; we are going to clarify some of this tonight." "This lake is safe all the way through mom." "How do you know?" "I know it all." "And you going to tell me more about it tonight, right? I just can't wait, do you know this?" "Oh, oh, we are better get teaching here." Jonathan said.

"Daddy wants all the kids to learn how to dive." "I wonder why?" "Mom, you are questioning too much." "I guess I do, I'm sorry."

All the kids were pretty excited about their day. It was almost eight o'clock when the last one fell asleep even though they were exhausted.

The time for the famous meeting finally arrived and the kids and I weren't too sure what to expect from Dana. I was afraid myself she might feel betrayed.

"So all of you, am I the only outsider here or what?" 'Mom.' Jonathan said. "You hid something from us too." "True, but this was because I wanted to surprise you."

'Well, this was quite a surprise alright.' Leah said.

"My Precious darling if the kids and I hid something from you, it was only and I mean it, for your own security, yours and the kid's." "Can you give me an example of this?" "I sure can." "Shoot then." "Well, don't shoot me with this one, but how can you tell anybody where the guns are if you don't know we have guns? So far since we got married, yours, mine and most likely the children's lives were spared because you didn't know. Not because you're not trustworthy, but because you didn't know. I can count five times for sure I survived because of the secrecy. Five times you saved my life, because you didn't know." "Can't you tell me now?" "Only if you wish my death." "I hate not to know, but I would hate worse losing you. This is serious stuff." "Yes sweetie it is, because you help saving your own and the kid's life every time you save mine." "This works out good then." "Exactly; especially if you don't know it all. Didn't you hear this before: 'The least we know the better?' Did you get your trust back now?" "Oh, I'm so sorry, will you forgive me?" "I don't have anything to forgive you Precious, this was just a normal reaction. The Kids have a surprise for you too." "Yes, they told me." "What?" "They told me they have something to tell me tonight." "Oh, ok, I like this better."

"Mom was fishing around to get it out of us dad, but we didn't say much." "I thought she didn't like fishing and especially not the worms."

"Precious promise me something now, would you?" "What is it?" "I want you to promise me to never try to get secrets from the children anymore, because too many lives depend on them."

Dana looked at all of us and she said:

"I promise. What a wonderful family I have Gaston. You brought me so much blessing when you came into my life. How can I ever pay you back?" "I still owe you Precious and I'll owe you through eternity."

"Mom I found a cavern and it would be the safest place to be in case of an evasion. Nobody has been there and by the look of it, we are the first ones to enter it. I think no one but the Lord can find us there if we are careful of course."

"This is wonderful, where is it?"

"Can I tell dad?" "Yes son, you can."

"You can't tell anybody mom though." "You can trust me." "It is almost across the lake and we can only enter it from underneath the water." "But I can't swim this far and not much under the water."

"This is why the scuba diving sweetie and the teaching to all the kids. We might never need it, but yet we might need it next week or even sooner."

"Can you teach me Jonathan in your spare time?" "I'd love to mom, but why don't you ask dad?" "Dad has enough on his hands as it is, this is why."

"Right son, in fact I have to go to town early tomorrow morning even though I hate to go and leave you alone." "We'll be fine dad, don't worry." "You're a good man Jonathan."

'Now, this is Leah's turn. She has a very good news too and thank you for your patience little sweetie.'

"Do you remember mom the digging for the worms?" "Yes I do, but what about them? I don't like them at all, yeack." "We were digging a tunnel for an emergency escape." "What do you mean Leah?" "As I am talking to you when everybody knows how to dive, we can swim directly from the bunkhouse to the cavern without being seen by anybody." "How?" "You already know about the false wall and the cave underneath the bunkhouse?" "Yeah." "Now in the bunkhouse's cave there is water that leads us directly to the lake and from there directly to Jonathan's cavern." "Man, you guys don't waste any time, do you?"

"We make a very good team Precious and I'm very thankful to God for all of you.

It's bedtime now though and there is a long day for me tomorrow. I'll be gone when you get up and if I'm not back by bedtime, you're not to worry. I could easily be gone two or three days. I want all of you to keep the diving training until everyone of you can make the cavern distance easily. No one under any circumstance can go near the tunnel or the cavern for security measures, until everyone can do this distance without being seen. We'll talk more about it when I'll be back. Kiss me good night now.'

"Dad, do I have to kiss you?" "You can shake my hand if you prefer Jon. Good night."

"Good night dad." "Good night little sweetie, I'm I getting a kiss from you at least?" "I'll always kiss you dad, good night." "Well, you know that Jonathan is a fine young man now, it is understandable."

I went to kiss little Sarah and Benjamin, the bully thinking it might be the last time I see them. With tears in my eyes, I took Precious to bed like I did on the wedding night and she responded just the same way she did then.

The bunkhouse

The main residence

Very warm in winter, very cool in summer

Boards to build cabines, bunks and the culvert

Chapter 9

It was only after a couple of hours sleep I left that morning at four o'clock, leaving behind me a pile of loved ones to go to the unknown on the Lord's call. At six o'clock I was in whatever was left of Kelowna. There was more desolation and oppression than anything else. People were beaten and killed by the hundreds. I walked in a group where they were beating mostly young children, women and older men and I told them to give their souls to the Lord. 'The Lord will deliver you from your enemies.'

When I took my carafe and I put it to their lips and I put a wet hanky to their foreheads a soldier came to grab me from behind and he fell dead before he could touch me. I was quite amazed by the incident, but I kept doing what I was doing when another one came to stop me.

The same thing happened to him. I looked up in the sky and I said as loud as my lungs could stand: 'Thank You Lord.' At that moment four soldiers with guns on hands surrounded me and one of them said: 'You're under arrest for murder and for helping these outlaws.'

There were some viewers around and some were shouting that I didn't do the killing and others who were saying I killed them both when they came to arrest me. I was taken to the courthouse to be judged immediately.

Helping the oppressed must be the highest crime these days. Here I was standing in front of a judge whom everyone could read hatred all over his face. I could read very clearly the number of the beast on his forehead. I was there to be judged for the highest crime in the world.

"You are charged with murder of two state's officers and for helping the outlaws sir, how are you pleading?" "I didn't touch any of them sir." "Guilty as charged."

The judge said knocking his desk with his little stupid hammer. 'Take him away.' He said motioning with his finger I was to have my head cut off. This must be the guillotine he was referring to. I thought I was going to find out soon.

He asked two police officers to take me away and when they came to grab me; they fell down right away on the floor totally dead cold. 'See what I meant, this is exactly what happened to the other two. He sent the two other officers who were there to take me as well. They came to grab me a bit shakily, but the same thing happened to them. There were people in the courtroom who shouted to the judge that I didn't touch them.

With the courage of a lion I looked at the judge straight in his eyes and I told him: 'I'm afraid you'll have to come and get me yourself by the look of things.' He got in such of a rage that his desk went flying off, he walked to the thick door and he passed right through it as if it was a piece of cardboard. I walked out of there free as a fly to the applause of the attendants who followed me outside.

Later on that day I passed by the Princess building and I found Denise there totally devastated and in tears.

"Denise, what in the world happened to you?" "Gaston, where have you been? I've been looking for you for ages. How are Dana and the kids?" She asked crying her head off.

"Are they still alive? I thought for sure that because you were believers you were all executed long time ago." "Dana and the kids, all the kids are safe and sound Denise." "When I saw in which condition her building was left, I thought for sure you were all dead." "Actually my dear friend, the Lord has been very good to us. But what happened to you? You look like you've been through hell." "I think I have been in hell alright." "Not enough to give your heart to the Lord though?" "My husband sold our baby and he took off with the money. He left me absolutely penniless." "I don't think you would want to eat your baby's price money anyway, would you? See Denise, if you were a believer and if you married a real one, this would have never happened to you. What you're living through is worse than death." "This is all I want to do now to die." "Now, now, why would you want to die when you could live happy forever?" "How can I be happy not knowing what happened to my child?" "The Lord is taking care of your baby and I'd say the only real chance you have to see him again is by giving your life to the Lord." "Do you really think so Gaston? I know you never lie. If Dana and the kids are safe, you must be doing something right. Can I see them?" "The only way you can see her again is by being a sincere child of God. There is no way I would take you or anybody else to her unless I was absolutely sure of this. The same thing goes for God's kingdom; no one can see it unless he's born again." "How do you do this Gaston? Is Dana one too?" "She sure is so and she's happy to be one too. How in the world can you be happy with your life the way it is now? How in the world would you want to live in the world the way you see it all around you? The way I look at it my family is already in heaven." "Oh Gaston please, take me there, would you?" "I love you very much Denise, but this is just not enough for me to take you to heaven or to Dana. This is something you'll have to do yourself.

I'll tell you what Denise, you meet me here in twenty-four hours and if you have met with the Lord, then I'll see what I can do, ok? And don't you think I wouldn't know the difference either. We'll take it from there. How long has it been since you ate?" "Four days." "Here's a hundred $." "Gaston?" "It's ok Denise." "Thank you." "That's nothing."

Then I turned around and I saw a little girl about six years of age all dressed in rags sitting on the steps of the crowned building. "Who are you and what are you doing here by yourself?" "I'm Sylvia and I've been looking for Dana and all of the other kids. I don't know my parents and I have been feeding myself out of the garbage cans." "When is the last time you've seen Dana?" "Almost a year ago." "Come with me, we'll get you something to eat and then you can sleep in my car tonight. What happened to your head?" "A man cut me with a knife and in the hospital they treated me. I lost a lot of blood, you know?" "Yes, I can tell that you are very pale."

I picked up a newspaper that is almost an inch thick and I quickly went through it. The whole court story was in there with all of the details. I wouldn't give much for the reporter's life, I thought.

Denise met me the next day at the named time and place. After she'd answered a few of my questions I was convinced she was sincere.

"Do you want to be baptised Denise?" "What ever it takes to go see Dana and go to heaven Gaston." "Ok, let's go to the lake right away."

We went down to the lake and while Denise was getting baptised, I notice Sylvia was lying down on the back seat hiding herself. When we came back to the car

I asked her why she was hiding and if she would like to get baptised too.

'I am terrified of water and I couldn't watch.'

Then I headed back to the property with the two of them when suddenly I felt that something was bothering me. I stopped the car and I told them: "I have to blindfold both of you. Nobody but me can see how to get where we're going." "You can trust me.' Denise said.

"Maybe so, but I'm not taking any risk Denise." "I don't blame you Gaston for being careful and protective." "This is for your own protection too." "I understand."

'You have a nice car.' Sylvia said. "I like it." "It has seen better days and better years."

The rest of the way was pretty quiet. When we got at the end of the little road, I sat both of them in the trailer and then I hid the car as usual.

'Fifteen more minutes and we'll be all reunited again.' Denise cried out:

"I can't believe I'll see Dana again." "Well, you will and she sure can use your help again also."

Dana cried for a whole half-hour and so did Denise. Jonathan who never said anything much about her to me before was in seventh heaven to see Sylvia again. All the other kids weren't too trilled about her though.

The little Johanne, one of the sweetest ran away from everybody and I went to ask her what was wrong.

'Sylvia is a bad girl and she's going to hurt Jonathan, I know it.' She said with tears in her eyes.

"Well, you and I can keep an eye on them, can't we? I'll tell you what, if you see something that doesn't seem right to you, you come and let me know right away, ok? Do we have a deal?" "Yes dad."

Then she shook my hand on that and she also gave me one of the most sincere hug there is. This girl is in love with Jonathan, I could tell. We'll have to keep an eye on this too.

Dana was more than happy to see Denise again and she told me I went a bit too strong on her with the Lord's thing and the baptism.

'You have to see my side of it too sweetheart.'

Dana was also very glad I brought Sylvia over and she admitted to me she knew about Jonathan and her.

'Keep an eye on her Dana, I don't want our boy to get hurt or into troubles.'

I had to go down again the following week, but this time I had a very bad feeling all the time I was gone. I had a few fights and I rescued kids and women who were mistreated, but a very strong voice was telling me I should go back home and the sooner would be the better.

Sure enough, when I arrived at the end of our trail I saw a school bus that shouldn't be there. I took a good look at the tracks on the ground and I could tell they were pretty fresh. I put the car away and I took the fourth trail, knowing they had taken the number two. Never before I had pushed the wheeler to its full capacity as I did then. According to the footprints they were two men and they were probably armed, but I didn't really have a way to know. I couldn't jeopardise my family safety either. At about one half of a mile before the campsite, I stopped and I left the machine there. I ran the rest of the way to find out there was nobody home. Everybody was gone. I went to look in the bunkhouse behind the false wall and I saw that all of the equipment was there. So they're not in the cavern, they must have been taken as prisoners. I don't really know how fast I ran, but in no time at all I was back at my machine and down the trail I went. The bus was still there when I arrived and not even taking the time to hide the four-wheeler, I ran to where one of my rifles was hidden. I grabbed it, I jumped in the car and I drove down the road. I couldn't believe my luck when I saw a huge moose in the middle of it. I stopped the car, got the gun out, loaded it and I shot the animal dead on the spot. I put my outfit on and I waited having my back turned toward where the bus would be coming from. Thank God I had time to drive the car into the bush, but not without a few dints and scratches, but I didn't really care.

Seven minutes later while I was cutting the animal the bus arrived. They must have been thinking I was an Indian or something like that anyway. I heard them shout to the occupants of the bus not to move if they wanted to live any longer. I heard them laughing when they came down of the bus and one of them said:

"This is a nice animal you've got there." "Yeah." Then within eight seconds both of them were lying down unconscious on the animal.

'This is the Defender.' I heard Dana tell the others.

"I've seen him before long time ago." "Did you see this mom?" Jonathan asked. 'Not even ten seconds.'

I got inside the bus and I walked directly to Sylvia and I pulled the Band-Aid off her forehead which let me see the six, six, six number very clearly. I searched for the device that led the two monsters to my family and I pulled it out from under her arm pit. Without a single word I invited everybody out of the bus except for Sylvia whom I pointed out to stay where she was. I waved everyone on their way back to where they came from. I heard Jonathan tell her mom that he wants to be like this man.

"He might just be a woman son, we don't know." "I don't care mom; I just want to be able to do the same thing."

Do you have any idea how hard it was not to hug my loved ones in a moment like this? Nothing required more strength in my entire life.

Right then I discovered Jonathan had the same strength. He had loved a girl without telling anyone, discovered she was a devil and let her go without a word and all of this under the age of seven.

I took the men's machine guns and I put them in the trunk of my car. I put the two mercenaries in the bus. I cut off as much meat as possible out of the animal and that too I put in the car. Next I pull the rest of the carcass off the road and I waited for them to get on their way. When I was sure they were gone, I drove back toward my family. I filled up the trailer with the meat and then I drove to the camp in the second trail. When I reached them at about half way through, I was received with nothing but excitement from everyone.

"Not all at once you guys. I can't get anything out of that. What is going on Dana?" "Two men kidnapped us and we were delivered by the Masked Defender." "Get out of here now."

'It's true dad, mom is telling you the truth.' Jonathan said coming to his mom's defence right away.

"This is the second time you don't believe me when I talk about the Defender." "I'm sorry sweetheart, but it is also the second time that what you're telling me about him is very hard to believe." "This is true too. Excuse me for getting upset." "I understand Precious. You are under a lot of pressure. Come on now; give me a hug, would you? How did they find us?" "As far as I can tell Sylvia was a traitor." "And I'm the one who brought her here." "Don't blame yourself Gaston, you had no way to know."

"We'd better get going here. Jonathan, you come with me and three boys to help me with the meat. We drove to the houses very quickly and Jonathan had nothing but praises about the Defender and how he wanted to learn more about self-defence now.

"I can teach you some more when you're ready son."
"Right away dad, I want to learn everything you know."
"Well, I'm glad you do son, we'll start tomorrow again.
Do you still remember what I taught you?" "Pretty much
I think. Can't we start tonight dad?" "We might have
time for a half an hour or so to go over what you already
know." "Alright dad!"

Then he gave me a strong hug and a kiss on the
cheek I was not expecting.

'Watch out son, I'm driving you know.' I told him
laughing.

We emptied the trailer in a hurry, washed it and I went
back to get a load of tired kids who were seated down
exhausted. When I came back the second time I gave
to Dana the newspaper to read. Denise and Dana were
arguing to decide between the two who was going to
stay with the kids.

'I'll stay.' Denise said, but Dana insisted she will be
the one who stays to the most dangerous spot.

"When you've finished reading Dana, can you
try to remember the night of the limousine, the night I
celebrated your birthday for the first time?" "Why?" "Just
try to remember everything, would you? We'll talk about
it later, ok?" "Ok." "I'll be right back sweetheart." "I know
you will Gaston."

I smiled to her and I went back home again detesting
every seconds of the way for having to leave her behind.
Within eighteen minutes I was hugging my Precious
Princess once more. I brought her home with the rest of
the kids and I told her I had to go back to the animal.

'I'd be better get as much meat as I could.'

I took two boys with me and when I got as close as a
half a mile from the moose one of them told me to look.
There were at least six wolves on it. So I quickly turned

around knowing I'll have to chase them away again. They were just too close to too many children.

On the news two days later we found out a school bus went down a ravine and the three occupants were found dead.

'God is in control.' I told Dana.

I appreciate every single day of peace there is. One day Dana said:

"Gaston, you'll have to do something about those ants, they are coming in the house by the hundreds now." "Where do you find them?" "I find them always around the sink. They seem to love your teacup and your teaspoon."

I took a plastic pail then and I heated up a spike, I made several holes all around it at three inches from the bottom. Then I put two inches of water in it and I added three tablespoonful of sugar. I mixed it all very good and I set it outside the kitchen wall. Within two days we couldn't find another ant in the house and in five days I counted seventeen hundred of the dead ones from the bucket. This was approximately half of what was in there. It was then I found out that ants were very bad swimmers. I made a similar trap to catch the mice and it works fine. Those were more bait for getting big fish.

March 2009

Everything at the campsite was pretty quiet for the longest time until one day a clever man I have to admit got behind me and he put a gun to my head. Well, maybe this wasn't too much of a smart thing to do.

'Get up very slowly. Any wrong move and you're a dead man.'

Things were spinning pretty fast in my mind. How come my seven Mutesheps didn't bark or they didn't howl? This is something they usually do when there is a danger near by. If this man wanted to shoot me he had a lot of time to do it. I sure didn't have much time for all of the answers to my questions though. In a super swift movement I spun around and I came down on his arm making the hand gun fly off, breaking his wrist and all of this before he could say another word. He's a big man and I knew I couldn't take any risk with him. After a second look at him I said:

"I've seen you before?" "This is the second time you've broken my arm." "Couldn't you learn your lesson from the first time? How's your jaw?" "As good as it could get, I suppose." "Why didn't you shoot me?" "I wanted to make it even with you." "What do you mean?" "I figured you left me my life that night and I didn't deserve it. You could easily killed me." "I don't kill people." "Is this because you're a Christian?" "No, I'm not. I used to be though. I used to be blind, but I became a Jesus' disciple. I just can't wait to meet another one. I never quit thinking about that night since. You could've given me away, but you didn't. Actually, you're the only one who knows who I am and for this reason I knew we would meet again. I never thought it would be this way though. So what you're telling me is you don't want to kill anyone anymore." "My plan that night was to take you away from this scene to protect you." "Why didn't you do anything for the dying man on the pavement?" "It was too late for him and if I did I would have been shot dead too. You left my car in a pretty bad shape and I laid there for three hours before someone picked me up. You've made a pretty big mess that night." "I thought I stopped a pretty big mess that night, if you don't mind me saying." "I think you're right too. Where did you learn to fight this way?" "I watched a lot of movies and I practice on guys like you." "I can see and I can feel this." "Does it hurt?" "Less than the last time." "How did you get here?" "On a horse." "Where is it now?" "At about a mile away." "What do you want to do now? You should be thinking about making it to the hospital." "They kill more people than they save nowadays." "I'll take you home and I'll try to repair this mess. I'll give you a bunk and in a few days if you're not getting any better we'll find you a doctor.

Can you shake hands with your left one?" "Does this mean you trust me?" "If I didn't I would have probably broken this one too. How old are you?" "Thirty-seven. Why?" "I have a wife and kids at home. There is also my wife's best friend who is your age. All of them are called: don't touch." "Are they both your wives?" "No fornication of any kind would be tolerated on my property, got it?" "It's clear enough, yes." "Your health probably depends on it. Let me feel your wrist. It's out alright. You're going to feel pain when you'll put it back in place." "I'll put it back in place?" "You don't expect me to fix everything I break, do you?" "No but, I don't know how to fix this." "I'll show you how, let's go. One more thing before we go. No one knows about me being the Defender or how I met you the first time and I want to keep it this way." "I got it." "Go get your horse now and don't take it between the house and the lake or he'll have broken legs too." "Don't tell me you break horses' legs too?" "Don't expect me to trust you at one hundred per cent either, for a while anyway."

When I got home before Al; I talked to Precious about our guest. She didn't like the idea of having a stranger around at first until I told her the good side of it if he happens to be who I think he is. When he got home I introduced him to all of the others and his eyes stayed on Denise a little longer than I would have liked it. Then I invited him to a shed to get his wrist fixed.

"How's the pain?" "Tolerable." "Keep your mind on Denise for now, it will help." "I like her." "She's got a husband. Hang yourself with your broken arm and use the other one to put it back in place." "This is cruel." "Maybe so, but it is the only way I know to get it back in place without a doctor and the quickest too, because you'll feel it when it gets there." "You're right, I got it." "Now I'll put a few sticks on both sides and I'll tape it. You should be just fine. Just don't go fight anyone yet, especially a defender."

We went back to our routine and Al happened to be a very good help. He is a hard worker and he and I took turns for going to town. I got to trust him completely with just about anything that concerns the security.

One day in June 2011, he came to me and he said he wanted to find Denise's husband.

"Why? You don't want to kill him, do you?" "Don't be ridiculous Gaston, I want to find out if he's still alive or not. Denise might just be a widow and not knowing it." "Ok private eye, good luck. You might find out the records are hard to keep up to date with the number of people who is getting killed every day." "I'll find one or the other." "I know you're capable, you found me."

Jonathan's training is pretty well completed now. He can jump higher than me, he can fall in every possible way and he can roll and spin as fast as a fish. I'm pretty sure now that he can beat an ordinary man and besides, no one else knows a thing about it, which is his strongest trump.

He got into the house one day and there was a man holding his mom from behind with a gun on her head. Dana yelled at him to go get his dad. He started to cry, he ran to them and he put his arms around her.

'Tell this wimp to shut up or I'll shoot him.'

Dana had her legs a bit separated to hold herself up. Jonathan pulled back his right arms and he hit him through her legs, well you know where. The man let her go making all kind of faces. Sonny boy screamed: 'Go get dad mom, he's at the well.'

When I came to the house I found Jonathan smiling, sitting on a chair holding the pistol and pointing out his victim on the floor with what seemed to me having a broken knee.

When Dana walked inside I noticed the astonishing look on her face. It was the exact same one I saw the night I made a man apologised to her. Jonathan and I burst out laughing. I went to hug my precious wife and I introduced her to one of the best Defenders to be; Jonathan, The Black Cat Lapointe.

Al came back with good news for himself and a bad one for me. The good news was that Denise's husband had been killed while stealing babies. Al had in his hands the article on the newspaper about it and also the death certificate. According to the law of man Denise was a free woman.

"I want to marry her." "Ok, now you need to find proof that you are single." "What?" "You heard me. You can't get married unless you can prove you are. You already told me you had three wives at home. What is the bad news Al?"

Then he gave me the newspaper.

'Gaston Lapointe is the most wanted individual in the western world. We have reasons to believe he is the number one Defender and the number one enemy of our king.'

It was my turn to go to town and I had to be even more careful than before, because there were fifteen years old pictures of me everywhere. I was surprised to find so many people to warn me and who wanted to hide me though.

Maybe, just maybe I thought there are more and more people who found out what hell is like now and they are looking for God and heaven.

On my way back home that day I came to a single car accident scene. There was a poor guy already dead in the wreck and the man's face was totally slashed. I pulled his wallet out of his pocket and I looked in it. Ron Lapointe March 13th 1946. I thought, what would my Lord do next? I pulled out my wallet too and I took a good look in it to make sure I didn't give any information I shouldn't give. Then I put it in the man's pocket along with a mask of mine.

When Al came back from his following trip, he brought me news they were celebrating my death. Have a good party I said, we'll see who gets the last laugh.

Shortly after this, Jonathan and I started to teach Benjamin and Al. The girls learned a few tricks too, but they are just like their mom way too feminine for this sort of things. Sarah is the funniest clown I have ever seen. No one can tell where she takes her ideas, but she can make us laugh to tears every time. Well, I have a little idea myself where they come from.

One night when lying down on the pillow Precious put me against the wall pretty firmly.

"Gaston, I didn't mean to, but I saw Jonathan and Al practising your art this morning and one of the moves he made was the same one I saw before from the Masked Defender. I also know that you taught Jonathan everything he knows. I also think you took way too much time in the washroom the night you celebrated my birthday for the first time, especially after you told me that every minute spent with me was so precious. Is it safe for you to tell me now?" "Do you remember you had mixed feeling that night too?" "This was you on the stage, wasn't it?" "It was me Precious." "And I praised him about how he could protect a woman." "Oh, you praised me too sweetie." "Was this you too with the police the night Sarah was born?" "They killed three innocent people that night." "What a guy you are Gaston. You sure can keep a secret." "Only when I have to Precious."

2013

Al and Denise have decided to get married. They came together to tell me one morning and I congratulated them.

'I think the two of you can really become one.'

Denise, still very pretty said:

"You approve Gaston? I didn't think you would?" "Al is a very fine man like there is none around anymore. Did you talk to him about the Isaac Tent?" "No, I thought you would." "It is your duty. Talk to him about it and then he can go hunt for a pastor and get baptised. Tell him not to bring any Antichrist or a false prophet over here though."

Al came back from his last trip with the news that no pastor would marry a couple of disciples unless they become Christians and get the mark of the system. Denise started to cry and Dana went to hug her. The two of them made a Tent with blankets that was pretty impressive.

'Gaston!' Al asked out of frustrations.

"Don't you think if you could baptise Denise, you can also marry her? It seems to me it would be even better than the laws of this country at this present time." "We need two witnesses, Denise has one and you need one too." "What about you?" "I can't do both." "Then I want Jonathan to be my best man." "He's too young." "I'm sure if he can beat a man and he can teach a cop he can also give one away." "He is pretty mature, but what do you ladies think of that?"

Both of them said laughing: 'It's alright.'

Now, this is serious stuff. Al you go and ask Jonathan what he thinks of it and I'm not going to influence him in anyway.'

The two of them became buddies both learning from each other. For Jonathan having police training on top of all the rest was I'm sure the best thing that could happen to him. Watching the two coming running and laughing was telling us everything we needed to know.

'I'm going to be free to marry the two of you at three o'clock this afternoon. Al, take your pistol and take your buddy here with you. Don't get lost, but I need six chickens for one o'clock at the latest if you want to give us a wedding meal. The rest of us, we have a lot to do until then, go now.'

Denise came to give me a hug that didn't lie. Al shook my hand and he said: 'Don't break it.' Then I hugged him too and I gave him a few good friendly slaps on his back.

This was a nice day. When the newlyweds walked towards the Tent after the ceremony, Benjamin asked:

'What are they going to do in there?' My sweet little Sarah told him: 'Al will put Denise on top of him and next year we will have a little baby with us to fill up the circle.' I could tell that my little story about the circles travelled a long way.

2017

We could hardly get news from the rest of the country anymore. Al found out though that my son Guy was doing a fine job in his living area. He is also a martial artist who learned the art of disguise and neutralising his enemies. It was said about him he could walk in front of you unnoticed right in daytime. I was by this news reassured about Marlène, his sister and other members of my family. I myself don't get any younger and I don't really feel my age except for my breathing. I cut down on my activities mainly to please my Precious Dana whom I love just as much as the very first day or more.

Al and Denise have a place on their own now at approximately two thousand feet from ours. They have a son and a young daughter now and they seem to be very happy with their lives. They never really quit being thankful to Dana and I. As far as I am concerned they owe me nothing and I told them this many times.

Jonathan has taken over most of my duties and he is more capable to fill them up now than I do. According to the reports I get he can help more people in one day now than I could in two. Benjamin is so strong that he has to be careful not to break someone's hand on a simple handshake. Leah and Sarah grew up to be absolutely beautiful and their only concern was to find a good prince in this world of desolation. All I can say to them is the Lord will take care of everything for them as He has done for their mom and I.

Jonathan reported a very good and funny one to me one time. He had sensed that something was wrong and he went at the end of our trail alone. I gave him heck for not taking Al along with him. On hearing this he asked me how many times I took someone with me. None I had to admit. He hid himself in the woods when he heard some motor vehicles coming towards the end of the road. There were two jeeps carrying eight soldiers. They stopped and they seemed to be discussing strategies. He could tell they had machine guns. Without wasting any time he called the moose. Being in a rutting season they came charging. Charging they did, not one, not two, but three of them did. They charged at the jeeps that weren't welcome in this paradise of theirs. They flipped those vehicles upside down with everyone in them as if they were feathers or toys. Before they could come back to reality Jon had taken all their firearms away, tied up their hands behind their back, covered their eyes and he drove them back to their civilisation in town.

'I don't know what they had dreamed about, but they sure got themselves into a nightmare. Maybe it was the hunted who got the hunters, it happens sometimes with bears too.'

In 2021 Johanne and Jonathan found the way to the Isaac Tent and I'm now the grandfather of three more. Jonathan told me he wishes to start training his oldest son soon.

In 2025 one morning I went to start the car to generate the power, but nothing happened. No matter what I tried nothing happened. I sent for Al and I asked him to shoot his pistol. He got it out and he tried to fire it, nothing.

"Are you sure you have a bullet in it?" "Of course I am." "Try another one."

After he tried a dozen of them I sent Jonathan to start the quad. Nothing there either.

'Go start the snowmobile.' Nothing there either.

"My friends, we are in the last stage of the present world." "What do you mean?" "I mean that all mechanisms have ceased functioning. We are back to the bows and arrows and horseback riding, this is what I mean. The end of pain is not far away. Jonathan knows where everything is, so from now on everybody, you should listen to him in everything he says, because he listens to the voice of the Lord."

'Dad.' Ben said.

"You're talking like you are going to leave us and you can still outrun me." "Ben, with you too my beloved son I'll rest on your strength. The Lord is getting ready to come and get me soon and take me to his beautiful home. I have done all I could do and I sure can use a rest now." "You can rest with us too dad." "Would you be selfish enough to keep me from my reward?" "I don't want you to go." "We will all be together soon and much better off than here where we fear every minute of the day for your life and for one another. I thought I did all I could do to prepare you for this mess down here and for Wonderland." "Oh, you did dad, it is just that I love you too much to let you go." "You have to keep being strong Ben, because you are the pillar of the family." "I thought Jonathan is." "Jonathan is the head and as you know all the parts of your body are necessary. Your two sisters are very bright and sensible and if you listen to them too, you'll do alright. I'm not gone yet and we'll have to talk some more about all this, if it's alright with you? How much can you lift now? I always wanted to have your strength, do you know this?" "I don't know why dad, I can't move very fast." "You're not likely to need to." "I can hold the back of the Lincoln up six minutes and the front three." "This is amazing Ben. What a gift from God you have." "I thought I got it from you and mom." "You should know by now that everything comes from God and will return to Him." "I have to go now dad, but I'm glad we had this talk." "Anytime son, I have so much time now that I don't know what to do with it and I feel helpless." "You feel helpless while you're still working ten hours a day. You'll never cease to amaze me dad, have a good day."

At bedtime that night Precious had many questions for me.

"Are you thinking of leaving my love? I heard you were talking like it's on your mind. I don't see how a man who's making love to his younger wife five times a week could even think this way." "I was told by an eighty-four years old man one time in front of his wife that if it was used normally or reasonably it is not likely to stop until you die. He said him and his wife were making it four times a week still. The very most appreciated compliment I've ever received was from this same old man." "What did he tell you?" "He told me I was as wise as an old man. I was twenty-three then." "Gaston, you're so strong and alert still I think you're going to outlive me." "I know what you're saying sweetie, but the years are there all counted no matter what we think or say." "I'm still your sweetie, am I not?" "Always and forever, you're my Precious." "Are you tired?" "I'm just fine my love." "I know." "Tease!" "I like that too. Gaston you're probably going to outlive me." "Just try to make it through tonight and then one night at the time, ok?" "The way it is, it's alright with me."

News were pretty rare since the abolishment of the mechanisms, the only ones that travel now are by mouth to mouth. Everything has pretty well stayed the same way until one day while I was jogging in May of 2028, I simply collapsed.

It was my Jonathan who found me. No wonder he has flair like The Black Cat he is. I told him I had a heart attack and I wanted him to go talk to his mom and send Ben over to pick me up.

'Now my days are all counted and I want to see the whole family together at once, because my time left would be too short otherwise.'

Ben was with me quickly and he carried his old man to the house almost a half a mile away slowly but surely.

I was laid on the couch on my demand simply because I didn't want to close my eyes on our bed.

'Give me five minutes with my Precious and then all of you can come in and each and everyone I want to bless you.'

"Don't go now Gaston, I still need you." "Sweetie, you are the very best thing that ever happened to me.

The thirty years we spent together have passed just like the most beautiful dream, but you and I know the dream doesn't end here. We'll meet again and surely sooner than you think, probably in the next chapter. Be happy for me, because today I will be meeting with the Lord who has been so gracious to put us together and to give us all we had. Can you smile to me, your gorgeous Majesty?" "You have always been a wonderful prince Gaston and I'll be missing you too much." "Please don't cry now sweetie and don't tell me to let you have it, not this time. Oh, oh, oh." "Gaston." "Please sweetie, call the others, would you?"

'Jonathan and his sweet Johanne, Leah and her prince, Sarah and her precious' smile, Benjamin and all of you come kiss grandpa good bye. Al and Denise; friends like you are very, very rare.

There is only one more thing I would say to all of you. I was poor and then I was rich, I've been sad and then very happy, I was weak and strong, I was nothing and famous, I was young and now I'm old, but the very best of all the blessings came to me after I gave my heart to the Lord. Precious." "Love!"

'It's over mom, let him rest now. He has done more than many men.'

Welcome to Wonderland

Chapter 10

Two years later, in 2030 Dana then fifty-nine was still lost without her Gaston. She was never really the same anymore. One time Sarah told her:

"Dad wouldn't come back mom, but we will all go and see him and the Lord one day." "I love you all very much, but I'm just completely lost without him."

Then one morning Leah found her mother smiling and lifeless in her bed. She got to the pearly beautiful white and gold gate which separates the good from the bad and then she asked for Gaston.

"How do you know him?" "He's my husband; this is how I know him." "When did he leave you?" "Two years ago." "What is your name?" "Dana. Aren't you guys supposed to know everything?" "We're not God who knows everything; we only know what He tells us. Besides, you don't want us to send you to the wrong Gaston, husband of yours, do you?" "No, no, I don't." "Well, you better calm down then, don't you think?" "I guess you're right. I'm sorry." "I think I got him now. Gaston Lapointe was born in October 1992, married Dana in 1999 and come to life in May 2028." "Wait a minute here, that doesn't add up. He was eighty-four when he left. He was born in March 1944." "Yes, but he was born again in 1992." "Oh, this is how it works?" "This is how it works and you will find him on the other side of this white wall over there. All you have to do is to follow the red light."

When she entered the pointed wall, she walked into a kind of labyrinth. There was a light to follow that led her to the right and then left, right and right and then left again, straight for a while, right and then left and straight out to the most beautiful environment possible.

This place is more beautiful than any human imagination could have done. Her smile is still the most beautiful there is. Her amazement is at that precise moment something absolutely unequal. What does look like a sky is a magnificent topaz dome. There are fruit trees further than your eyes can see and all the grass is nicer than the nicest golf course you have ever seen. The weather is always even. There is no more of God's madness, meaning no thunder and no lighting. There is no river on earth as beautiful as the one that crosses the land from East to West. On each of its sides there is nice sand whiter than snow. The rocks and the stones laying on it are diamonds, pearls and rubies of all sizes more beautiful than anything I have ever seen. They are there for everyone and no one wants them more than the other. The sidewalks are made out of soft gold pleasant to our feet. All the animals I knew on earth as being ferocious like the lions, the tigers, the cougars, even the bear are smiling to us and come to lie in front of us to make either a pillow or a footstool. Fairly quick Dana found out there was no danger in them.

A young man went towards her and he asked her what she was looking for.

"I'm Dana and I'm looking for Gaston, my husband. Can you help me to find him?" "I'll do my best to help you Dana." "What is all this that we're looking at?" "This is one of the mansions Jesus was talking about. This is your new home." "What is your name young man." "You can call me Love like everyone else." "Oh, just wait a minute now, you are a gentle and handsome young man, but there is only one man I would call Love and this is Gaston I'm looking for. I was told I would find him on this side of this wall and the only one I can see here is you. I just won't be happy if I can't find him." "Do you always cry this easy Dana? For one thing there is no time here, so when you say wait a minute, this doesn't fit in this environment. All we have here is space and eternity and I'm pretty sure there is only a little bit of space between you and Gaston. I'll help you find him and if you want to I'll introduce you to his mother and his three young brothers." "Are you really? I'd love to." "You finally pronounced my name Dana." "Oh, I didn't mean this and you know it too." "Come and follow me, they will be delighted to meet with you at last." "Oh my God, she looks so much like you Looove."

'Did you call me Dana?'

'No Lord, You know Dana has this habit to say; oh my God all the space.'

"Be careful Dana, the Almighty is quick to answer. Every space you call on Him, he's right there with you. At any space of the eternity you need Him and for any reason, He answers you immediately." "Looove, don't you have another name I could be more comfortable with?" "I do, but I like this one the best and this is how I like to be called."

"Would you excuse us Gertrude for a space; I need to speak to this young man here about something?" "Certainly Dana."

Looove, can I talk to you aside for a sec?" "A space Dana. We have no second, no minute, no hour, no day, no week, no month, no year, no century, not even a millennium and no time, we only have space." "Looove, tell me why is it that Gertrude looks so much like you?"

"We all are kind of brothers and sisters in Jesus, don't you know this?" "Oh, ok."

"Hi Gertrude." "Hi Dana, I'm happy to finally meet with you. I heard so much about you that I had to put some space between Gaston and me. Here are his three young brothers. This is Ghyslain."

'Hi Dana, Gaston is right you are Lovely.'

'This is Jean Yves.'

'Hi Dana, Gaston and Ghyslain are right, you are Lovely.'

'And this is the youngest and is name is Joseph. They were all very young when the Lord took them and they were spotless.'

'Lovely huh, you guys are right, she is the loveliest of all.'

"Space or time young man, I can't wait any longer. Are you or are you not going to help me to find Gaston?" "Yes, I will help you Dana. Didn't you think of asking Jesus about where Gaston is? I'm sure he would tell you right away." "Now, why didn't I think of that myself or before?" "Simply because there isn't an ounce of selfishness in you Dana, that's why. Now close your eyes and call on the Lord Jesus. He'll be right with you. I'll be back shortly." "Oh, don't go away, don't leave me alone please." "I'll be near you, don't worry, but you have to meet Jesus on your own this space."

"Jesus, can you come to my help?" "Yes Dana, you called me for sure to this space and here I AM." "This quick my Lord?" "You're not ready yet Dana? I can come back some other space." "No, no, Lord Jesus, it is just I didn't expect you to answer me this quickly." "All of my Father's children are very important to me and to Him. What did you want Dana?" "Lord I was told at the gate that I would find my beloved husband Gaston on this side of this white wall and he is nowhere to be found. I met with his mother and his brothers, but I didn't meet Gaston yet. I thought this was supposed to be paradise and it wouldn't be heaven to me without my Gaston." "Well, I think we're going to do something about this situation, won't we?" "I sure hope so Lord Jesus." "You've been on trial long enough now." "On trial?" "I'll tell you what Dana, you go see Gertrude privately and she will tell you how and where to find your Gaston." "Oh thank You Lord Jesus, thank You very much." "Dana don't you ever forget that I'll always be here for you as I AM now. I promised it thousands of years ago and my word is true and it never fails." "I know this Lord, Gaston told me." "Go see Gertrude now and be happy and be blessed for the eternity I promised you."

So as she was told Dana went to see Gertrude and she asked her for a private audience.

"Hi Dana.' Gertrude said joyfully.

"I Gertrude." "I can see that you're still a bit concerned." "Yes but Jesus sent me over here and he told me you would help me to find Gaston." "Come in and sit down, I'll tell the boys to get some fish for our dinner." "Excuse me Gertrude, but don't you think they are a bit too young for this?" "Dana, here there is no more pain, no more danger, no more worries and you'll get used to it too. The fish they want will gladly jump out of the water to be our meal today. Tomorrow a deer will come and lay down for us and be delighted to do so. There is no wilderness in the Lord's kingdom and no need to fear anything. After lunch we'll go on horse or lion or tiger's back riding as soon as Gaston is back, if you want to." "Gaston back, Gertrude this is why I'm here. Jesus said you would help me to find him. You don't think he is a bit too old for back riding Gertrude?" "Gaston is not too old for riding more than the children are too young to fish. You love him, don't you Dana?" "More than anything, he has been so good, so loving, so faithful one could only love him. He is with us, isn't he Gertrude?" "Dana my girl, God erases from our memories all the ones who aren't with us and if Gaston wasn't with us we couldn't remember him." "He's all I'm thinking about so he must be with us." "Gaston had a lot of integrity Dana and he loves you very much, in fact the only one who loves you more than he does is the Lord Himself.

You're about to hear the rest of the story my dear Dana. You see, Gaston has so much love for the Lord, for you, for me and for everybody even his enemies that the Lord decided to change his name."

Dana continued and she said:

'Now his name is Love. But he is so young.' Dana cried out.

"You were young for him too one day and he didn't mind this. This certainly didn't stop him from loving you. He is like he was at twenty-seven years of age and I am like when I was at twenty-two. How old were you Dana when he met you?" "I was twenty-six then and I was full of hope. He filled all my expectations and more. Do you think Gertrude I can be like I was then?" "I don't see why not Dana, the two of you would make an awesome couple. You didn't see how you look yet, but you are about to see this." "He told me once the Lord wouldn't separate us. He was right wasn't he? It would be awesome to be like I was then for him." "He loves you no matter what, but you have to feel good about yourself as well. I'll tell you what Dana, you go to the river, send the boys home with their catches and look yourself in the water."

Dana did as she was told and she quickly looked herself in the glistening water and she remembered her younger years.

"Oh my God!" "Yes Dana, you called me?" "No, yes, no, yes, yes, my Lord, I want to thank You for everything.

No wonder we call You Father, Wonderful, Almighty, only You can do so much in so little space and in so much space. Again Lord, thank You."

Looking herself one more time in the water a second image appeared beside her in the water.

"Love, is this you? Gaston, how wonderful it is to be back with you." "Hi Precious Princess. Welcome to Wonderland. At this moment a one thousand musicians band started to play and a chorus of ten thousand Saints and Angels began to sing; Precious Princess of Wonderland.

Welcome to Wonderland to you Precious Princess.
You've accepted the Lord, the Lord accepted you.
Now you're here in his land and forever you'll rest.
What you're seeing is for you cause you've believed the truth.
This is the Promised Land given us by the Lord.
Pure water and white sand, you will never be bored.
All you will ever need is here for you to take.
All those beautiful things were put there for your sake.

2
You will never get hurt, you will never get scared.
All the bad of the earth got caught in Jesus' care.
You'll never be hungry and you will never thirst.
Forever be happy, cause you put Jesus first.
Forever and ever you're a child of our King.
Come to the Lord's supper, He'll tell you everything.
And He'll give you the crown, you deserve all around.
All the diamonds, the gold, the rubies and the pearls.

3
Then you can sing with us to princes and princesses.
Whom have carried their crosses so now too they can rest.
Others have washed their robes in the blood of the Lamb.

Let us welcome them all to this beautiful land.
For the eternity you'll have immunity.
No one can take away what it is yours to stay.
The bad have been destroyed nothing is left but joy.
Peace and love all the way, promised milk and honey.
Part spoken

Will you sing with us to the princes and princesses?
Will you carry your cross so you too can rest?
Did you wash your robe in the blood of the Lamb?
Will you be welcome in this beautiful land?
Will you have immunity for the eternity?
Will you have all those things no one can take away?
Will you be destroyed with the bad or live forever in joy?
Will you live in peace and love all the way with milk and honey?

1 and 4
Welcome to Wonderland to you Precious Princess.
You've accepted the Lord, the Lord accepted you.
Now you're here in his land and forever you'll rest.
What you're seeing is for you, cause you believed the truth.
What you're seeing is for you, cause you believed the truth.

"Love, how could you wait this long to make yourself known to me?" "This was the Lord's idea. You will never be bored in his kingdom. Didn't you notice something else too about you and me?" "What do you mean Love?" "There is no more passion, meaning there is no more pain, no more worries. We have only peace and love." "Yes Love and I love it." "So do I. If you want to come with me we can sit on a hubcap and travel all over, discovering the entire universe. We can hook ourselves to a shark and travel through all of the seas discovering all their infinities. We can also sit inside a whale like brother Jonah did for as long as we like it. If we need anything we can call on to the Lord and in a wink of an eye He'll answer us." "This is wonderful." "This is the Wonderland I one day talked to you about, the wonderful kingdom of the Lord. No money could buy; it is the most wonderful gift of all. The everlasting and happy eternal life to whoever believed in the Lord Jesus and follow his teaching, the Lord of lords, the King of kings, the I Am who I Am, The One and only from the beginning until the end."

'Someone called, Love and Lovely?

'This is Michael.

"Hi." "Whatever you do or wherever you go the two of you, don't forget the Lord's Supper." "We wouldn't miss it for the universe or even for the heavens." We said at the same time.

'Who's alike speaks alike.' Lovely said with her lovely smile. At the same space we hugged each other and something extremely strange happened. It is not easy to describe, but it was like a mild electric courant that went through us from our hair to our toenails.

"What was this Love?" "I don't know, but it was the most wonderful feeling I ever experienced." "Same here Love. I remember that making love was good and relaxing, but it was nothing in comparison to this." "You're right Lovely, no breath taking and no sweat either. It must have been another one of Jesus' tricks. I told you that you wouldn't be bored in here." "Yes Love you did and I am very comfortable with your name now and I love mine as well." "This is a lovely name for a lovely woman and I love you both Lovely."

"Thank You Lord for this beautiful book You gave me." "No, thanks to you Gaston, I told you that you would do it."

Endless story, eternal life